"What a delight Suzanne Woods Fisher's latest novel is! *A Season on the Wind* is multifaceted and thoroughly enchanting. By the time I finished the first chapter, I was cheering on each of the central characters, was invested in their goals and secrets, and was anxiously turning pages to see what happened next. I've always loved Suzanne's distinct, relatable voice. She has a gift for enabling readers to feel like they're part of the story—so much so that they don't want to leave the world she's created. *A Season on the Wind* is everything a novel should be—engaging, heartfelt, bold, and charming."

Shelley Shepard Gray, *New York Times* and
USA Today bestselling author

"Sparks fly in a lively tale about the Audubon Christmas Bird Count in Amish country. *A Season on the Wind* overflows with warmth and conflict, laced with humor, and the possibility of rekindled love."

Amy Clipston, bestselling author of *The Jam and Jelly Nook*

"*A Season on the Wind* is a compelling read, an enjoyable volume that entertains on a quiet evening, or under a shade tree on a warm spring afternoon. Suzanne Woods Fisher calls our attention to the lives of bird-watchers and birds, both rare and common, that grace the pastoral hills of Pennsylvania. An endearing visit with our Amish friends, with a side order of birds and human nature."

Cheryl Harner, president of the Ohio Audubon Society

A
SEASON
on the
WIND

Novels by Suzanne Woods Fisher

LANCASTER COUNTY SECRETS

The Choice
The Waiting
The Search

SEASONS OF STONEY RIDGE

The Keeper
The Haven
The Lesson

THE INN AT EAGLE HILL

The Letters
The Calling
The Revealing

THE BISHOP'S FAMILY

The Imposter
The Quieting
The Devoted

THE DEACON'S FAMILY

Mending Fences
Stitches in Time
Two Steps Forward

THREE SISTERS ISLAND

On a Summer Tide
On a Coastal Breeze
At Lighthouse Point
The Moonlight School

A SEASON on the WIND

SUZANNE WOODS FISHER

Revell

a division of Baker Publishing Group
Grand Rapids, Michigan

© 2021 by Suzanne Woods Fisher

Published by Revell
a division of Baker Publishing Group
PO Box 6287, Grand Rapids, MI 49516-6287
www.revellbooks.com

Printed in the United States of America

Library of Congress Cataloging-in-Publication Data
Names: Fisher, Suzanne Woods, author.
Title: A season on the wind / Suzanne Woods Fisher.
Description: Grand Rapids, Michigan : Revell, a division of Baker Publishing Group, [2021]
Identifiers: LCCN 2021004407 | ISBN 9780800739508 (paperback) | ISBN 9780800740603 (casebound) | ISBN 9781493431946 (ebook)
Subjects: GSAFD: Love stories.
Classification: LCC PS3606.I78 S45 2021 | DDC 813/.6—dc23
LC record available at https://lccn.loc.gov/2021004407

Unless otherwise indicated, Scripture used in this book, whether quoted or paraphrased by the characters, is taken from the King James Version of the Bible.

Scripture quotations labeled MSG are taken from *THE MESSAGE*, copyright © 1993, 2002, 2018 by Eugene H. Peterson. Used by permission of NavPress. All rights reserved. Represented by Tyndale House Publishers, Inc.

Published in association with Joyce Hart of the Hartline Literary Agency, LLC.

Baker Publishing Group publications use paper produced from sustainable forestry practices and post-consumer waste whenever possible.

21 22 23 24 25 26 27   7 6 5 4 3 2 1

Life is long enough for one more chance at a rare bird.

James D. Watson

Meet the Cast

Penny Weaver—Single Amish woman, age thirty-five, moved to Stoney Ridge from Big Valley, a much more conservative Old Order Amish church, to live in her late grandmother's home. Manages Lost Creek Farm's guesthouse (where birders come to stay while birding), and also manages her young brother, Micah.

Micah Weaver—Amish teen, age eighteen. Has developed quite a reputation in the bird world for his remarkable ability to spot and identify birds, especially rare birds. Starting a business as a field guide for avid birders.

Ben Zook—A twitcher. Non-Amish man (though he had been raised Plain), age thirty-seven, renowned author and photographer of birds. Made his mark in the world of birding with his debut book, *Rare Birds*. Has come to Lost Creek Farm in hot pursuit of a "vagrant," a bird seldom seen in North America.

Natalie Crowell—Cousin to Ben, age thirty-one, lives in Philadelphia, has worked in interior design until her life imploded recently. Accompanies Ben to Lost Creek Farm at his invitation. Has no interest in birds whatsoever.

Trudy Yoder—Young Amish girl, age fifteen, avid birder.

Shelley Yoder—Trudy's older sister, age eighteen. Has a beautiful singing voice. Avid attractor of male devotion, including Micah Weaver's.

Boyd Baldwin—Non-Amish veterinarian to Stoney Ridge, thirties, love interest of Natalie's.

Hank Lapp—One-of-a-kind Amish man. Ageless.

Roy King—Amish widower, late thirties. Heart is set on Penny Weaver.

Zeke Zook—Elderly Amish man, father to Ben. Suffers from Alzheimer's disease.

David Stoltzfus—Wise and wonderful bishop to the little Amish church of Stoney Ridge.

White-winged Tern—A vagrant bird that has been blown off course during fall migration. This Eurasian bird, seldom seen in all of North America, has chosen Stoney Ridge for a lengthy stopover, creating quite a stir. It has a sly knack for eluding birders.

Birder's Glossary

accidental: a bird that shows up where it shouldn't (aka casual)

bins: binoculars

casual: birds that fly from wherever to a wrong place (aka accidental)

chase: to chase after a reported rarity

chick: newly hatched baby bird

clutch: eggs in a nest

dip: going after a particular bird and missing it

dray: squirrel nest

fledgling: a young bird with wing feathers large enough for flight

jinx bird: a relatively common bird that has managed to elude a person's life list despite repeated attempts on their part to find that species

LBJs (little brown jobs): a blanket term for drab songbirds that are difficult to distinguish

lek: a patch of ground used for communal display in the breeding season by certain birds

lifer: a first-time sighting for a birder

nemesis bird: a species that constantly eludes a birder

rookery: a breeding colony

snags: dead trees

spark bird: a species that triggers a lifelong passion for birding

twitcher: a hard-core birder who goes to great lengths to see a species and add it to his or her list

vagrant: bird straying well outside of the regular ecological range

whitewash: excrement outside of nest

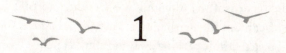

1

Penny Weaver stayed so still that the field sparrow in her yard didn't seem to know she was there. It was better in the early morning, when she could see the solid color on his proud chest. In this late-afternoon light, a field sparrow seemed like an ordinary Little Brown Job. After he flew off, she crossed the yard to the old milking stable that her brother Micah had converted into a guesthouse with the help of a few men from their church.

Inside the guesthouse, Penny took one last look around. On a whim, she had cut a handful of late-blooming chrysanthemums from the garden and put them in a mason jar to set on the small table. The guesthouse was made up of two small bedrooms, a tiny but functional bathroom, and a sitting area with a woodstove. Against the wall, near the table, was a kitchenette of sorts: a sink, and a mini refrigerator and microwave with power provided by a generator. It wasn't fancy, certainly nothing like these Englisch strangers were probably accustomed to. But it was clean, tidy, warm . . . and the strangers had asked the bishop, David Stoltzfus, for a place to stay while birding with Micah. She had to remember that, especially if they were the complaining type. *They* had asked.

If this worked out, it might provide needed income. The bishop came up with the notion of adding a guesthouse at Lost Creek Farm for birders, to encourage longer guiding trips for Micah than the usual one-day outings. "This could be a good thing for Micah," David had said. "It could be just the thing to bring him out of his shell. And it's good for Stoney Ridge too. Micah's eye and ear for rare birds seems to be God's means to bring blessings to our town."

It did seem as if the Almighty was working overtime lately to bring Micah out of the shadows. Last January, he'd spotted a Black-backed Oriole pecking away at Penny's kitchen feeder. The Black-backed was a stunning cousin to the Baltimore Oriole, but this one lived in central Mexico. It was only the second time the Black-backed Oriole had been spotted in the United States. Ever. That little bird created a major attraction during its two-month stay, drawing bird lovers from all over the country.

As if that wasn't enough, in early March, Micah spotted a Roseate Spoonbill. While it wasn't hard to notice—goodness, it stood nearly a yard tall, with pink feathers like flamingos—where Micah had found it *was* remarkable. An overlooked, hard-to-get-to creek that ran along the northern edge of town. It had been nearly fifty years since the last Roseate Spoonbill was spotted in Pennsylvania. Why it had traveled from Florida—remaining for nearly a month in a creek so insignificant it had no name—was a mystery. Then again, that's what made birding so intriguing. Birds didn't always act or play according to the rules.

And now, in mid-November, Penny's brother had sighted the White-winged Tern, a vagrant bird, rarely seen in all of North America. Suddenly it seemed that birders everywhere knew the name Micah Weaver.

She heard a noise outside and peeked out the window. The sound of a car coming up the long, steep drive always startled Penny, so different a sound than the gentle *clip-clop* of a horse pulling a buggy.

Opening the door of the guesthouse, she spotted the dark brim of Micah's hat as he peered around the edge of the barn. She let out a sigh. That boy. Nearly nineteen and still so shy. He was as gentle in nature as he was tall in height.

She hoped David was right to add this whole venture of hosting birders at Lost Creek Farm to Micah's field guiding. She hadn't slept well last night, tossed and turned, anxious. It wasn't typical for Penny to feel unsettled, which only made her even more uneasy.

She smoothed down her apron, tucked a stray strand of hair inside her prayer cap, took a deep breath, and crossed the yard to greet the guests. A small man climbed out of the driver's side of the car and waved his arm, smiling.

"Welcome. You must be the man coming to find the bird," Penny said. An awkward silence followed. Something seemed off. What had she done wrong?

"Um, my name is Natalie Crowell. My cousin is the birder."

Oh no! Penny realized this man was actually a woman with a startling haircut. Crewcut-short like a man's, spiky on top, white-blonde. "Welcome to our farm. Lost Creek Farm. It's where my brother Micah and I live. Micah is the field guide you've come for. And I'm Penny." She was babbling now, nervous, embarrassed.

Out of the passenger side of the car, another person emerged and popped his head over the top of the car. "I'm the one you were told about. Don't feel embarrassed. People confuse us all the time."

"Very funny," Natalie said. She pulled her big purse out of the car and turned to Penny. "Ben's my cousin, but we look nothing alike."

That did not need pointing out. Ben had longer hair than Natalie's—thick, dark brown, wavy. He raised his arms onto the top of the car, folding them, leaning forward slightly as he cupped his elbows, and as he did, Penny's stomach dropped.

"The name's Ben Zook. I've come to see that White-winged Tern that everyone in the bird world is buzzing about. I sure hope it's not a one-day wonder."

Penny's heart gave one huge thump and then started beating wildly.

It was *him*.

Her Ben Zook.

Even after two decades, she would know him anywhere.

She'd always known that one day, somehow, somewhere, they'd meet again. And here he was. He was here for a bird.

Of course the Lord would entice him back home with a bird. A rare bird. Just as birds found their way back over land and sea, so God had found a way to bring Ben Zook here.

Ben walked around the car to greet her, holding out his hand to her. His movement was quick, graceful, and Penny suddenly remembered that was his way. He was tall, so tall she had to raise her chin to see his eyes. He was so fine to look at that she couldn't help but stare at the sheer wonder of him. His deep voice made Penny think of a waterfall, fast-moving and fluid, unable to hold on to yet so mesmerizing.

Ben Zook was *standing* just a few feet away from her!

Still dumbstruck, she gazed at him, then at his offered hand. *Do something, Penny! Pull yourself together.* But she couldn't budge. His eyes registered no recognition of her. Not a flicker. Penny could see she was a complete stranger to him. Eyes couldn't lie. And still, she couldn't move a muscle.

Ben dropped his hand with an awkward smile, then turned away to take things out of the car. He opened the trunk to pull out suitcases, handing one to his cousin. He paused, leaned one hand against the car, swayed a little, and suddenly folded to the ground like a rag doll.

~

Ben felt a gentle touch on his forehead before his eyelids could open. He came to slowly, as if he were waking up from a sweet dream, so sweet that he didn't even want to be roused. He couldn't remember what he was dreaming about, only the mood it evoked.

It covered him in calm; his soul was settled, utterly safe. He could scarcely remember ever feeling that way.

Wait. He did remember. He was a little boy, maybe five or six years old, sick with some dreaded childhood illness like chicken pox, and his mother had put her cool hand on his hot forehead. Just like now.

Eyes opening, he blinked up at her. This woman wasn't his mother. And he wasn't six years old. And he had absolutely no idea what had just happened.

From somewhere far away, he heard warbling sounds, and the world started slowly coming back into focus.

"Ben. Ben! Are you okay?"

The warbling sound belonged to Natalie. Ben lifted his head, then pushed himself up on his elbows. "Was ist los?" *What happened?*

A Plain woman, the one who had touched his forehead, leaned back on her heels beside the car, a stricken look on her face. "Sie is bletzlich umechdich warre." *You fainted suddenly.*

"Zwaar?" *Truly?* Argh. Not again. He felt himself color and shrugged, feigning nonchalance. "I had a bout of the flu recently. Still recovering, I guess." He tried to get himself up and felt two large hands under his arms, hoisting him to his feet. Still a little unsteady and more than a little embarrassed, Ben leaned one hand on the car, brushed himself off with the other. *What a way to meet people.* He turned to face the man who helped him up and realized this must be Micah. Tall and thin, more so than others had described him, but still a boy, Ben could see that. His eyes, mostly. They remained downcast, shy and reserved, even as the two shook hands. "So you're Micah Weaver. I'm Ben Zook."

The boy gave a brief nod. Just a brief, awkward nod of greeting, despite the fact that Ben had traveled a long distance to meet him. Over the last few years, Ben had heard Micah Weaver's name circulated around the Pennsylvania birding community, always with a sense of awe. Apparently, the boy had an uncanny ability

17

to spot birds, especially migrating ones blown off course during storms. Ben hoped Micah Weaver would live up to his reputation. He had a book manuscript due in, one that was on hold, waiting for this White-winged Tern.

Ben Zook had only two loves in his life. Books and birds. In a stroke of good fortune, he'd stumbled onto a way to cobble together those two loves into a career. He wrote books about rare birds. The market wasn't exactly mainstream, but there was a steady and faithful market for it, and for that he was grateful. As Natalie often pointed out, he'd bought himself a job. Happily it was work that he loved.

Penny Weaver, the woman who had first seemed frozen in shock at the sight of Ben, snapped out of her odd stupor and jumped into action. "Micah, would you take their luggage to the guesthouse? You must be thirsty from your travels. If you'll follow Micah to the guesthouse, I'll bring you something to refresh you."

Ben glanced at the Plain woman as she hurried off to the main house, half walking, half running. Scurrying. Just the way he remembered how Amish women moved. Quick, purposeful, no-nonsense. He felt strangely touched by her care for them, two strangers, until he remembered that this was a business arrangement and he owed her a sizable check for her hospitality—regardless of whether or not he was able to photograph that rare bird. The bishop had made that clear. He had retained Micah's help to find that bird, effectively stopping other birders from hiring him for the duration.

Micah lifted all their luggage like it was made of cotton balls and was halfway to the guesthouse as Ben reached into the trunk of the car to retrieve his optical equipment bag. That, he hadn't let Micah touch. He didn't let anyone touch it.

"Ben, are you all right?" His cousin looked at him with concerned eyes.

"I'm fine, Natalie. I just need some water. I didn't drink enough today."

"You spoke in tongues to Penny Weaver."

He scrunched his face in disbelief. "What?"

"You did! And she understood you too. It was freaky."

Oh no. Could he have spoken in Penn Dutch? No way. There was no way. He hadn't used the dialect since he left the Amish as a teenager. Hadn't spoken a single word of it.

"Well, believe it or not, you did." She looked around, sniffing, scrunching her face at the smell. "What reeks?"

He chuckled. "That is the sweet aroma of farm life." When her eyebrows knit together in confusion, he added, "Fertilizer." When she still looked puzzled, he added, "Manure on the fields."

"Oh."

That was common knowledge for a man who spent his childhood less than a mile away. A man who might've easily become an Amish farmer himself, were it not for his father.

But Penny Weaver and her brother Micah knew none of that, and he had no intention of telling them. He wouldn't lie, but he believed the past belonged in the past.

Besides, Ben had always loved change. After growing up in a town that never changed, he loved it even more. Stoney Ridge, in his opinion, was the kind of town that was better to come from than to stay in, but he wasn't really the staying type. He was a man on the move, all the time. Like a bird in that way, migrating eight months of the year.

He doubted there was anyone left in Stoney Ridge who might even remember him. So many, like his mother, had passed on, or moved away. Maybe that was the real reason he felt he could return at last. He could be here, could bag this rare bird, yet remain anonymous. He could stay on the fringes, irrelevant to a community that only cared about their own.

Then again, maybe he would've followed that bird anytime, anywhere. It was an extraordinary find—the first sighting of the Eurasian species in the United States this year and the first-ever reported in Pennsylvania. It was his nemesis bird. A bird that continually dipped him. "Fische un Yaage macht hungrigen Magen," he murmured. *Fishing and hunting make an empty stomach.*

He clapped his forehead. Why in the world did *that* saying pop into his head? It was one his father often said. The mind was such a strange thing. And how it affected the body—that was strange too.

The last year or so, Ben had felt a world-weariness that dampened his enthusiasm for most everything, even birding. He hoped this super rare White-winged Tern would snap him out of his funk. Assuming . . . the Micah Weaver kid could find it again. The way he slipped out of sight after dropping off their luggage in the guesthouse, Ben got a funny feeling he was as elusive as the bird.

～

Trudy Yoder. *She* was the one who had told Micah about the White-winged Tern. He'd taken the word of a fifteen-year-old girl. Stupid, stupid, stupid!

Trudy was absolutely positive she'd seen it, described it in great detail—startlingly specific. She'd never been wrong before. As annoying as Trudy could be in practically every way, she knew her birds. So Micah took her word for it without verifying the find with his own eyes and posted it as a confirmed sighting on the Rare Bird Alert. Then he added his own name to the confirmation.

News of the vagrant, spotted by Micah Weaver, traveled like wildfire.

That was when Micah got the first jab of guilt to his gut. A few days later, the moment lost even more of its shine when his sister Penny told him that a twitcher was coming to the farm, an author on bird books, expecting Micah to locate this rare bird like he could snap his fingers and it would appear. Paying him handsomely so he wouldn't take other birders out in the field. Micah had been out at dawn every morning, out again each twilight, regardless of the weather, trying to locate that bird. So far, nothing.

As a birder, he was honor bound to tell the truth. It was a cardinal value among those who loved birds. If you cheated about finding a rarity, who did you cheat? Even more important, he was honor bound to tell the truth because he was Plain. It was woven into the very fabric of his soul.

The whole thing made Micah feel sick to his stomach.

Why had he taken Trudy Yoder's word for it? He knew how easy it was to misread birds. He'd done it himself, many times. He certainly knew better than to post it on the Rare Bird Alert as a confirmed sighting, adding his name. In truth, only Trudy had seen the bird, so it should have remained an unconfirmed report. He should never have attached his name to it.

So what made him do such a shameful thing?

Because his reputation as a crackerjack field guide impressed others, especially Trudy's older sister, Shelley Yoder, who sang like an angel and looked like one too. Because spotting rare birds was easy for him, unlike getting words out from around his twisted-up tongue.

It was a sinful thing, a worldly thing, to act like he was a big somebody. But, as he well knew, it was even worse to be a nobody.

Micah Weaver, Bird-Watching Log

Name of Bird: *Green Heron*

Scientific Name: *Butorides virescens*

Status: *Common bird in steep decline*

Date: *March 5*

Location: *Farm pond on Beacon Hollow*

Description: *Adult male. Small and stocky with a daggerlike bill, thick neck, hunchbacked body, slender yellow legs. Velvet-green back and crown, a chestnut neck and breast.*

Bird Action: *Crows harassed the Green Heron as it performed display flights around its territory.*

Notes: *A migrant to Pennsylvania, the Green Heron is easy to overlook, shy, solitary, and secretive, skilled at concealing itself in its wetland surroundings. It lives around small bodies of fresh water—pond, marsh, river, creek, lake—and its diet is mostly fish. The Green Heron is one of just a few bird species that use tools. It drops feathers or insects or twigs on the water's surface to lure in fish. Pretty smart.*

During courtship display, the male loses his dignity. He stretches his neck forward and down and snaps his bill shut, or points his bill upward while swaying back and forth. He puts on a bird dance. This actually happens.

What female could resist?

2

It had always been a mystery to Penny why she felt such a powerful attachment to Ben Zook, from the moment she'd first laid eyes on him over twenty years ago. He still had an effect on her, a visceral effect. Her hands trembled and her stomach quivered, and she must've peered out the big bay kitchen window a hundred times to see if he was really, truly there, in the guesthouse at Lost Creek Farm.

When Penny was twelve, she'd spent a summer here on the farm with her grandmother, who taught her everything about birds. How to be so still as to become part of the bird's world. How to listen to a bird's distinctive call and song. How to identify birds by observing small details, like how its bill was shaped. That summer, she also taught Penny how to draw birds, using her keen eye and memory.

In the afternoons, her grandmother enjoyed a lengthy nap, so Penny would finish her chores with plenty of time left over to slip outdoors. She would hike up the ridge behind her grandmother's house, and there she found a world of birds to explore, all kinds.

She searched for new birds to report back to her grandmother: the Downy Woodpecker with its fine hairdo, a magnificent thatch of a red crest. The small Black-capped Chickadee, which was living proof to Penny that you didn't have to be big to be bold. The Blue Jay, a bit of a bully, but even more strikingly beautiful than the meek and timid orioles and tanagers.

It was during one of those afternoon hikes when she first laid eyes on the young Ben Zook. She was late heading home and took a shortcut, clattering down a steep embankment, startling a young man who was chopping up some trees downed in a recent storm. He had the most arresting face: high, sculptured cheekbones; a long narrow nose; wide-spaced eyes. Peeping under his straw hat was thick brown-black hair, the color of freshly plowed earth. His skin was milk pale. She couldn't take her eyes off him, wondering how she would draw such a face.

He tipped his head. "What's your hurry? You gonna scare the birds right out of the sky."

"No, I'd never do such a thing," she said, all earnest.

He pushed his straw hat back on his forehead. Blue eyes, she noticed. As blue as an Eastern Bluebird. Fringed with dark lashes. "Why not?" he asked.

"Because"—she couldn't stop studying his face—"I just wouldn't do anything to hurt a bird."

A wide smile spread over his face, and she couldn't help but smile in return. If a man could be pretty, he was. Clearly Plain. He probably knew her grandmother. Even still, she doubted her grandmother would want her to be talking to a grown man, even a Plain man, but especially such a pretty one. She backed away, gave him a curt nod, then ran up the hill to take the long way home.

The next day, she tried the shortcut again, and there he was, still hacking away at the fallen trees.

He paused and looked over his shoulder. "Hey, it's you again. You don't live around here, do you?"

She shook her head. "Just staying with my grandmother for the summer."

With a final stroke, he cut off a limb, then turned toward her. "You got a name?"

She crossed her arms behind her back, rocked left to right twice. "Penny."

"Penny . . . like the money?"

She nodded.

"Penny . . . like for your thoughts? Or a penny saved is a penny earned? Or penny wise and pound foolish? Or better still . . . ," and then he sang a few lines from a song that started with someone named Penny Lane. He laughed. "Guessing from the blank look on your face that you've never heard of the Beatles." He laid his saw against a branch. "I could have fun with your name."

She stared at him, mystified. No one had ever teased her about her name before.

"Ever heard this one? What did the quarter say to the penny?"

"I don't know."

"You don't make much cents." He grinned. "Get it? C-e-n-t-s."

She tucked her head, hiding her smile.

He gave her a crooked grin. "Call me Ben." He picked up the limb and tossed it on the woodpile. "So, Penny, I've seen you more than a few times, scaling that ridge like a mountain goat. Whatcha doing up there in the woods?"

He'd noticed her? "Me? I like to . . . go looking for birds."

He gave that crooked smile of surprise. "There's plenty of birds right here. Just go sit over by that martin house. It's a regular airport. Birds coming in and going out all day long."

She jabbed her thumb in the ridge's direction. "Different kinds up there."

"How so?"

"Well, there's an eagles' nest. Bigger than a buggy."

"You're pulling my leg."

"I'm not. Just saw it a few minutes ago. Eagles like to nest near water."

"There's no water up there."

"There is. A pond."

He wedged the saw into a tree branch. "Let's go."

Her eyes went wide. "Now?"

"Now. I want to see this mysterious pond. And I want to see a bird's nest that's supposed to be bigger than a buggy."

She hesitated, knowing her parents would disapprove. Yet there was something about this young man that she instinctively trusted. He seemed so terribly . . . sad. Even when he smiled, it never quite reached his eyes. So she pivoted and led him back up and over the ridge. He followed her quietly, and it felt strange to be leading a grown man somewhere. She didn't stop until they came to an overlook.

"Look." She pointed. "There it is."

He stared at the pond, enamored. "I've lived here all my life and never knew it was here."

"Might be new," Penny said. "There's a beaver's dam down that way. I call it Wonder Lake."

He gave a little snort. "More like a swamp." He tented his eyes with his hand. "But I'll grant you this. It must be a paradise for birds."

"There. See the eagle parents?" From this vantage point, they were nearly eye level to a dead tree in the middle of the pond that housed the enormous eagles' nest in a fork of its branches.

Ben's jaw dropped. "Well, I'll be. Son of a gun. You weren't fooling. That's bigger than any buggy I've ever seen."

He leaned against a rock, so Penny followed suit. She pointed out which was the mother eagle, bigger than the father. "They had an eaglet, but—"

"An eaglet?"

"A baby bird. They're called eaglets until they're fledglings. That's when their feathers start coming in. Anyway, they had just one, but it died."

"Oh. That's sad."

"People say that birds don't have emotions, but I think they do. Earlier today, the mother eagle sat on the edge of her nest and her husband tucked his head under her beak, like he was trying to comfort her. It was real . . . sweet. And sad. Sweet and sad."

"Bittersweet. That's the word for it."

"A bittersweet story." She gave a little shrug of her thin shoulders. "Every bird has a story."

"Every bird has a story," he echoed. He turned to look at her and watched her for a long while. "From now on I'm going to call you Penny-wise."

She rubbed the tops of her knobby knees. "I expect they'll be leaving the nest soon. No reason to stay."

His gaze went to the nest, fixed on it. "No, I suppose the reason to stay died along with the chick."

They watched awhile longer, until he said, "We'd better get back. Lots of work to do before the day ends."

"You're cutting up all those trees? All by yourself?"

"All by myself." He pushed himself off the rock. "My father likes to say"—he dropped his voice an octave and shook his chin like a billy goat—"bad thoughts and feelings, they come out with the sweat."

Penny couldn't imagine any bad thoughts and feelings needing to be expunged from such a beautiful, kind, gentle person like Ben Zook.

Many times that summer, she would take the shortcut to see if Ben was working on those dead trees. Most times in the afternoon, he was. When she saw him, she would step out of hiding and stand still, waiting for him to spot her. He would slowly turn around, as if he sensed she was there, and his face would light in a smile. Even his eyes. "Well, hello there, Penny-wise. What bird did you spot on this fine afternoon?"

He would swing his ax to wedge in the tree limb and tag along after her, always keeping a respectable distance. Songbirds he was familiar with—martins, robins, bluebirds, finches, cardinals—but she showed him birds he'd never seen before or, more likely, had never noticed. A Red-bellied Woodpecker, a White-breasted Nuthatch, a Tufted Titmouse with its peachy-colored flanks.

Ben Zook was so easy for Penny to be with. He would talk a

little, ask a few questions, but mostly he seemed to be genuinely interested in the birds. He talked a lot about the eagle parents, about losing their chick. She taught him all she'd been learning about eagles from her grandmother: eagles mated for life, both parents cared for the eggs and the chicks. When the chicks became fledglings, the parents started tearing up the inside of the nest so it wasn't quite so warm and cozy for those babies. Time to go, they were telling their fledglings. Time to make your own way.

One afternoon, they were sitting on what Penny called the resting rock, a large flat rock that overlooked the eagle nest. She'd been telling him about spark birds, that first bird that sparks an interest. When you get bit by the bug.

"Eagles," he said, eyes fixed on the large stick nest. Leaning forward, he rested his elbows on his knees and folded his hands. "Those are my spark birds. That's the moment I fell in love with a bird."

She looked at his profile. *Him.* Ben was her spark bird. That was the moment she knew what true love felt like. She was only twelve, but she knew. It had something to do with the way Ben listened to her, the way he looked at her. With great respect, as if her thoughts mattered.

The last time she saw Ben was the day they'd come back down the ridge after she'd shown him a Sandhill Crane, a precious rare bird in Pennsylvania. He told her to hold on, went to his wheelbarrow, and pulled out a pillowcase to hand to her.

"What is it?"

"Sunflower heads. Dried. From the garden. I thought you said most birds like 'em."

She opened the sack and her heart started to race. A gift. He had given her a *gift.* "Thank you, Ben," she said to him, her tone serious.

"You're very welcome, Penny-wise," he said, serious in return.

She looked up at him. "I'm leaving tomorrow. Back home in time for school. My father's coming to get me."

He seemed a little disappointed, but maybe she had just hoped he'd be sorry to hear she was leaving. "Well, I'll never see another bird without thinking of you, Penny-wise. Thank you for teaching me about them." He doffed his hat. "Keep looking for the rare ones." He went back to pick up his wheelbarrow and pushed it toward the barn. She watched him go, watched until he disappeared inside the barn door, and asked the Lord for a gift. She prayed that one day, when she grew up, Ben Zook would be her husband. He was the only one she would ever want. He was a once-in-a-lifetime man. A rare bird.

Penny didn't return to Stoney Ridge after that summer, but she never forgot about Ben. She never could. There was just something memorable about him, something that touched her heart. Then one spring day, when Penny was nineteen, she happened upon a bookstore. In the window was a display featuring books about birds. One, she noticed, was a book about rare birds written by Ben Zook. There was a picture on the back of the book. It was him. Her Ben Zook. She bought the book and fell in love with him all over again. Since then, she'd bought every book he'd ever written.

When she'd first returned to Stoney Ridge last fall, she discreetly inquired of Ben's whereabouts. She found out that he'd left home a few years after that summer they'd met and had never returned, not even for his mother's funeral. She took a meal to his father, out of kindness, and when she saw how lonely he was, how cast adrift he seemed, she started to visit him regularly. When the bishop learned that she was making those visits, he asked her if she would be willing to make meals for him, and do some housekeeping, laundry, and cleanup, for a wage. The bishop told her that Zeke Zook ran most people off his property, sure they were stealing from him, but he seemed to trust Penny. She would've helped Zeke Zook even without being paid, because she felt close to Ben when she was caring for his father. Being there, in Ben's childhood home, knit her heart to him. She imagined him running up and down those stairs as a boy, sitting at the kitchen table as a teenager, crossing the yard to the barn as a young man.

And now Ben Zook was here—still such a beautiful man with a tender affection for birds. He was back in Stoney Ridge at last. And staying on her property. She peeked out the window one last time, saw that the lights had gone out in the guesthouse, and so she went to bed. But she barely slept.

Her spark bird was back.

So quiet. Ben had forgotten how quiet life could be on an Amish farm. Now and then, familiar sounds would puncture the silence: the bark of a dog, the bawl of a dairy cow, the *clip-clop* of a horse and buggy along the road. Gentle and comforting sounds, especially compared to hearing gunshots blast away in the night while he was in Honduras recently.

He glanced at his watch. Past seven. He rolled out of bed and went into the bathroom, flicking on the light. He looked in the mirror. His eyes were bloodshot and his face raspy with beard stubble. The flu bug he'd been fighting since he'd returned from Honduras was back in full force, churning his belly.

He went into the living area to get a glass of water. The refrigerator had been stocked with some basics. Enough to make a sandwich for dinner together last night, and eggs for breakfast this morning, but he would have to get to a store. Then again, maybe Micah Weaver would help him find that White-winged Tern today and he'd be able to leave Stoney Ridge behind. The thought cheered him.

No sound came from Natalie's room, so it was safe to assume she was still asleep. It pleased him that his cousin had agreed to come with him, and even more so that she was able to rest, to truly rest. When she picked him up yesterday, she'd looked worn down. He worried about her. She'd taken it hard, that divorce from Joel the jerk. Natalie had asked him to please stop calling Joel a jerk, so he tried not to say it aloud. But Joel was a jerk. What kind of a man broke his wedding vows for another woman and made it sound like it was nothing more than turning in a car for the latest edition? A jerk.

He'd never been crazy about Joel. The guy was always dropping names, trying to impress. Still, Ben knew that his bias had little to do with Joel and everything to do with his loyalty to Natalie. Second cousins, but she'd always been like a little sister to him.

Ben grabbed his coat and binoculars, and opened the door to sit on the stoop, listening for birdsong, identifying their calls and songs before he could spot them. His favorite way to start the day.

He noticed Penny Weaver over on the side yard, hanging a brightly colored quilt on a clothesline. Almost as if she sensed he was there, she turned around, lifted her hand in a hesitant wave, then hurried into the house, as if the mere sight of him made her flustered. She had a slightly bewildered look, or maybe it was just the way she looked at him, as if he were a rare bird that had flown in to land at her bird feeder. Or maybe this was the way all Amish looked at those who weren't part of their clan. It occurred to him that he'd never been on the outside looking in before. He'd stayed away. Until now.

Today. Today was the day he would find that elusive bird. He rose, maybe a little too fast, and had to hold on to the porch railing for balance. First, he would have to track down the elusive Micah Weaver.

Micah Weaver, Bird-Watching Log

Name of Bird: *Bald Eagle*

Scientific Name: *Haliaeetus leucocephalus*

Status: *Low concern*

Date: *February 21 (first sighting this year)*

Location: *Wonder Lake*

Description: *Nesting pair*

Bird Action: *Male and female repairing nest from winter damage*

Notes: *Penny says this Bald Eagle nest—an aerie—has been at Wonder Lake for over twenty years, possibly longer. Today both eagles kept adding materials to it, but the female was in charge of where the sticks were placed. Each time the male brought something in—sticks for the outside or moss to line the inside—he would proudly set it in place. The female would wait patiently until he flew away and then move his latest acquisition to where she wanted it. Pretty smart lady.*

3

Micah had risen before dawn to continue his search for the White-winged Tern. He had stopped at the neighbor's phone shanty to check the Rare Bird Alert, hoping there'd been a sighting of it. Nothing, though there was a confirmed report of a Caspian Tern hovering around Blue Lake Pond, and he wondered if the White-winged Tern might be found nearby, especially during feeding time.

It occurred to him that Trudy might've mistakenly spotted the Caspian Tern, and if so, then he would seem like a complete fool to other birders. And if that wasn't enough to make him feel terrible, he worried he was growing prideful.

Three hours in the cold morning air weren't wasted: he spotted a Snow Goose that had been reported on the Rare Bird Alert but unconfirmed, a Long-billed Dowitcher, and a Black-crowned Night-Heron. He even saw the Caspian Tern, but not its distant relative, the White-winged Tern. The morning cheered him up, because after seeing the Caspian Tern, he had confidence that Trudy would know the difference between it and the White-winged Tern. Cousins, perhaps, but very different.

On his way home, he drove down a certain tree-lined road, and his horse, Junco, slowed to a walk as they passed the Yoders' farm. It was their habit. Micah came down this road each time he was out in the buggy even if he was heading in the opposite direction. He was always hoping for a glimpse of Shelley Yoder. Once she happened to be coming out of the phone shanty just as he passed, and when he tipped back the brim of his hat, she waved, giving him a friendly smile. That lifted his spirits for the rest of his day. One smile from Shelley Yoder could do that to a man.

Micah ran a hand along his whiskerless chin and peered out the side window for a sign of Shelley, but the farm looked deserted. He gave the reins a little shake, and Junco recognized the signal to pick up his pace into a fast trot. Micah's stomach rumbled. It was just as well that Shelley wasn't around. He was hungry as a bear and needed a shower.

And suddenly, running across the road to greet him was Shelley's younger sister, Trudy. He yanked on the reins, and the light buggy he was driving slewed to a stop, nearly running over Trudy and raising a whirlwind of dust. Normally, Micah took great pains to avoid Trudy, which wasn't easy, considering he was courting Shelley. Trying to, anyway. He hadn't gathered enough courage yet to ask her to go anywhere with him. But he planned to. Trudy, on the other hand, had a knack for being ever present. She found Micah wherever he happened to be, badgering him with endless questions, but she never stopped talking long enough for him to get the answer out.

She ran to his side of the buggy, a huge smile wreathing her face. "Look, Micah! Look what I found today." She held out her cupped palms to reveal a tiny hummingbird nest. "I don't think it's a Ruby-throated nest. Could it be a Rufous?"

He took it from her to examine. Too small a nest for a Rufous.

"I found it on a tree branch."

He gave her a sharp look.

"Now, don't give me that look. The branch was knocked down during yesterday's rainstorm."

"Any s-sign of the White-winged T-tern?"

"Nope. Haven't seen it since last week. Have you spotted it again?"

He shook his head, his eyes fixed on the nest in his hand. He passed it back to her.

"I'll let you know the minute I spot that White-winged Tern. The very minute, I'll come running. I know it's still here."

"How?"

"I just feel it in my bones." She frowned, peering at the nest in her hand. "You don't suppose . . . could it be? A Calliope?"

Slowly, he nodded. The Calliope Hummingbird was an accidental for Pennsylvania. Rare, but now and then, one or two would be spotted. It was unusual for it to breed here. "G-good find."

She smiled. "I thought so too." Her small eyebrows drew together, as if tugged by complicated thoughts. "At first I thought it might be a Bee Hummingbird, it's so small, but then I remembered that a Bee Hummingbird is the size of a bee, and they live in Cuba, which is far, far away, so I knew it couldn't be—"

Micah's grip on the reins shook a little and Junco jolted forward. He glanced in the mirror to see Trudy, staring at the nest like it was made of gold, still talking a blue streak. He wondered when she might realize he'd left. That girl could talk a gate off its hinges. He had to smile at the sight of her. Skinny as a rail. Brown hair wisping out of her prayer cap like feathers. Dress too short, she looked like a sandpiper with those long, skinny legs. Her eyes were dark, too big for her small, freckled face. Plain in the plainest sense, that was Trudy Yoder. She was nothing like her sister Shelley. It was like comparing a brown sparrow to that Black-backed Oriole that had come for a long stay at the farm.

A monarch butterfly crossed right in front of him, narrowly missing a collision with the buggy's windshield. Micah was impressed at how it veered out of the path so quickly. Monarchs were the only butterfly that migrated like birds, though different from birds in that they required successive generations to migrate. This one was probably the third in the line from far-off Mexico, where the monarchs gathered each winter. This one, he thought, would probably make it all the way from Canada to Mexico where its great-grandparents started off in the spring. Watching it out the buggy's open window, he wished it a safe journey.

～

Slowly, Natalie opened her eyes. The room wavered before her, hazy from sunlight streaming around the edges of the window shades. Where was she?

Then she remembered. She was somewhere on an Amish farm in the middle of nowhere with Ben. She shut her eyes again. Why had she agreed to join him on this lark?

Because her life was at a dead end. A complete stop. DOA.

Twenty-four hours ago, she was on the window seat in the kitchen, her legs curled underneath her. That's where she spent the bulk of her days, mostly staring out the window, watching the rest of the world carry on with their lives in a way she couldn't seem to do.

She was definitely not coping well with her grief, not in the way her cousin Ben—more like the brother she'd never had—expected her to be by now, not in the way she should be if she wanted to move on with her life.

In the midst of that surge of self-pity, Ben called from somewhere in Pennsylvania, where he'd been tracking migrating birds for a book. "Natalie . . . glad you picked up. The Rare Bird Alert said they think there's been a sighting of a vagrant over in Lancaster County. An unusual find. I'm driving back to your place to pack a few things, then planning to head over there."

She rolled her eyes. Ben and his birds. Then it struck her that he said he was going to head over to Lancaster County. Was he serious? She couldn't imagine he would ever, ever choose to return to the place he'd left behind. "Ben, slow down. Have you thought this through?"

"Thoroughly thought out. There's an Amish kid I've heard about who's supposed to be the best field guide in the state of Pennsylvania. He's the one who spotted this bird."

36

"An Amish farm. An Amish boy. All to find a silly bird that can't find its way home."

Silence. "There's nothing silly about birding, Natalie."

Oh yeah there was. "And you think that going back to an Amish farm is the way to do this?" *After how you felt when you first left? You vowed to never return.* Natalie well remembered.

"Here's an idea," he said, ignoring her objections. "How about if you come along with me?"

She sat straight up. "No way. If you recall how my life is a complete disaster, then you'll remember that I'm trying to find a job before my house gets foreclosed on."

"I'll give you the money you need to hold on to your house. There's no way I'd let it get foreclosed on."

Sweet, very sweet, but not practical. Not a lasting solution. Not when you're thirty-one years old, newly divorced, and deeply in debt. She couldn't expect Ben to keep bailing her out. She had to get her life figured out. "I'm pretty sure there's a job offer in the works. The interview went really well." Extremely well.

"That's great, Nat. Good for you. So . . . I'm planning to stay on this Amish farm while I'm out in the field, looking for this White-winged Tern. My publisher delayed my manuscript deadline so that I can add the story and photographs."

A *ping* from Natalie's computer indicated an email came in. She just had a feeling about this job—this would be the one. Jumping up from the kitchen seat, she bolted to her computer on the dining room table. Half listening to Ben ramble on about this bird that got blown off course in a storm, she read the email.

Natalie, I'm sorry to inform you that we've offered the design position to someone else. We feel you're overqualified for what our firm needs. Best wishes to you.

Overqualified, Natalie thought. *Last week I was told I was underqualified.*

Her shoulders slumped. *When will I ever catch a break?*

"Still there?"

Her cousin's voice jolted her back. "Still here."

"So what do you think? Want to come?"

"Want to come . . . where?"

"To the Amish farm. It'll be nice and peaceful and relaxing. Just a couple of days." He paused. "I'd really like your company, Natalie."

There was something in his voice that made her realize that for all his nonchalance, this trip wouldn't be easy for him. Her eyes flicked back to the email. "Yeah. Sure. Count me in."

And that was how she ended up on this Amish farm with that pungent tang of sour manure wafting through the air. She pulled the covers over her head and rolled over to go back to sleep.

～

Life was all about the constructive use of time: minutes until water in a kettle boiled, hours until the sun dried the laundry hanging on the clothesline, two days until Zeke Zook expected Penny to come by with a hot meal and kind word. Like all the women she knew, Penny was a person of activity, moving purposefully through every waking moment.

She turned off the stove burner and covered the large pot of cherry jam she'd been stirring. Her face was flushed from the heat of the stove, her dress and apron splattered with pink spots. This morning, she had awoken with a memory that Ben Zook had liked her cherry jam. More than liked it, he had raved about it. Whenever she had made it each springtime, she'd thought of him. Of bringing it to him on that summer day and how pleased he'd been, opening the jar right then and there to scoop it out with his finger. He'd pronounced it the best cherry jam in all the world over.

What a strange thing memory was. A certain smell, or taste, and touch of the breeze, and Penny was a young girl again. There were times when she wondered if this was a trace of the image of God placed in each human being—the ability to hold memories. To hold on to the feelings they evoked.

She wondered if Ben Zook might remember her after a taste of her cherry jam.

She shook her head. Foolish girl, she told herself, though at thirty-five she was hardly a girl. What was to be gained by trying to connect to Ben? She didn't know. She just couldn't help herself. It seemed as if decades had peeled away and she remembered the sheer joy of being with him up on that ridge, sharing her birds with him.

And suddenly, there Ben Zook was. She saw him through the kitchen window, peering through his binoculars at the humming-bird feeder she had hanging outside her kitchen. She wiped her hands on a dishrag, pushed some wisps of hair under her prayer cap, and hurried to the window to see what he'd seen.

At the feeder, Penny saw a male Ruby-throated Hummingbird, hovering. Then it darted away, off to find another food source. She saw Ben's binoculars drop to his chest, so she opened the door.

He walked toward her, giving her a charming smile. "Do you see the Ruby-throated Hummingbird very often?"

"Oh, I do." She tried to sound nonchalant, though her insides quivered like Jell-O. "They return each year to the same area."

The little bird whizzed past them again to hover near a potted salvia plant near the kitchen door and their eyes followed it like a magnet. "I was crossing the yard to your house when I heard it first. That buzzing sound of its whirling wings. The ears always come first. Most folks think watching birds starts with the eyes, then the binoculars. They're wrong. The ears come first. Listening, that's what bird-watching is all about."

She had taught him that! Long ago. Perhaps he *did* remember her.

"I don't mean to bother you . . . um . . . I'm sorry. I forgot your name."

Oh. So maybe he didn't. "Penny. Penny Weaver."

"Ah yes. Penny Weaver, that's right. I should remember that, seeing as how I've come here for a young field guide named Micah Weaver."

"Micah is my brother."

"Yes. I remember that. By the way, where is he?"

"He went out looking for the bird this morning."

Ben frowned. "I missed him?"

"He left before dawn. I thought he'd told you." She should have double-checked that with Micah.

"Let him know, please, that I'm looking for him. I'd like Micah to take me out to see it as soon as possible. As soon as he returns."

"I'll tell him, but it's hard to say when he'll be back. I know he wanted to be sure to identify the bird's general location for you." She looked up at the blue sky. "We've had such a mild autumn that there's an unusual variety of migrants lingering on their stopovers. It's been a birder's dream come true."

"Yes. Yes, exactly." Ben rubbed his forehead, as if a headache was coming on. "Then, let Micah know I want to go out in the field with him tomorrow morning. Even if he doesn't find the tern today, I'll help him find it tomorrow."

"Tomorrow? But that's Sunday. The Lord's Day. Micah won't work on the Sabbath."

For a moment he said nothing, and his mouth took on a tight, stern look. Then he sighed. "I forgot. Monday, then."

"Tomorrow is an off-Sunday, but next week, you'd be welcome at our church."

"No." He paused, and something almost like yearning appeared in his blue eyes. Just like that, the look was gone, swallowed up. "No, but thank you for the invitation." His gaze shifted to the road. "One other thing, is there a grocery store nearby?"

"There's a Bent N' Dent just up the road."

"Amish?"

"Yes."

"Guess I'd better get there today, then, and not tomorrow." His mouth pulled up at one corner, but it wasn't quite a smile.

It occurred to her that he was trying to be friendly. She thought she should try a bit of friendliness herself. He was a guest at her farm, after all. Penny fiddled with her hands, searching for a subject. Then she smelled it. "Jam! Um . . . I'm in the middle of making cherry jam. I'll bring a jar to the guesthouse, if you like."

"No kidding? I haven't had cherry jam . . . well, it's been so long I can't even remember. Thank you. I'd enjoy it." He stared at her in that intense way of his, and she could feel the color building in her cheeks. "Is there a Mr. Weaver?"

"No."

"So, you and Micah, you're on your own, then?"

Slowly, she nodded. "He's my brother."

"I see. I'll let you get back to your jam making." He took a few steps, then pivoted. "Penny, do I make you nervous?"

"Nervous?"

"You seem a little flustered around me."

She touched the back of her neck. "Do I?" Of course she did! He made her feel a dizziness in the pit of her belly, the kind of feeling she'd get when the horse and buggy went around a downhill curve too fast. Dangerous, but exciting.

He grinned. "There's no reason to be nervous around me." He lifted his hands in the air. "I'm entirely harmless." The hummingbird came back again for more of the potted salvia's nectar, and they both watched it feed, one flower to another to another, its wings beating so quickly they were almost invisible. In a voice so gentle it nearly hurt, he said, "Do you ever wonder if birds feel joy?"

"That I don't know," she said, forgetting her unsettled feelings for a brief moment. "But I know they give joy."

Their eyes locked. Penny was the one to turn away first.

She slowly backed through the open door, closed it, then leaned against it and squeezed her eyes shut. She *was* nervous. Flustered too. Everything about Ben made her trembly inside. She had never thought she'd see him again . . . and here he was, staying at her farm. Wonders never ceased.

But that look in his eyes when she'd invited him to church sent a chill right down her spine. Ben Zook had wandered far, she knew that, but now she understood he had also wandered far from his faith. Surely God must be at work. A rare bird had brought Ben Zook back. This, she thought to herself, would be interesting. For just as the songless hummingbird had found a way to be heard, God always found a way too.

Micah Weaver, Bird-Watching Log

Name of Bird: Ruby-throated Hummingbird
Scientific Name: Archilochus colubris
Status: Low concern
Date: May 30
Location: Penny's hanging hummingbird feeder near kitchen bay window
Description: Adult male. Long wings and bill, ruby-red throat, white collar, emerald-green crown, back, and forked tail.
Bird Action: Chased away other hummingbirds at the feeder.
Notes: Only hummingbird to breed in Pennsylvania. Nests are very fragile and don't last past a single breeding season. The nest is made of feathers, twigs, and bits of leaves, then spider silk is threaded to bind the nest together and anchor it to the foundation of the tree. The bird lays two eggs, each about the size of a coffee bean. The nest has a spongy, velvety floor, with elastic sides that curve slightly inward like a cup. This clever design protects the eggs from falling out. Later, the nest can stretch as the young chicks grow.

Pretty astounding engineering feat by a tiny bird that weighs less than a nickel.

4

Natalie knew she should get up. Throw off the covers and face the day. *Time to make a new plan, ol' girl, cuz the old plan sure didn't work out.* It still baffled her how things started so well and went so sideways.

Natalie and her husband Joel had created a successful house flipping business. Early in their marriage, they had attended a land auction on a whim and ended up buying a foreclosed-on dump of a house in a historical neighborhood in downtown Philadelphia. A true eyesore. They spent all their spare time, energy, and money turning it into a showplace. The final result was stunning, so much so that it was featured in a local magazine. It caught the attention of a local cable television host, Sophia Parker. She asked the couple to do a complete makeover of her city townhouse, sharing stories and videos of the ongoing renovations on her morning talk show.

Almost overnight, Natalie and Joel had more work than they could've ever imagined. But they loved it. They were passionate about it. Joel handled the construction side of the business, Natalie handled the design side. Looking back with hindsight, she could see they were getting spread too thin. The demands on their time were constant. Any romance in their young marriage was fading away; they were reduced to worn-out roommates who coexisted, exhausted and drained. Yet it didn't occur to them to turn down a new project. Instead, they hired more helpers.

Why didn't they ever say no? The answer, she heard a little voice inside her say, was that it seemed as though there should be, could be . . . more. They added more and more branches to their business—home staging, design services, construction crews, tradesmen. Even then, it didn't feel like enough. And the bottom line was that they loved it. They both loved their work.

Over a year ago, when a film production company contacted Joel for a television pilot, they never even had to discuss it—they both jumped at the chance. Unbeknownst to the production company, they'd had a few setbacks and were late on vendor payments for the last few months. They weren't entirely sure that, this month, they could make payroll. If the pilot were picked up, this television series could be the golden ticket they desperately needed.

They were *this* close. *This* close! And then it all fell apart.

Just before filming, they found out that their controller quit without notice and left town. As they scrambled to fill his role and responsibilities, Joel discovered evidence that he'd been siphoning money from the company. A lot of it.

Exhausted, anxious, upset, Natalie and Joel tried their best to get through the making of the pilot, but even Natalie could sense it fell flat. By Sunday evening, the director—a woman who looked like she was barely out of high school—pulled Joel aside and said they just didn't translate well as a couple onto film. But, she said, would he consider doing a pilot alone?

Joel didn't even consider saying no.

Nor did he say no, a few months later, to leaving Natalie in order to move in with that director, either.

At least Natalie still had her house. She loved her little house, the first house she'd redesigned. The place where it all began.

With a sigh, she kicked off the covers and got up, grabbed her robe, and went to get coffee in the mini-kitchen. The door leading outside was left slightly ajar, and she saw Ben sitting on the step. "Morning."

He shifted. "Good morning to you. Sleep okay?"

"I woke in the night a lot. It's so quiet here."

"So quiet."

"How are you feeling today? You know, after fainting yesterday. You still look pale." Pasty white, in fact.

He frowned. "Just got up a little too fast, that's all."

She refilled his mug with coffee. "Ben, I've been thinking. I should probably head back to Philadelphia. As soon as you catch that bird, give me a call and I'll come back for you."

A look of alarm covered his face. "Give it a chance. I think you might be surprised at how good it can feel to get a little fresh scenery. I won't need more than a few days to find that bird, assuming this warm weather holds up. And assuming Micah Weaver turns up."

"He's gone?"

Another frown. "Left before daybreak."

"Why does it matter if the weather stays warm?"

"Migrating birds linger if there's food resources. In the spring, they hurry along to their breeding areas. But in the fall, they can take plenty of sweet time to head back to where they winter." He glanced at her. "Stay."

"It's just . . . I really should be job hunting." But it wasn't just that. This was the first time she'd been overnight from her house since the divorce, and she felt a pull to return, like it was the only place she felt safe.

"You shouldn't be working for anyone else. You could be your own boss."

Not this again. Natalie spun around to return the coffeepot to the stove top. Ben wanted her to brush herself off and get back in the saddle. How could she do that when she was still on the ground, wondering how she'd allowed herself to get bucked off the horse in the first place?

This last year, facing one hard thing after the other, her creative spark had been doused, stifled, like water poured on fire. She had no new ideas, no interest in designing, no desire to shop. Not even to *shop*. Her favorite thing.

"Just give some thought to staying, okay? I'm going out for a bit. There's a grocery store down the road. I'm going to pick up a few things."

She watched Ben walk to the car with keys in one hand, binoculars in another. That was Ben. What must it be like to have such a single focus? To have never been attached to anyone, only to his passion for birds.

A couple of times a year, Ben would appear from wherever he'd been to use Natalie's house as a base to meet with his publisher and do whatever it was a bird author did. Their mothers were cousins, although Natalie's branch of the family tree had left their Amish roots long ago. One day Ben appeared on Natalie's mother's doorstep, determined to never return, so they took him in, no questions asked. Natalie helped him get ready for his high school equivalency test, then encouraged him to try junior college along with her. They became like siblings to each other.

Natalie took a sip of coffee and appraised the guesthouse. The interior was a cheerless place. Roomy but spartan, airy but ordinary, and nothing matched. Not the wooden chairs around the table, not the dinner dishes nor the flatware. It felt as if everything in this big house came from a grandmother's yard sale. Bland. Plain. Drab.

Natalie wondered if blandness was an Amish woman's lot in life. Her burden to bear. No choices, no creativity, no unique personality. No color. A black-and-white world, like her wardrobe.

Natalie felt that way herself, of late. She didn't like the feeling. In fact, it was awful.

She refilled her coffee cup and peered out the window. Birds of all kinds sailed and dipped in the sky above. She smiled. Ben's version of Heaven.

Something brightly colored fluttered and caught her eye. She leaned closer to the window to look far to the right. Billowing in the breeze was a row of colorful quilts hanging on a clothesline.

Intrigued, Natalie walked out the door and into the yard to get a better look. Her breath caught, first in surprise and then in wonder. Each hanging quilt was more beautiful than the one before it. Jewel-like colors in geometric designs, sparkling in the sun almost like diamonds. She stared at them, mesmerized. Entranced. The quilts were such a disconnect, a mismatch, to all the plainness, the black-and-whiteness that she'd seen at Lost Creek Farm since she'd arrived. Micah's acute shyness. Penny's dreary clothing. The guesthouse's spartan simplicity.

Something about those quilts broke through Natalie's depression, her self-pity, her gray cloud. Something inside her bubbled with joy. She smiled. Maybe she would stay.

Ben followed the directions of Penny Weaver and drove to the Bent N' Dent to stock up on some groceries. Walking up and down the dimly lit aisles brought back a flood of memories from his youth. The modest business had a new owner, but it had once been a store his family frequented. Though when Ben was a boy, he'd never see boxes of cereal or bins of candy—*so* much candy. There wouldn't have been refrigerated cases full of paper cartons of pasteurized milk, not with all the dairy farmers in the area at that time. Even still, there was much that was the same about the place. The smell of dried spices, for one. As a boy, he imagined himself in India whenever he came in the store, breathing deeply of exotic scents.

As a man, he'd been to India, many times. It did not smell of dried spices.

Walking down the canned goods aisle, he now understood the name of the store. Each can on the shelf had a dent or torn labels.

Then he came to an entire shelf of tin cans with no labels at all. They were being sold for a dime. He picked one can up and shook it. Peas? Corn? Something small and loose and watery. He tossed it in his shopping basket, smiling at the thought of Natalie's shocked face when she unpacked the bag of groceries.

"Well, SKIN me for a POLECAT."

Ben froze.

"If it isn't BEN ZOOK."

That *voice*. That loud voice. He looked up to see a thin, flinty man staring at him. One eye stared, anyway. The other one drifted to the left. He looked older, but still much the same. Unforgettable. The one and only Hank Lapp. "Hello, Hank."

"SO the WANDERING BIRD has COME HOME AGAIN."

Ben glanced around the store. There weren't many in it, but a middle-aged man at the register—the store owner?—watched them. "Hank, could you lower your voice?"

"WHAT do you MEAN? I'M PRACTICALLY WHISPER-ING." His belly exploded with a laugh so loud, so ribald, that the rest of the store took note.

Ben noticed the store owner continue to appraise him with a curious look on his face. He set the basket down. "Let's go outside for a moment."

On the porch, Hank sat down in a rocker and pointed to the other rocker. "I recognized you THE MINUTE I saw you. SAME BEN." He whipped off his black hat to reveal wild white hair and raked a hand over his head. "SAME ME. SNOW on the ROOF but FIRE in the FURNACE."

Reluctantly, Ben eased into the rocker but didn't quite relax. Nothing like Hank, whose body seemed molded to the chair. He had a hunch Hank spent a lot of time in that chair. "So, Hank, how have you been?"

"OUTSTANDING! Married late in life to a catch, a REAL catch. EDITH YODER FISHER LAPP. Paradise on EARTH, that's what our marriage is. WEDDED BLISS."

Ben's jaw dropped. Edith Fisher? Now Lapp? Ben had always been terrified of her. Everyone was. He cleared his throat. "Well, good for you, Hank. Funny, I always took you for a devoted bachelor."

"I WAS. Running fast until EDITH caught me!" Hank laughed, as if he'd made a great joke.

Hard to imagine Edith and Hank together, but Ben felt an unexpected tinge of envy at Hank's obvious happiness.

"WHAT ABOUT YOU? Not Plain, I see." Before Ben could say anything, Hank added, "I thought you'd COME BACK for your own mother's funeral."

Ouch. Hank might not have intended it, but he hit the bull's-eye on a sore spot for Ben, a great regret. The Amish bury their dead within three days. Ben was in Brazil, and by the time he learned of his mother's death, two weeks had passed. The shame he felt had yet to pass. Attending his mother's funeral was the last gift he could have given her. Maybe the only gift. "I was in South America, doing research. I didn't get word until it was too late." A wave of weariness wafted through him. He took a minute to let it pass, glad he was seated. Yesterday's fainting spell alarmed him. He couldn't shake this flu bug.

"SO you've flown BACK to the NEST."

Ben shook his head. "Just a visit. Real quick. I'm after a rare bird. Bag the bird and away I go."

"A RARE BIRD? You need to talk to—"

"Micah Weaver."

"THAT'S HIM." Hank tapped his head. "BEST BIRDER AROUND. He's got the TOUCH. Folks think he may be a little . . ." He frowned. "Mopskopp."

Stupid? "Why would anyone think that?"

"'Cuz of the WAY he TALKS, o'course."

But Micah didn't talk yesterday. Said not a word. Maybe that's what Hank meant. "While I'm in Stoney Ridge, I'd like to keep my . . . presence . . . quiet."

50

Hank stared at him.

Ben thought it was a stare, anyway. Hard to tell. "You understand, don't you?" It wasn't easy for Ben to leave. It was even harder to stay.

Hank leaned forward in the rocker and slapped his knees. "LIKE a BLACKPOLL WARBLER."

Ben's head jerked up. "How's that?"

"They WANDER a long way from HOME. But somehow they ALWAYS get back to where they're MEANT to be." He rose. "Well, Edith always says, you can TAKE the MAN out of the PLAIN, but you can't take the PLAIN out of the man." He doffed his hat. "Your SECRET'S SAFE with me. GLAD you're back, BEN." He took a few steps, then pivoted. He sauntered down the steps and over to a mule hitched to a cart. He hopped into the cart, stood in the front, picked up the mule's reins, and started down the road.

Suddenly Ben had a flashback of being a boy, watching Hank drive a mule in a cart all over town. He smiled at the memory, a smile that came from his heart.

The door opened and the store owner crossed the threshold, leaning against the doorjamb. "One of a kind, that's our Hank Lapp."

"Isn't that the truth," Ben said.

"I'm David Stoltzfus," he said, offering his hand to Ben. "I believe we spoke on the phone. You're the birder who was looking for Micah Weaver."

Ben rose and shook his hand. "If you're the man I spoke to on the phone, then I suppose that means you're the bishop."

"That's right." David smiled, a gentle smile. "Welcome to Stoney Ridge. Please let me know if there's anything we can do to help you while you're here. Anything at all."

Tears pricked Ben's eyes and he had to look away. He hadn't expected this. The kindness in this man's eyes. Meeting up with Hank Lapp. He hadn't expected to feel welcomed. Another wave of weariness hit him, like a hard punch to the stomach, and he had to sit down, fast, before he passed out again.

～～～

Natalie wandered all around Lost Creek Farm while waiting for Ben to return from the grocery store. It was tidy and well-kept, and she thought she'd ask Penny if she could take photographs. She knew photographs were taboo among the Amish, though she was never clear on why. She had walked all the way down to the road when a horse and buggy turned into the driveway. Micah!

She waved him to a stop. "Hi there. Mind if I hitch a ride up the hill with you?"

She didn't wait for Micah to respond but hopped right in beside him. He looked a little surprised, but then he made a clucking sound with his teeth and the horse started up again.

"I'm Natalie. You're Micah, right? The field guide?"

He grunted.

"Ben is crazy about birds. Like . . . over-the-top crazy. He follows birds all around the world. Writes loads of books about them." She waited for a response from Micah, but none came, so she picked up where she left off. "I bet he's been to nearly every country in the entire world. All to find birds." She glanced at him. "You must feel the same way about birds."

He made a sound that could have meant anything.

"Ben's here for some special bird, he said. A rare bird, he called it, though it seems like most of the birds he chases after are rare birds. This one was . . . oh, I can't remember its name. What was it . . . ?" She let the end of her thought dangle open for him to finish off, knowing he knew the answer.

Eyes on the windshield, he said, "White-winged T-tern."

She slid another glance at him. "That's it. Exactly right. Sorry, I'm not a bird person. One bird is the same as another to me."

Micah didn't respond, but she knew, from the way his eyebrows shot up, that he was appalled. Ben always was, whenever she made that remark. It was the truth, though. Birds were birds. "Ben said it's the first time that a White-winged Tern has been sighted in the United States."

At that, he shook his head. "F-first t-time in P-Pennsylvania."

"Oh, right. Ben's been working on a book about birds in Pennsylvania. It's kind of nice, having him stick around for a while. He's usually not around for more than a couple of days." She moved her hand in the air like an airplane taking off. "Then he's gone again."

Micah glanced at her now and then, just enough so she knew he was listening. He didn't seem to mind her talking. Nearing the crest, the horse slowed down quite a bit. "Should I hop out? Maybe I'm adding too much weight for the poor horsie to pull."

A smile tugged at Micah's mouth. "Nah. Junco can g-git lazy."

Natalie grinned. She was finally squeezing more than a grunt or a single syllable out of him. He seemed nice, this boy. "I thought I'd ask your sister if I could take pictures of the farm. Not of the people, of course. I realize that. But do you think she'd mind?"

He gave a slight shake of his head.

"There's a client in Philadelphia who is crazy about the Amish. Certifiably *crazy*. I'd love to show her pictures of Lost Creek Farm. She would swoon." To call Sophia Parker a client as if Natalie was in the middle of a project with her, well, that was stretching things quite a bit. But she had been a client once, and she had been happy with Natalie. Happier with Joel, that Natalie remembered too.

It had always struck Natalie as ironic that Sophia felt so drawn to the simple lifestyle of the Amish when her own life was anything but. Earlier this morning, when Natalie was staring at those beautiful hanging Amish quilts, it dawned on her that Sophia might be influential in helping Natalie find a job.

Nearing the top of the driveway, Natalie was surprised that Ben and her car were still gone. "What time do you think it is? My cell phone gets no reception. Nada."

He peered up at the sky, then held up two fingers.

"Two o'clock? Already? He left hours ago."

Micah pulled the buggy to a stop near the guesthouse.

As she hopped out, she turned to him. "Thank you, Micah. That was my first buggy ride. I'll always remember it."

"Schlecht g-gfaahre is b-besser as gut geloffe."

She scrunched up her face. "Huh? What does that mean?"

"A b-bad ride is b-better than walking."

She laughed. "That wasn't a bad ride. A little bumpy, that I can't deny. But you're a fine taxi driver. Most excellent."

He blushed, which she thought was charming.

Beyond him, she saw a pickup truck head up the steep driveway. "Who's that?"

Micah turned to see. "Our v-vet."

Out of the pickup truck emerged a tall, broad-shouldered man with hair the color of summer hay. He waved his hands in the air to catch their attention. "Micah, there's a fellow at the Bent N' Dent who passed out. He's okay now. He's over at Dok Stoltzfus's. Says he's been staying here. They sent me to fetch his cousin and bring her down."

Natalie lifted her hand. "That'd be me."

"You? You're his cousin?" The vet hesitated and gave Natalie a quick up-and-down glance. "My cousins sure don't look like that." He flashed her a dazzling smile.

Natalie shrank back. Was he flirting with her? He was rather attractive, she noticed, in an outdoorsy lumberjack way. About her age, maybe a little older.

His eyes were still on Natalie. "I'll take you down to Dok's."

"I'm coming too."

They all turned to see Penny Weaver, hands gripped together, worry on her face. "If there's room in the truck, that is. Ben Zook is staying in our guesthouse. I feel a little"—she cleared her throat—"responsible for him."

"Of course, Penny," the vet said, his voice gentle. "Plenty of room for you." He strode toward his truck and opened the door to the cab, bowing with a flourish of his hand. "Ladies, my chariot awaits."

~

Penny's stomach twisted and turned on the drive, though some of that probably had to do with Boyd Baldwin's bouncy truck. She sat between Boyd and Natalie, and it occurred to her that, knowing Micah, they were never introduced. "Natalie, this is our local vet, Boyd Baldwin. Boyd, Natalie is staying in the guesthouse with her cousin. He's here to find a rare bird."

His left hand on the wheel, Boyd leaned around Penny's middle to offer a handshake to Natalie. "So this guy is your cousin?"

"Yes. More like a brother."

Penny listened carefully, wondering about Natalie's family. Wondering about Ben's family. Did he have a wife? Any children? She wouldn't ask, though. She would not ask. "Should we call someone about Ben?" she asked.

"No," Natalie said. "I'm all he has."

"Which is quite a bit," Boyd said, and Natalie turned to look at him, just as he looked at her. And in that moment Penny, stuck in the middle, sensed something flash between the two of them. She felt a smile tug at her lips, like she had found herself accidentally caught in the middle of something private.

Interesting, Penny thought. She'd always thought of Boyd as a Great Horned Owl, wise and cautious. Farmers loved him for his soothing manner, animals settled quickly at the sound of his voice, low and calm, his movements slow. In a farming community, few people were trusted more than a local veterinarian. Boyd, more than most. He came at any hour he was called, and handled each animal, big or small, with the utmost care.

Maybe that deliberateness, Penny wondered, was why he hadn't married. Boyd was known around Stoney Ridge as a dedicated bachelor. *If only he were Plain* started many conversations among the women of Stoney Ridge, followed by a shrug. But Plain or not, they all counted heavily on him.

As soon as Boyd pulled into Dok's parking lot, the three hurried inside to the waiting room. Ruthie, Dok's receptionist, looked up from her desk. "She's with him now in the examining room."

"Is my cousin okay?" Natalie asked.

"Dok's running some tests. She'll let you know more." Ruthie hesitated. "But yes, he's conscious and talking and wants to go home."

Natalie let out an exaggerated sigh of relief and plopped in a chair. "Thank God. I can't lose him. Not now."

Funny, Penny thought. *I was thinking the same thing.*

Micah Weaver, Bird-Watching Log

Name of Bird: Blackpoll Warbler

Scientific Name: Setophaga striata

Status: Endangered

Date: September 20

Location: Thicket of spruce trees along ridge overlooking Wonder Lake

Description: Adult male. Small songbird. Thin pointed bill, black crown, white face, black streaking on back and flanks. Yellow legs.

Bird Action: Foraging for food like it hadn't eaten in days, which it probably hadn't. Guessing it was on a brief stopover on its southern migratory flight. A warbler being a warbler, it didn't stick around long.

Notes: The Blackpoll Warbler isn't really a dazzler, but it makes the longest overwater journey of any songbird. Its roundtrip journey is 12,400 miles!

It winters in Puerto Rico, the Lesser Antilles, and northern South American countries—Colombia, Venezuela, Guyana, and Brazil. Not surprisingly, it needs to eat enough to double its body mass in preparation for migration.

Each spring, it makes a daring nonstop journey across the Atlantic Ocean to reach breeding grounds in the boreal forests of Canada—

A Season on the Wind

a journey that takes only two to three days. That little bird must feel like it's been shot from a sling.

In the fall, it's not in such a hurry to return. It's raised its young, food resources are plentiful. Making stops along the way, it might take as long as six to eight weeks to return to its winter grounds.

Unbelievable for a bird that doesn't weigh much more than an empty soda can.

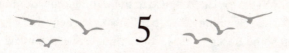

5

Waiting for medical news was awful, just awful. The clock on the wall slowed to a crawl. Natalie couldn't bear the thought of anything being seriously wrong with Ben. He was active and fit, healthy as an ox. She couldn't even remember him having a cold or a headache or a cavity. Something, though, seemed a little off lately. He tired easily, and there were times he seemed to break out in a sweat for no good reason, like a fever had come and gone. She'd suggested he go to the doctor while in Philadelphia, but he refused. So stubborn! Stubborn as a mule.

The handsome vet had gone over to the Bent N' Dent. Had to get something, he said. Natalie wondered if he'd come back at all—he must have better things to do than sitting in a waiting room with Penny and her. But a few minutes later, he returned with a brown paper bag and held it open to Natalie. She looked up curiously.

"Fern Lapp's Apple Cider Baked Donuts," he said. "The world's best."

"Well, in that case, I'll try one." She picked up a donut and took a bite, chewing it slowly, savoring the flavor. "Wow," she said. "I didn't know a donut could be this good."

"Welcome to the Amish." When he grinned, his eyes crinkled at the corners.

She couldn't help but smile in return. His eyes were blue. Too blue. Nothing could be that blue.

~

Penny had edged herself next to the waiting room door in order to make herself unobtrusive, but it also gave her a vantage point to watch and observe, her favorite things. She was intrigued by the interaction of Boyd and Natalie. If she thought of Boyd as an owl, Penny would choose a Sun Conure parrot for Natalie with the rainbow covering its body. Red, yellow, orange on their heads, chests, and wings. Green and blue on their tails and flight feathers. They could be as loud as they were brightly colored, and they weren't shy about vocalizing to express their mood. She'd read all about Sun Conures in one of Ben's books.

Natalie wasn't loud, though, other than that shocking spiked-up hair. But her moods, Penny sensed those were quite transparent. Earlier today, while she was out hanging laundry, Natalie joined her. She loved the colorful quilts and had all kinds of questions about them. She volunteered intimate personal information that Penny found to be rather appalling, yet at the same time fascinating. Natalie had been depressed since her divorce, she told Penny. Her creativity had been stifled. Quenched. On top of everything, she was facing a mountain of debts.

Penny didn't even know how to respond. Such openness made her uncomfortable, though there was a part of her that envied it as well. The Amish were such notoriously private people.

Just then Dok Stoltzfus emerged with Ben behind her, a sheepish look on his face. Penny remained in her chair, letting Natalie fuss over him, though her eyes took him in, appraising his condition. He seemed fine, clearheaded, standing tall, definitely embarrassed.

Before Dok said a word, Boyd Baldwin rose and went to the door. "This is a family affair. I'll be off. I've got calls to make."

Penny saw him give one last look at Natalie, wiggling his eyebrows, before he went out the door.

Then Dok took charge. She looked at Natalie. "You're his closest relative?" She barely gave a nod and Dok plunged right in. "I won't get the results from a blood test until Monday, but I'm fairly certain he's gotten malaria from a recent international trip."

"But I thought you could only get malaria in Africa," Natalie said. "You hadn't gone there recently, had you, Ben?"

"Honduras," Ben said. "I must've gotten bit by mosquitos."

Dok held up a finger. "All it takes is one."

Natalie gave Ben a gentle jab with an elbow. "You never complained about feeling sick."

He rocked his hand back and forth. "Good days and bad days."

"Malaria is curable, right?" Natalie said.

"If it's been caught early, diagnosed properly, and treated correctly," Dok said. "And I think it has. I'll start him on a course of antimalarial drugs. And he'll need a lot of rest."

"That settles it," Natalie said. "Bird or no bird, Ben, we should get you back to Philadelphia."

No! Not yet. Penny's gaze fell to her lap, where she was gripping and releasing, gripping and releasing, small handfuls of her apron.

"I can't go," Ben said. "I'm *this* close to that White-winged Tern. I'm not leaving until I see it. It'll only be here for a short time. As soon as I find that bird, I can finish up the book and send it off to the publisher. Then I'll rest."

"Mr. Zook," Dok said in a warning voice, "you can't push yourself. Malaria can be chronic and have lingering consequences, like anemia. Parasites can nest in the liver and avoid getting killed by drugs and recur whenever they feel like it and keep a person below par for the rest of their life. I don't mean to frighten you—" She paused. "Well, frankly, yes I do. Malaria is nothing to mess around with. I'm serious about getting complete rest. At least one solid week of no physical activity."

"Listen to your doctor." Natalie poked Ben with her elbow. "Ben, we need to get back to Philadelphia. Frankly, I need to get back and keep job hunting. Your publisher will understand."

"He won't. I've already delayed the manuscript for this bird."

Lord! Penny quickly shot up a prayer for help. *You didn't bring Ben home again just to have him leave. Please don't let him undo the good work you've been doing.* "He could stay."

Dok, Natalie, and Ben swung around to look at Penny, sitting quietly by the door.

"Lost Creek Farm," she said, trying to sound nonchalant when her throat felt dry as a desert. "It's a good place to recuperate. Quiet and peaceful."

"We can't ask that of you," Natalie said.

Oh yes, you can. You most definitely can. Penny looked from Ben to Natalie, unsure of what more to say. "Micah and I, we can look after him."

Ben's eyes flitted uncomfortably from Penny to the doctor. Penny thought he might be debating which excuse to use. But then he surprised her by saying, "It would be a big help to me."

"Penny," Dok said, "are you sure?"

"I'm sure."

A smile of relief covered Ben's face. "This way, as soon as I'm up to it, Micah can take me out to see the bird." He clapped his hands. "Sounds like a plan to me. I promise not to cause you any extra trouble. You can charge me double for the inconvenience."

"Charge him triple," Natalie said, frowning. "And the doctor has to give him the green light before he starts chasing birds."

Dok lifted her hands in surrender. "As long as Penny keeps an eye on him, I'm satisfied."

Oh, Penny planned to. She definitely planned to.

Ben turned to Natalie. "Then let's be off. Back to Lost Creek Farm."

"Sounds fine to me." Penny barely held back a smile. *Thank you, Lord.*

After returning to Lost Creek Farm, Natalie made sure Ben went to his room to lie down at the guesthouse, then she hurried to the big house to give Penny Weaver a list of instructions. She sat at the kitchen table, drinking a cup of tea, and warned Penny to not let Ben trick her into thinking he was well. "Don't let him leave this farm without the doctor's permission."

She was surprised at how readily this young Amish woman agreed to everything she asked of her. So kind, she thought. Ben was a stranger to Penny Weaver, yet she couldn't be more solicitous. There was a lot to be said for those qualities. Natalie felt good about leaving Ben in this woman's care.

She also inwardly congratulated herself on not volunteering information about Ben's Amish background. He'd asked her not to, but her mouth was sometimes faster than her thoughts. Most times, actually.

And then Natalie set out for Philadelphia. As she drove down the steep tree-lined driveway, she glanced in the rearview mirror at Lost Creek Farm, with its big house set on top of the hill. There was a soft buttery glow coming from the kitchen window, and gray woodsmoke whirling up through the chimney. The sun was just starting to reach the ridge, streaming down the hill and radiating across the rolling hills in the distance. It looked like Heaven to her. Ben was recuperating in a little slice of Heaven.

Suddenly, she didn't want to leave. As she drove down the one-lane road, that familiar wave of self-pity returned to her, and she almost turned the car around. But she didn't. She knew she needed to move on, to forge ahead and make a new life for herself, but knowing it and doing it were two entirely different things.

Before Natalie left Stoney Ridge, she stopped to fill her car up with gas and was surprised when Boyd Baldwin pulled up beside her in his rumbling truck. He jumped out and took over pumping her gas.

"You seem to have a knack for being in the right place at the right time," she said, trying very hard not to smile.

"Small town living." He finished pumping her gas and returned the handle to the lever. "Time for a cup of coffee?"

She hesitated. It had been a long time since a man had flirted so boldly with her. While she definitely found Boyd Baldwin to be attractive, it didn't make any sense to fan the sparks of romance. Not here. Not now. Not with a vet to Amish farmers. "I . . . um . . ."

"Have a jealous boyfriend?"

She shook her head.

"You're in the Witness Protection Program?"

A laugh burst out of her. "No . . . nothing that mysterious. I'm heading back to Philadelphia. Just thought I should get on the road."

He glanced over at the coffee shop across the street. "Seems like that's an even better reason to get a shot of caffeine." He leaned in a little to give her a gentle nudge with his elbow. "It's only coffee. Not a marriage proposal."

Right. Of course. She was taking this too seriously. She took everything far too seriously. "Then, I accept. The offer for coffee, that is. Just a quick cup, though. I really should be off."

They sat in the coffee shop and talked for three hours, until the manager brought out the floor mop and they took the hint that he wanted to lock up and go home. Natalie felt dazed by Boyd, dazzled, all the way until she reached I-76. Then she came to her senses, shaking off any consuming thoughts about the handsome veterinarian. Yes, he was kind and thoughtful, interested in everything about her, so easy to talk to. So content with his life. So bright and happy. At one point during their lengthy coffee visit, she asked him what his secret to life was.

Every day was a new day, he told her, so yesterday really shouldn't matter. Even better, there was no point in worrying about the future.

A lovely theory. Not exactly realistic, but lovely. She'd never been around someone who had such an impenetrable optimism.

And those eyes of his, the way he listened to her with such bright interest. Those blue, blue eyes.

She shook off the image of those eyes. Oh, for Pete's sake. What was she thinking? She had a career to resurrect. A reputation to regain. She had a house of her own waiting for her in Philadelphia. She belonged there, not here.

~

Using the moonlight as a guide to cut through neighbors' fields, Micah trudged home from the youth gathering, thoroughly discouraged. Tonight, he had promised himself he would talk to Shelley Yoder. All afternoon, while Penny was at the doctor with the twitcher—whom Micah was studiously avoiding—he'd stood in front of the mirror in the bathroom and practiced what he wanted to say, over and over, deliberately choosing specific words with hard consonants so that he could deliver them smooth as silk. He hated that he couldn't speak well, hated that he had to force words out, oftentimes ones that weren't even close to how he felt or thought. They were just words he could say with ease.

"There's a vagrant bird on the ridge," he'd planned to say. "I could take you to see it sometime."

He hoped Shelley liked birds. He didn't really know.

A sigh escaped his lips. All through the volleyball game, the barbecue that followed, the singing that followed the barbecue, he had waited patiently for a moment to cut in and talk to her, ask her if he could take her home.

There was one point when he thought she might be looking at him. After they'd gathered for the singing, the boys left the table to warm their hands by the dying fire, while the girls remained at the picnic table. A lantern in the middle of the table glowed, casting off shadows.

Nate Glick told an off-color joke, and the boys all laughed. Micah pretended to laugh, pretended to be one of them. But he wasn't. The laughter caught the attention of the girls, and Shelley looked over at them, her eyes wide. He saw a small smile spread on her lovely face, and he felt his heart pound, smiling like a fool back at her. Then he realized she wasn't looking at Micah but at Nate Glick.

He saw her leave in yet another fellow's buggy.

This was the way it always went. Shelley was the prize, the girl every boy wanted. The girl he wanted so badly it made his chest hurt.

An owl hooted from a nearby tree and Micah instinctively froze, eyes scanning the trees to locate the sound. Another owl returned its call. All thoughts of sorrow over Shelley vanished as he stood in the dark, listening to those deep hoots of longing. They nearly echoed in the still night air.

"Ain't it grand?"

Micah jumped out of his skin. "Trudy! What are you doing out s-so late?"

Trudy stood behind him, eyes fixed on the trees. "Tracking the owls. I heard 'em calling to each other from my window and just had to come find 'em."

"Are you c-crazy? You should b-be in b-bed."

"No crazier than you."

Micah shrugged. He couldn't argue that. There'd been plenty of times that he'd lie in bed and hear a night bird calling, and two minutes later, he'd be outside with his binoculars, searching for a glimpse of it.

"There she goes." Trudy pointed to the tree just as the owl took off, wings spread, flying silently through the sky. "I think she wants to go check out this boy owl. Make sure he'd be worthy of her."

He gave her a look of doubt. This was an unlikely time of year for mating, though the warm weather seemed to be throwing everything off. Besides, birds didn't always follow the rules.

She shrugged. "It's the way of nature. The female gets a say-so. I was just reading about the Sedge Wren. If the male isn't a good nest builder, the female makes him build it all over again. As many as twenty nests!"

"It's a f-family t-trait. Wrens make d-dummy nests."

"Zwaar?" *Truly?*

"The f-female will choose one of the male's d-dummy nests, f-finish it off herself, and lay eggs in it."

"I think you know just about everything there is to know about birds, Micah." Trudy released an exaggerated sigh. "Nature always gets it right. The male bird is the pretty one. He has to prove himself. Not the female." She backed up a step or two. "Well, I'd best be getting home before anyone notices I'm gone." She disappeared into the fringe of trees that lined the field, as silently as she'd arrived.

Micah waited for a while to see if the owls might keep talking, but it seemed that Trudy was right and that the male passed muster for the female. Even an owl had better luck at love than he did. The night sky went quiet again, and he went on his way.

Micah Weaver, Bird-Watching Log

Name of Bird: *House Wren*

Scientific Name: *Troglodytes aedon*

Status: *Common, stable*

Date: *March 22*

Location: *Wood stack against the house*

Description: *Wren pair. Male and female look alike. Thin, slightly curved bill. Small, gray-brown, slender, long tail that cocks up when perched.*

Bird Action: *Male filled every cavity in wood stack with sticks, building dummy nests. Female picked one twig structure as preferred nest and filled it with grass, leaves, and moss. Laid seven eggs.*

Notes: *House Wrens might be common, but that's because they're shrewd. First, House Wrens are very comfortable around humans. They'll nest in any cavity they can find—which is probably why somebody first named them a "House" Wren. Second, the male will build multiple "dummy" nests to attract females. Scientists can't agree on what benefits the dummy nests create—possibly roosting sites or predator decoys? Or just to impress females with nest building skills? What they do know is that wren pairs with dummy nests are more successful in surviving and raising offspring than wrens* without dummy nests. So whatever the reason, it works.

Third, House Wrens may look harmless, but they're actually saboteurs. The males, in particular. They are constantly hunting, defending territory, and destroying other birds' nests. Sneaking up to a bluebird, finch, or swallow nest, the House Wren male will pierce the eggs, then trash the nest. Vandals.

If you think these drab-looking LBJs barely rate a yawn . . . have another think.

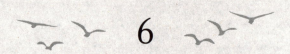

6

Ben stacked his hands behind his head and closed his eyes, too edgy to sleep, too tired to get up. He'd been feeling far more ill than he let on, not to Natalie, not even to the doctor— who turned out to be the bishop's sister. He'd fought what he thought was the flu for weeks now, pretending it was nothing. Ignoring moments when he felt as if he had the chills. Knocking back aspirin when struck by a splitting headache. Hardly eating anything but bananas and sweet tea because his stomach couldn't stop roiling. Mostly, just feeling blah. Bleak and blah. Bleary and weary.

Now that he knew it wasn't just a lingering flu but malaria, exhaustion overtook him. His fight was gone. All he wanted to do was sleep.

He'd spent the last two decades of his life completely absorbed in his work, traveling from one location to the next to chase birds, crafting one book after another. Everyone in the bird world knew the name of Ben Zook after his debut book, *Rare Birds*, hit the shelves when he was only twenty-two. He'd had more success, made more money, than he ever could've imagined. Yet without good health, well-being slipped away. Nothing much mattered.

He hadn't done much more these last couple of days other

than rest his weary bones and eat Penny Weaver's good food. He was grateful that he had dropped like a stone at Lost Creek Farm and not at Natalie's small house in Philadelphia, where he would have starved. Each day, Penny brought home remedies to the guesthouse—ginger tea, turmeric biscuits—anything to aid his recovery. She'd been remarkably, unnecessarily kind. After all, he was a complete stranger to her. If only the White-winged Tern would be so kind . . . and make an appearance.

Restless, he got out of bed and went to the window. A sudden shaft of moonlight lit the grass where a deer stood, still as a statue. A young doe, by the look of her. His eyes swept the yard. Usually, if there was one deer, two or three were nearby.

A light flickered in the second story of the big house and he wondered who it belonged to—Penny or the mysterious Micah? They called it the big house, but it wasn't really big, not like most Amish farmhouses that kept growing and growing to accommodate many generations of a large family.

He thought he saw a silhouette of a woman's figure move past a window upstairs. Why was she awake at two in the morning? Was she one of those people who couldn't sleep much? These last few days, he found his thoughts drifting often to wonder about Penny Weaver. When he first met her, he wrote her off as a typical Amish woman, a composite of all that had frustrated him about the Plain life. Timid and shy, unquestioningly submissive, lacking her own opinions or independent thoughts. One might be tempted to think, looking at Penny's kind gray eyes and innocent face, that she had no spunk. Though he barely knew her, he'd seen enough to conclude that his first impression was wrong. She had spunk. She had spirit.

And today it struck him that she was quite attractive. Maybe not by conventional standards, but he thought her appeal lay in her naturalness, her unfeigned openness.

In a culture that highly valued marriage, in which single men and women were marginalized . . . why hadn't Penny Weaver married?

She must have had plenty of choices. He wasn't sure how old she was—midthirties, maybe? A spinster by Amish standards.

A wave of weariness swept over Ben; his stomach rumbled in distress. He closed his eyes, frustrated with being helpless. He had a vagrant bird to chase down! He thought about giving up on the White-winged Tern. The way he was feeling, weak as a newborn lamb, he couldn't chase anything, anywhere.

What else could have grounded him but a bout of malaria? It must be how a bird felt when its wings were clipped. Trapped. Caged. Peering through the bars at the life going on outside the cage. And of all places, on an Amish farm, less than a mile from his childhood home. This was the last place on the entire planet that he wanted to be laid low, stuck in bed.

And yet, it was soothing here.

Earlier in the evening, he'd noticed a small fire not far from the big house. Alarmed, he peered out the window and realized it was actually a firepit. Penny and Micah sat around the fire in Adirondack chairs, drinking something steaming hot in big mugs. He lifted the window slightly and heard them talking to each other in Penn Dutch. Watching them, he felt an ache in his gut that had nothing to do with malaria.

He released a strained sigh. Just as he exhaled, a downstairs light appeared in the big house. He squinted, trying to see what was going on over there, his eyes fixed on the bay window of the big house's kitchen. Too far away to see. He grabbed his binoculars and adjusted the dials to peer at the house.

He saw Penny Weaver seated at the kitchen table, chin tucked low, something in her hand. Was she writing? No. Not by the way she moved her hand.

Hold on. If he wasn't mistaken, he thought she was sketching. Drawing? An artist, among the Amish? His interest in Penny Weaver ratcheted up a few notches.

Good grief, he was becoming one of those whackos who spied on his neighbors.

Penny drew only at night.

Whenever she couldn't sleep, she would draw. On her mind was a Pied-billed Grebe she'd been watching since spring. She and Micah had spotted it as it built a floating nest on Wonder Lake. She couldn't quite forget it, about how it had adapted to its surroundings. Such a funny duck-like bird, with its short heavy bill. It was less social than other grebes, rarely seen in a flock.

She wondered what Ben Zook thought about Pied-billed Grebes, about their unusual floating nests. About their choice to be alone, living away from their kind.

Actually, she wondered what Ben was doing now—if he were sound asleep, or if he lay there in the dark like she'd been doing, staring at the ceiling. She had finally pushed back the covers, sat up, turned on the flashlight, and gone downstairs to draw.

From a bottom shelf in the pantry, she took the lid off a large box. On the top was her sketch pad, thick with drawings, and her treasured supplies. Charcoal pencils, erasers, pen and ink, watercolors, brushes. Underneath were Ben Zook's books, every one he'd ever published. Pad in hand, she went to the table and struck a match to light the lantern. As she sat at the table, she laid out her pencils next to her and opened her sketch pad, flipping to a blank page. She loved these quiet moments, the sky dark, when the world was still. Sketching away, she felt what she called a small degree of euphoria.

Long ago, Penny had made the mistake of forgetting to hide her sketches before her mother hosted a comfort quilting. One of the quilters was the wife of a minister, and she must have seen them. The very next day, the deacon had paid a call, all stiff and stern. "Art is an individual expression of pride," he said. He told her to throw her drawings away. Burn them, he suggested.

Properly shamed, Penny had understood the warning that the deacon was giving her. He'd have her on her knees confessing her sin of pride if she didn't listen to what he was telling her. She listened. But she didn't throw her drawings away or burn them. Nor did she stop drawing birds. She just did a better job of hiding them.

Penny felt, deep in her heart, that the Lord God forgave her flagrant disregard of the deacon's warning. She didn't believe that God had wanted people to act more like robots rather than people with free will, with differing abilities and talents and interests. The deacon was correct in saying that art was an expression, but for her, it was an expression of worship. Whenever she drew winged creations, she sensed God's pleasure. His delight in how she noticed tiny details, how she observed the variety and uniqueness of birds.

Penny might only be thirty-five years old, but she had lived long enough to realize that the church Ordnung was a living thing, changing from one bishop to another. She'd observed enough church leaders to know that some were better than others. She chose to make up her own mind about weighty matters, like drawing birds. But she did so quietly.

In the morning, Penny carried a breakfast tray over to the guesthouse. Before Ben's cousin Natalie had left for Philadelphia, she'd gone over the things Ben would need in her absence, but Penny had trouble concentrating on what she was saying—Natalie had the longest red nails Penny had ever seen on an Englisch woman. And the thickest, blackest eyelashes too. A little like spiders' legs.

Natalie had seemed to sense Penny wasn't listening, because she repeated herself: three meals brought to Ben each day, make sure he took his medicine, don't let him talk Micah into a bird chase. Penny had to smile at that last request. As if she could stop either of them.

"Please hold on to receipts and keep a list of any expenses," Natalie had said. "You'll be paid for your troubles."

As if Penny considered Ben's convalescence in her guesthouse as trouble. Not hardly! She considered having Ben Zook trapped in her guesthouse with a bout of malaria as a gift from above. It was like nothing she could ever have imagined to ask. Over the last few days, she would look out the window and see him resting in the porch rocker, and her heart would catch anew with awe and a shiver of excitement to think he was here.

What was the Lord up to? Something wonderful.

As Penny neared the guesthouse, she noticed the door was left ajar, and she could see Ben sprawled on the couch, sound asleep. She set the breakfast tray on the small table and turned to leave, but stopped, pivoting. She tiptoed a little closer to Ben and looked at him for the longest time. She wanted to reach out and smooth the lock of curly hair that had fallen on his forehead. She didn't, of course, but she wanted to.

Suddenly she realized Ben's eyes had opened and he was smiling at her. She backed away, mortified to be caught.

"Checking to see if I'm still alive?"

"Your cousin, she gave me a list of things to do for you." That was the truth, though it felt like a lie. An excuse. And in a way, she supposed it was. "I wondered . . . is there anything I can do for you today? Anything you need?"

He rose to an upright position, stretched his arms, dropped them in his lap. "Maybe a cup of coffee?"

She poured him a cup from the carafe, studying him from the corner of her eye. She wondered how many countries he'd been to, how many rare birds he'd followed. "So you were in Honduras recently," she said as she set the coffee carafe near him on the side table. She watched him take slow sips, his eyes downcast. She worried it wasn't quite as hot as it was when she set out from the big house. "I would imagine you saw a breathtaking variety of birds while you were there."

When he didn't respond, she looked up to catch the surprise that lit his eyes. "So you like birds too?"

Did she *like* birds?

"Of course I do," she said, a little more coldly than she intended. It galled her that he had no memory of her. Who was the one who taught him about birds, so long ago? Who was the one who had showed him the eagles' nest and sparked his love of birds? Did he truly not remember her?

"I've always thought most Amish birders were men. There's a longstanding joke among them that birding is hunting without the guns."

Interesting. She wondered if Ben meant to let that bit of familiarity slip. "There's lots of women birders among us. You'll have to meet the bishop's wife, Birdy. She's almost as knowledgeable as Micah. But my brother is a marvel in the field. He knows their sounds, their songs and calls, their behaviors, their patterns. He could recognize birdcalls before he could talk."

Ben stared at her hard with a frown between his eyes, as if she were a puzzle he was trying to piece together.

"Anything else you need before I go?"

He suddenly looked a little woebegone and her heart softened. "Company. It's a little lonely." He motioned toward the kitchen chair. "Would you mind staying awhile? Share a cup of coffee?"

Oh my. No, she didn't mind at all. She didn't mind a bit.

~

Ben felt a little bit of life returning to him in the afternoon. He put his lunch plate on the tray, along with the empty carafe of coffee from breakfast, and decided to walk it over to the big house. Slowly. The brisk air felt good in his lungs as he made his way across the yard. He stopped near the bird feeder to watch a red cardinal help himself to Penny's birdseed. The wind kicked up, swirling around him, making him wish he'd worn a hat, when suddenly a delicious smell wafted by. His eyes moved to the big bay window in the kitchen, and he saw Penny standing in front of the stove. He allowed himself to drink in the sight. For a split second, Ben Zook imagined that he belonged here, that she was his woman. Imagined a boy just like Micah as his son. The brief fantasy was sparked not by Penny Weaver nor by her brother Micah but by all Ben Zook had walked away from in his life. Being here, it churned the waters.

She turned suddenly, noticed him through the window, and he realized he'd been staring and became self-conscious. He lifted the tray as the reason he happened to be standing there, gawking at her like a fool.

She opened the door and stepped out onto the stoop. "You didn't need to bring the tray up."

"Well, I—" His words fell away as he abruptly lost his train of thought. Her eyes were bright, as if with happiness, her cheeks were pink from the heat of the stove top, and tendrils of chestnut-colored hair had escaped from her prayer cap. "Fresh air. Exercise. As good as medicine." He passed her the tray. "Something sure smells delicious."

"Roast chicken and potatoes." She stepped closer to the door. "I take a hot meal over to—" She stopped abruptly. "To a man down the road who lives alone."

He wondered if it was the tall, heavyset fellow whom he'd seen once or twice already, trudging up the hill to pay a visit to Penny. "Lucky guy," Ben said, feeling his face heat. He nodded and left, not wanting her to see him blush. Another malarial symptom— those unbidden flushes of heat.

Or was it?

It wasn't *her.*

Good grief. It could've been any half-decent-looking female and his reaction would probably have been the same. An autumn day, a warm kitchen, a chicken roasting in the oven. It wasn't *her.* It wasn't because of Penny.

A gust of bitterly cold wind smacked him in the face, blowing away such stray thoughts.

Day by day, Micah felt a tight knot of pressure building in his chest, and it was all his own doing. Not only had he promised Ben Zook a glimpse at the White-winged Tern, which was probably halfway to Cuba by now, but he had also promised the local Audubon president that he would be the official count compiler for the Christmas Bird Count in Stoney Ridge on the third Saturday in December. It was the first time Stoney Ridge would participate in the CBC, and Micah had to organize volunteers and give them specified routes through designated fifteen-mile circles, counting every bird they saw or heard all day long. So far, the only three volunteers were Trudy Yoder and Birdy Stoltzfus, whom he trusted, and Hank Lapp, whom he didn't. That man was chock-full of bird facts, always wrong, and always willing to share.

A lot was riding on how well Micah's teams performed during this CBC. He knew there was a bias against the Amish because they didn't use technology, nor fancy gadgets to call birds. He knew his growing reputation as a field guide was on display, and even though he was sharply aware of the dangers of thinking he was somebody, he also wanted to do well in this work. God had given him a love of birds, and a place to live where he could spend his days locating birds. He sure didn't want to go back to Big Valley, and Penny didn't either. This was an important year for the two of them. Micah wanted it to work. With his whole heart, he wanted this to work.

And up to now, it was working. This afternoon, since the twitcher was still stuck on the couch with malaria, he took an older married couple out birding. They had come all the way from Philadelphia to view migrating raptors. When they called to ask if he had time to take them out in the field, he had told them about Hawk Mountain, north of Reading. That was the place he recommended to the enthusiastic couple. Considered the best place in the world for hawk viewing, it was where he would have gone, and had gone, many times.

But this couple had heard of Micah through another birder friend, and insisted that whatever he could find for them, raptor-wise, would suffice. So yesterday, Micah had gone out alone to check on a stopover spot, a little-known area—rich with resources—where exhausted birds, after flying all night long, would rest and refuel. It was a difficult hike to but worth the effort. Yesterday, he'd spotted a Bald Eagle and a Broad-winged Hawk. And a few songbirds bold enough to hang around raptors, which always gave him a smile.

Today, somehow, the secret stopover spot yielded a bonanza. A Golden Eagle, two Bald Eagles, Ospreys, Red-tailed Hawks, Red-shouldered Hawks, Sharp-shinned Hawks, an American Kestrel, and a Peregrine Falcon. The birding couple was over the moon with happiness. They'd never seen a Peregrine Falcon in the wild. They gave him a generous tip, insisting Micah was the world's best birder. He wasn't. It was all God's creative handiwork that brought such pleasure. Micah was only pointing it out.

~

The sun was nearly setting when Penny saw Roy King head up the hill carrying a bucket. She wiped her hands on the dishrag, set it on the oven holder, and went outside to meet him. She reached him at the top of the drive. Though he had a round, boyish face, he was a big man, shoulders broad and blocky, straining the seams of his dark coat. His hair was too long, stick straight, with black bangs that longed for a trim. Dear, kind Roy. He needed a wife.

"Chestnuts," Roy said, lifting the bucket. "You said you hadn't been able to find any, and I happened upon a tree."

Knowing Roy, he had searched high and low for those chest-nuts. Last week after church, she'd made a casual remark about being unable to find chestnuts in Stoney Ridge, and he had noted it. Remembered. "Thank you, Roy. I'd given up looking for them. Micah likes to roast them over the firepit." She waved an arm toward the house. "Would you like to come in for a cup of tea?"

"I need to get back." A streak of pink colored his cheeks. "I wondered if I might be able to take you to the auction on Saturday."

Penny made a funny little jerking movement. "I . . . can't be away from the farm for a full day. Not with our guest feeling so poorly. I've been preparing meals for him. Three a day."

Hurt crumbled the hope in Roy's dark brown eyes, and Penny had to look away. He must have known, of course, that she'd say no. She always said no.

For a long moment Roy said nothing. "I thought you said the guests would be Micah's responsibility. That they'd be coming for his birding trips."

Over the summer Roy, along with Luke Schrock and Teddy Zook, had helped Penny and Micah make accommodations at the guesthouse. "The man is sick, Roy. He has malaria. And don't forget he's paying Micah for the field trips, and paying me room and board to stay at the guesthouse. He's got every right to expect homemade meals."

"It's just that you'll soon be tangled up in an outsider's troubles. Next thing you know—"

"What?" she said, her head held erect. She wasn't a child who needed a warning.

He lowered his head. "I just think you ought to be careful, that's all."

She thought this warning had more to do with the fact that she had turned down his invitation to the auction. Roy, like Penny, was fairly new to Stoney Ridge, and had zeroed right in on her, the very first moment they'd met. He was a widower with two young daughters, and Penny knew she seemed a suitable candidate to fill that emptiness in his home. This wasn't the first time Penny had been ardently pursued, but she always responded in the same way, with gentle refusals. The unsettling thing about Roy was that the more she turned down his invitations, the more determined he became.

Roy kept staring at her with his big brown, pleading puppy-dog eyes, searching her face, trying to see into her heart. Again, Penny had to look away.

He lifted the bucket. "Would you like me to put it somewhere for you?"

"I'll take it."

She accepted the bucket from Roy, and to her surprise, he'd been holding something behind his back with his free hand. He whipped out a bouquet of purple asters, the last of the season, and handed them to her before walking away. Sniffing their sweet floral scent, Penny turned and realized Ben had been watching them through the guesthouse window. The weight of his gaze warmed her skin like the heat from a fire. Abruptly, as if he'd been caught spying, he turned away from the window.

Her breath held. Her heart tripped over itself. Her skin flushed with excitement.

Oh my.

Micah Weaver, Bird-Watching Log

Name of Bird: *Pied-billed Grebe*

Scientific Name: *Podilymbus podiceps*

Status: *Low concern*

Date: *March 2*

Location: *Lost Creek*

Description: *Nesting pair, small brown waterbird (between a robin and a crow), large blocky head with chunky thick bill, small body. Pigeon-sized, brown color, with a chicken-like beak.*

Bird Action: *Grebes are part bird, part submarine. They're famous for striking courtship displays. I've seen them race noisily across the surface of the water, but today I saw something more sedate. The male and the female faced each other some distance apart, and stared at each other, making soft trills. Then they both dove underwater, coming up with their bills full of weeds, paddling with their feet to stay upright.*

Notes: *Less social than most grebes, Pied-billed Grebes are rarely found in flocks. Nests aren't on land, but on the water. They're built from the bottom up—little bowl-shaped platforms of plant material that become a floating mass. Both parents help to build the nest. They dive for decaying plant material, picking it up from the bottom of the lake, piling it on. The nest* gradually sinks so they just keep adding on to it. The decaying plant material gives off heat, which helps to incubate the eggs.

Most people think a Pied-billed Grebe is a duck. It's not (it's a diving bird). It doesn't have webbed feet, yet it can rival any duck as a speedy swimmer.

And that's if you're lucky enough to spot this shy bird. It gets grumpy. It cannot stand people.

7

Two days of heavy rain followed. Just as well, Ben figured, watching the water stream off the roof. With a little luck, the White-winged Tern would wait out the rain. Birds were smart that way. Migration was dangerous; they knew they needed the assistance of wind blowing in the right direction. They took all the help Mother Nature provided.

Ben knew he could probably learn a little something about that from birds. It was difficult for him to receive help from Penny Weaver. It had nothing to do with her—she was actually quite different than he expected. After she finally stopped acting so flustered around him, he found her to be extremely interested in his work. She peppered him with questions, and it was only after she left that he realized he'd done all the talking. That wasn't at all typical of Ben. Normally, he kept himself to himself.

Each morning, he did greet her with one question: Did Micah think the White-winged Tern had left to join its feathered friends in the south?

Each morning, Penny responded with some variation on the same answer for him. "The Lord is creator of all things. If he can manage all of nature that surrounds us, then surely he can manage a little wayward bird. He'll keep that bird here for you." She said it with complete confidence, as if she had a direct line to the Almighty. She said it so earnestly that he almost believed her. If only.

He wondered where she'd gone today. Several times, about this time in the afternoon, he'd seen her carry a casserole dish out to the buggy, held with potholders so he knew it was still hot, and away she'd go, not returning for a few hours. He figured she was taking a meal to that beefy guy who trudged up the driveway every few days. The one who left his big shoes at the door of Penny's kitchen before he went inside. Penny's suitor.

Good grief, he was tracking her whereabouts like a crazed stalker.

Ben felt noticeably better today, less of his insides turning on him, less of that wiped-out exhaustion, and he hoped tomorrow he'd feel even better, especially if the rain stopped. Dok Stoltzfus told him to expect the antimalarial drugs to make a difference by week's end.

He'd been there several days with nothing to show for it. For the first time he realized the usefulness of being constantly busy—it allowed him no free time to think about things that bothered him. Unlike now. His mind kept spinning with memories, long buried but coming to life, unbidden. They appeared in his dreams, they filled his waking moments. Strangely, Penn Dutch kept coming back to him in bits and pieces.

Recollections from his childhood were happy ones. His brother, Levi, was always, always in those. Ben woke this morning to an image of milking the cows in the barn as dawn broke. Tugging him out of the haze was his father's deep voice, singing a hymn, the sound lifting to the rafters. Levi would pick up the melody, Ben would add his own version of harmony.

Wasn't that the way it always was? Levi, trying so hard to stick to the rules. Ben, ignoring them.

With sudden, aching intensity, he missed his brother.

The rhythmic *clip-clop* sound of an approaching buggy made him push himself off the couch to see who might have come to visit

Penny Weaver. He saw two people in the buggy, and as it crested the top of the hill to come to a stop, he recognized them.

Hank Lapp and his wife, Edith.

Ben watched, partly amused at the sight. Hank was trying to help Edith climb out of the buggy while sheltering her with an umbrella and making a mess of it. He kept getting in her way until she batted her hands at him to make him back off.

But they didn't head to the big house to see Penny. They marched straight to the guesthouse and Ben's amusement quickly changed to annoyance. And a mild panic. He had told Hank he didn't want others to know he was here. If Edith knew, how long before his father would know? A bad feeling rumbled in his belly.

"HELLO, HELLO! BEN! You in there?" Hank knocked on the door as loudly as he spoke.

Ben plastered a smile on his face and opened the door. "Hank. I see you brought your wife. Hello there, Edith." Everything was silent for three long seconds while Edith fixed Ben with a disapproving glare, magnified by her glasses. He felt his hackles rise, the way they did when he was just a small boy in church, wiggling too much on the bench, and Edith would point a long finger at him.

Her chin drew in, creating two folds beneath it. "It's a bit cold out here in the rain."

"So it is," Ben said, opening the door wide. "Come on in. I can make some tea."

"I'll do it," Edith said. "You'd better sit down. You look like something the cat dragged in."

Did he? He'd been feeling a little better until Edith said that. He moved some of his papers off the old green couch and closed his computer. He doubted Edith would approve. From what he remembered of her, there was little she approved of.

Hank plopped down into the corner of the couch, legs sprawled, his lumpy boots tracking mud all over the braided rug. "Well, this is downright COZY." He pointed to the computer. "YOU MUST

BE getting A LOT DONE. The RAIN. THE BAVARIA and all."
Hank's sheer presence raised the temperature of the room.

"Malaria," Ben corrected.

"BEN, I've got a JOKE for you."

Oh no.

"A skeptic asked THREE men, 'So what would you do if some-one gave you TWO COWS?' The Quaker said, 'I'd give BOTH of mine to charity, and expect my REWARD in Heaven.' The Hut-terite said, 'I'd give my TWO COWS to the colony, and they'd keep my family in milk.' BUT NOT THE AMISH MAN. He said, 'I think I'd keep ONE of my cows, and TRADE the other for a BULL.'" Hank reared back and hooted with laughter, so much so that it brought on a coughing fit.

Despite his annoyance at their intrusive arrival, Ben felt a trickle of amusement, both at the joke and at Hank's enjoyment at the telling. Edith remained sober-faced, though she'd probably heard that joke plenty of times before.

Edith handed them each a mug of hot tea. She eased down in a chair across from Ben and fixed her eyes on him. He felt as if he were suddenly a boy again, and she'd caught him doing something wrong. She'd always served up judgment, swift and clear. "Ben, you'll probably want to see your father."

"Probably not," Ben said, but thought, *How's never?* He shot a glance at Hank. "Have you told him that I'm here?"

"NO, SIRREE. YOU told me not to, and I'm a MAN OF MY WORD. Right, Eddy?"

Then why, Ben wanted to ask, *did you tell Edith? And why are you here now?*

Edith ignored Hank and continued to stare at Ben with a look that said, *Listen up.* "Your father isn't well. Not well at all."

Mid-sip, Ben stilled. "Old age catching up with him?"

"WORSE. HE has the OLD TIMER'S DISEASE."

Edith frowned at Hank. "Alzheimer's. Dok thinks he's got the Alzheimer's disease. Easily confused. Can't remember things."

Everything about Ben tightened. For years, he didn't care about his father, didn't care what might happen to him after his mother passed away. And yet, in that moment, he felt as if his heart was beating frantically like a trapped bird. "How long has he had it?"

"Awhile now," Edith said. "He's still living on his own, but that's got to change. He's not able to care for himself. He won't let me come in his house at all. Refuses all my offers of help. He never was an easy one. Impossible, in fact. Quite the orneriest man I've ever known."

Ben didn't disagree.

Edith's beady eyes reminded him of a raptor's, coming in for the kill on an unlucky field mouse. "Seems as if the good Lord has brought you back to the fold just in time." She gave him a little flex of her lips that didn't quite make up a smile.

Ben felt a pressure growing in his chest, a heavy weight. No way. There was no way he was going to stay and take care of his father.

He rose to his feet, rubbed his stomach, and feigned an expression of acute pain. "I'm feeling a wave of malaria striking again. I'm sorry to cut this visit short." It was the best excuse he could muster, but it worked.

They hurried to leave, Edith especially. Hank lingered to express his sympathy. "I KNOW all about THOSE DIGESTIVE DISTURBANCES. I get them WHENEVER EDDY makes SPICY FOOD."

Once the door shut behind Hank, Ben sank back on the green couch, his muscles quivering, his mind agitated. He squeezed his eyes shut. So his father wasn't well. Alzheimer's disease. He shouldn't care, he didn't care. But he did.

This rare bird chase was tangling him up in things he had no business with. He had to get out of Stoney Ridge, fast. The rare White-winged Tern would just have to be left out of this book. But even in his frustration, he knew he didn't have the energy to manage a bus ride all the way to Philadelphia. He would have to wait for Natalie to return.

Bird or no bird, he was leaving.

88

Three days a week, Penny delivered a hot meal to Zeke Zook, Ben's father, and stayed to do some light housecleaning and provide some company for him. She took his dirty clothes back home with her to launder.

When David Stoltzfus asked her to provide those services for Zeke, insisting to pay her out of the church fund, he warned her about him. The man had a reputation for being cranky and quarrelsome. It didn't take long for Penny to discover it was a well-earned reputation.

She also recognized that Zeke was desperately lonely, too proud and too stubborn to ask for help. He just seemed so lost to her, so alone, and her heart took pity. Then she started to notice that he would be watching for her arrival, and come outside to meet her buggy, no matter the weather. He grew sullen when the time came for her to leave. Knowing that he looked forward to her coming helped soften her feelings about him, because it wasn't easy for her to spend her time with a grumbling grouch—even knowing that grouch was Ben's father.

Now and again, Zeke would speak of his wife but never of his son Ben, and Penny knew not to bring up his name. This was the Plain way, especially for the older generation. Those who were shunned were meant to have a taste of life away from God, away from fellowship. No one could actually live without the loving comfort of family. It was the same as what happened when a sheep left a fold. Shunning was meant to bring one back, not keep them away. But so often, all it did was keep them away. Far, far away.

Penny wondered time and again why Ben had left. What drew him so far from home? What made him never want to return?

A few months ago, she'd asked Micah to set up a bird feeder outside of Zeke's kitchen window. She thought he might enjoy watching the birds come and go, and he seemed to spend most of his time sitting at that kitchen table. At first Zeke acted as if it was all pure silliness and nonsense, until a bright red male cardinal came to the feeder. He didn't move or make a sound, but she could feel something change in him. She looked at him, into his eyes. That one flashy bird had caught his attention and held it. "That cardinal is your spark bird, Zeke. That's what it's called when your interest in birds is first sparked." She snapped her fingers. "And the flame ignites."

"I don't know about that," Zeke said gruffly. But the cardinal, it had brought a light in his eyes when he'd seen it, a warmth.

Penny had to laugh. A flashy red cardinal, of all birds. She would've thought Zeke Zook would disapprove of red feathers, even if it was the Lord God who made them.

Micah was soaked to the skin. Trudy Yoder had rushed over last night to tell him that she'd seen the White-winged Tern not two hours earlier up at Wonder Lake. If it weren't almost dark when she'd appeared at the kitchen door, he would've set out to find it. Instead, before the sun rose the next day, he made his way up the muddy ridge trail to find that bird. That elusive, exasperating bird.

He spotted a flock of Snow Geese and two Tundra Swans, and he checked on the hidden Pied-billed Grebe nest that he and Penny had discovered getting built last spring, and found it abandoned, nearly disintegrated. That's what happened when you built a floating nest.

But there was no White-winged Tern where Trudy said she'd seen it, not at Wonder Lake, not anywhere nearby. That bird! Nimble enough to continue dodging him.

Whenever he thought about Ben Zook in that guesthouse—a twitcher among twitchers—knowing the man was desperate to go out birding, knowing that as soon as he felt up to it, he'd be shadowing Micah, knowing he had come here just because of him . . . it made Micah's insides twist up.

He *had* to find that bird.

~~~~~

Penny heard a knock on the kitchen door and opened it to find Ben, holding out an empty coffee cup. She blew out a startled breath. Seeing him standing there, right on her doorstop, she felt her heartbeat give a hitch.

"I'd love a cup of coffee, if there's any to spare."

She spread a hand on her chest, willing her pounding heart to still. "I didn't expect you to be up so early." She took the coffee cup from him. "I'll fill it. The coffee's just about ready. There's nothing worse than waking up without coffee. Would you like to come in?" She bustled inside, so excited she forgot to hold the door for him and it closed on his face.

Unoffended, Ben opened the door and crossed the threshold, one hand on the doorjamb. "I hoped Micah might be here."

She thought Ben held himself gingerly, as if a little unsure of his steadiness. "Long gone." Standing by the coffee maker, she watched the last remaining drops of coffee drip into the pot. She filled his mug, steam rising from the dark liquid. A heavenly scent. She felt herself calming as she set her mind to a simple task. "Last night someone spotted the White-winged Tern, so he made haste to see if it was still there this morning."

"Just last night?" Ben's voice surprised her with its strength. "Where was it spotted? How long ago did Micah go? Which way did he go?"

She spun around to see his eyes wide, his face animated. "You mean you'd head out after him?"

"Just point me in the direction."

She burst out laughing, long, unrestrainedly, resting an arm on the countertop.

"What's so funny?"

"You're barely able to stand up straight, and yet you'd risk your health to catch sight of a rare bird." She shook her head. "You and Micah are going to get along famously."

"If I can ever find him."

"Oh, he's around. Don't you worry. When the time is right, he'll help you find your bird." She crossed the room to hand him his mug. He didn't say anything, just looked at her with those clear blue eyes. He was feeling something, she was almost sure of it. She saw his chest rise and fall under his coat, as if he, too, were short of breath.

He leaned back against the door. "Mind if I stay for a while?"

Pleased, she pointed to an empty chair. "Sit. We can talk while I tend to breakfast." She was more than pleased—she felt herself blushing. Quickly, she averted her face and turned to her cooking. "How do you like your eggs?"

He took off his coat and hung it on the back of the chair. "Scrambled."

"Scrambled it'll be." She kept her back to him as she tended the eggs, cracking a few into a bowl to whisk them, adding a small amount of milk from a pitcher.

"Penny, you're always asking me questions. I have a few for you."

She froze. Was he starting to remember her?

"Why are just you and Micah living at Lost Creek Farm? Aren't there more Weavers?"

"Oh yes. Plenty. They all live over in Big Valley. Micah and I, we're the youngest."

"But there's quite an age gap."

"I was the youngest of eight until Micah surprised my mother—who was already a grandmother many times over—with his arrival. A late-in-life blessing, we called him."

"So how old were you when Micah was born?"

"Seventeen. In a way, I sort of helped raise him."

She glanced over at him, noticing his worn jeans and a waffle-knit shirt pushed up at the forearms. He'd stretched out his legs, crossing one ankle over the other. Relaxed. He hadn't shaved, and his scruffiness made him just a little bit rumpled. While he sipped his coffee, his eyes downcast, she chanced a longer look. Goodness, he was handsome. She took notice as if she planned to sketch his face. High cheekbones, wide-set blue eyes framed by those dark eyebrows, that distinctive Roman nose. It wasn't the Plain way to take such notice of one's physical attributes, but she couldn't help herself.

"Have you lived here a long time?"

"About a year."

He looked at her, folded his arms, and cocked his head with a knowing smile. "Really? Why, that's no time at all."

"This is my grandmother's farm. She passed a year ago and left it to my mother. That's why we've come. To care for it." There was much more to the story as to why she and Micah had landed at Lost Creek Farm, but that would have to wait for another day. Too much, too soon.

"It's quite an inheritance from your grandmother."

"Yes, the farm . . . and so much more than that. She gave me an inheritance of loving birds. She's the one who first started us on the bird-loving path. Micah and me, we're the bird lovers in the family. There's better birding here than where our folks live."

"Better raptors than Big Valley."

She glanced at him again, still whisking. This man knew his birds. "Yes. Micah loves raptors best." This was nice, Penny thought. Talking comfortably, sharing their lives. For a brief moment, it felt as if they had done this kitchen routine a hundred times before. This had been the life she'd always imagined, always hoped for. They were in Penny's kitchen, sitting by the bay window, watching birds alight at the feeder, sharing a cup of coffee in the morning, talking over the day.

"Natalie's due in soon." His voice was expressionless and oddly measured. "When she comes, I'm going to head back to Philadelphia with her. Even if I haven't seen the White-winged Tern."

She practically dropped the bowl of eggs as she jerked around to face him. "You'd leave without seeing the bird?" *Isn't that why you're here?*

"I think I've been here long enough." He took a sip of coffee as calm as could be, as if he'd just told her it looked like rain today, and not anything momentous like he was leaving. "Every bird has a story. Ever heard that saying?"

She wanted to throw an egg at him. *I'm the one who told you that saying!*

He took another sip of coffee. "I suppose this one's story will be that it dipped me."

Go on, then. She turned to the counter, whipping those poor eggs so hard they splattered on her apron. *Leave without finding what you're looking for. Turn your back on everything good God is holding out to you.* She lifted the bowl to pour the eggs. The eggs hit the frying pan with a sizzle, sending the smoky scent of hot bacon grease throughout the kitchen.

As soon as the eggs were done, she scooped them onto a plate, next to three strips of thick bacon, and buttered toast slathered with cherry jam. She sliced a grapefruit in half, not even bothering to section the fruit, set the plate in front of him, and returned to the stove to turn off the flame. She didn't say a word, mostly because she was afraid of what he might say next.

When she returned to the table to refill his cup of coffee, she saw he hadn't picked up his fork. Hands on his thighs, he was openly staring at the food on his plate.

"Something wrong?" Her tone still had a stubborn edge to it.

He startled, and their eyes met, and in his eyes, she saw something vulnerable. Almost childlike, as if scrambled eggs, bacon, and toast were wondrous things. In that split second, he reminded her so much of his younger self. Full of pent-up emotion, full of sadness. Her vexation eased off, her heart softened, melted.

"No," he said, in a far-off voice. "No, everything's fine."

Calmer now, she filled a plate for herself and sat across from him. He waited to eat until she sat down, even dipping his chin and closing his eyes as she did during a moment of offering silent thanks to the Lord. He asked her a few polite questions while they ate, complimented her cooking, noticed the birds at the feeder with interest, and even offered to help her clean up afterward, but she refused his help. His sagging eyelids over breakfast revealed his fatigue. As she filled the sink with soapy water, she watched him walk slowly to the guesthouse, almost like a petulant little boy with his chin tucked low, as if he didn't really want to leave the big house.

So why would he leave? How could he go without at least trying to find the bird he'd come for? And what about his father? Penny hadn't mentioned that she knew Zeke, but neither had Ben. Would he leave without seeing his father? Then there was the biggest question of all, the one that kept needling her: How could Ben not have any memory of her?

She was so tempted to tell him, to ask him, but knew better than to speak. She was waiting for the Lord's go-ahead on that, and it hadn't come to her yet.

What did she expect him to say? *Of course I remember you, Penny-wise. How could I have ever forgotten? You made a permanent mark on me.* Obviously, she hadn't. Not like the one he had left on her.

Ben's visit left Penny in a state for the rest of the day.

~

Whenever Ben thanked Penny, she brushed it off as if she'd done nothing. But it wasn't nothing. Such a simple, humble breakfast, yet Ben felt nearly overcome by the sight and smell and taste of it. It evoked memories of all the breakfasts his mother had served, just like that one. Ben always thought the first sip of coffee was the best sip. He took his time tasting Penny Weaver's coffee, smelling its rich scent, observing the quiet interior of the home. The coffee was excellent. Everything inside the kitchen was in order. Plain, clean, simple, and comforting.

And that cherry jam! He never remembered cherry jam tasting so delicious. He had to hold himself back from grabbing a spoon to finish off the entire jar, it was *that* good.

More than a little reluctantly, he made himself leave the warm kitchen and go back to the empty guesthouse. Nearly there, he pivoted to look back at the big house, astonished. *She'd* done this, he realized. She had quieted the tumult within him, at least for a little while. Given him a sense of inner peace. This woman he scarcely knew.

Closing the door to the guesthouse, he flopped on the couch, trying not to overanalyze his strange circumstances. So many memories kept bubbling up, moments long forgotten. Images ran through his mind like a film reel, almost as if he could see himself from a distance, as a bystander. It was the good memories, the happy ones, those were the ones that took him by surprise. Those hard, difficult ones, those he had no trouble recalling.

The one that kept returning to him lately was the pivotal moment in which he left home. The familiar sadness moved through the room like a cold breeze and grasped his heels, as if trying to drag him down. He set his elbows on his knees and dropped his head into his hands.

Ben was sixteen years old. The farmhouse had finally emptied after his brother Levi's funeral. His father closed the door on the last visitor and turned to Ben and his mother. "Levi's name will never be spoken of again."

His mother said nothing. She just turned and left the room. Ben heard her weary, defeated footfalls on the stairs. He watched his father add another log to the woodstove, as if it was just an ordinary night.

His father had asked Ben to make sure the barn door was closed before he went to bed. Outside in the dark, he stopped for a moment and looked at the moon, listened for night birds. He kept thinking he ought to be feeling something. Sorrow or shame, something, anything. But nothing. He felt nothing.

He saw the downstairs light in the farmhouse go out and knew his father had gone to bed.

Like it was just an ordinary day. But it wasn't, and there never would be another ordinary night in this home.

Something snapped inside of Ben. He couldn't be here, couldn't stay one more night under his father's roof. He saddled his horse and took off.

He rode all the way to his cousin Natalie's house, seventy miles away near Philadelphia.

His throat locked up when she answered the door. He couldn't say anything, because once he did, he was afraid everything would pour out. Natalie looked past him and saw his horse, eating the grass right out of her front yard. She threw open the door. "You'd better come on in."

~

Natalie hadn't left the house since Saturday after she returned from Stoney Ridge. She planned to get out, she even set up a coffee date with a friend, she showered, she dressed . . . but then she received a call from the bank that she was overdrawn again and her brief enthusiasm to rejoin the world fizzled out. She canceled the coffee date with her friend and changed back into her yoga clothes. She'd have to go out soon because her refrigerator was nearly empty. But not today. She sighed. Another DoorDash meal day.

Natalie curled up in a blanket on the couch and closed her eyes. Her financial situation was growing dire. Six months ago, she would've blamed Joel for it, for everything, but in the last couple of days, she had started to realize that she was part of the problem. They both had this strong motivation to achieve, to make something of themselves. At first it was the glue that bonded them together, and later it became the poison that broke them apart.

The ring of her cell phone startled her. She grabbed it to check the caller ID before answering, just in case it was the bank with more bad news.

Boyd Baldwin. The vet to the Amish. The handsome, charming man who seemed to be pursuing her. Natalie couldn't quite explain the feelings she had about him. He had called her each night since Sunday, and they'd talked for hours like they'd known each other forever and yet were just getting started.

It rang and rang.

He deserved better.

She declined the call and set her phone on silent.

Micah Weaver, Bird-Watching Log

Name of Bird: Northern Cardinal

Scientific Name: Cardinalis cardinalis

Status: Low concern

Date: Pretty much every day

Location: Penny's bird feeder (filled with sunflower seeds, a cardinal's favorite)

Description: Male, brilliant red with black mask and throat. Large, long-tailed, with a short, very thick bill and a prominent crest.

Bird Action: Perched on the feeder to use its bill and tongue to extract sunflower seeds by crushing the shells.

Notes: Cardinals don't migrate, so this bird sticks around all year long. Most live within a mile of where they were born. A male Northern Cardinal is the one that gets a lot of attention. (He's the state bird of seven states.) Apparently, he's responsible for more people opening up a field guide than any other bird. All due to those dazzling red feathers. Unlike most birds, the male Northern Cardinal doesn't molt into a dull plumage, so he's easy to spot against a snowy background. Yet despite his charming appearance, he's one of the toughest birds in the world. Very territorial—even with his girlfriend. He mates for life.

The female Northern Cardinal is pretty amazing in her way. Only a few female songbirds sing. Mostly it's the males who croon, trying to woo a girl. The female Northern Cardinal will often sing while sitting on her nest. Most likely, she is telling the male to bring food to the nest. Pronto.

Both males and females will attack their own reflection in a window, mistaking it for an adversary intruding in on their territory. Pretty birds, but not so smart.

8

The next morning, Ben woke early, feeling better, less exhausted than he had in weeks. Maybe Dok Stoltzfus did know what she was talking about. He heard a door slam and rose from the bed to peer out his bedroom window. The horizon was just starting to lighten up, the sky slightly purple, and in the dimness of dawn he saw Micah striding away from the house.

He jerked on the window sash until it slid open. "Wait! Wait for me!" Then he hurried to get his clothes on, his boots, his coat and hat. He grabbed a chunk of Penny's apple bread from yesterday for breakfast. In his haste, he nearly forgot his optical equipment bag.

Micah was waiting for him outside the guesthouse. Ben sensed the boy's hesitance even before speaking. "I want to come with you. Wherever it is you're going, I want to come." Even in the pale morning light, the look of discomfort on Micah's face was obvious.

"P-planning to h-head up to the r-ridge. It's a l-long haul."

Ben scraped a hand over his whisker-roughened jaw. "I'd like to join you."

Micah's wide gray eyes, so like his sister's, were full of uncertainty. "You're up t-to it?"

"Don't worry. I won't slow you down." More kindly, Ben added, "If I can't keep up, I'll turn back. I promise."

The boy accepted this and started off again, Ben trailing behind him. Micah's legs were so long that Ben had to take two steps to match his one. He was breathing hard and had a feeling he'd pay later for this impulsive hike at dawn, but he'd come to Stoney Ridge for Micah Weaver and the White-winged Tern. If he couldn't have the bird, at least he'd get a chance to see why birders kept talking about this boy wonder.

Micah strode behind the big house, straight into the woods that led up a steep ridge. To Ben's surprise, he strode at a measured and moderate pace, noticing birds as he walked. He hoped Micah wasn't going slow for his sake, but if so, he was grateful for it. Ben was puffing, his heart pounding, his legs aching, but he wasn't going to miss this chance.

"Think we'll see the White-winged Tern?"

Micah only shrugged.

"Has it gone on its way?"

He hesitated, then shook his head.

"So you think it's really still here?"

Again, the boy shrugged, but gave a slight nod.

If that was about all Ben could get out of him today, that the bird was somewhere nearby, he was satisfied.

"Do you have a favorite time of the year?"

"M-March."

"Why March?"

"Listening is b-best in M-March."

"Wendell Berry said that a proper human sound . . . is one that allows other sounds to be heard."

Micah stopped for a moment, as if he was taking that thought in. It was the first time that the boy seemed interested in something Ben had to say. "The Q-Quakers call it quiet time. A time to listen to G-God and his creation as we p-participate in the unfolding of spring."

Ben looked at him in surprise. Micah quoted it like a recitation, with hardly a stammer. Natalie had said his stuttering seemed pretty pronounced. "Well, how about that. You're a regular chatterbox."

"I'm n-not much for s-small talk."

"So I noticed."

"W-what's your f-favorite t-time of the year?"

"Autumn, I think. Starts in August with hints of the coming fall. Birds take their sweet time migrating back to their winter spots. And it's not just the birds, but there are colors that only October can offer."

Micah made a noise of approval and turned to start up a steep ridge, so steep that Ben wondered if he'd made a mistake, because by now he was starting to wear out, huffing and puffing and growing overheated. But then they came to the top of the ridge and sat on a large flat rock to rest. Below them lay a pond in the shape of a figure eight, rimmed with marsh. An ideal setting for migrating birds to rest in a stopover, and for some, perhaps, to stay and nest.

"Wonder Lake." Micah shrugged. "M-more like a m-marsh."

Micah peered through his binoculars, then handed them to Ben, pointing to a dead tree in the middle of the pond. Ben's breath caught. It was a Bald Eagle's aerie, a nest, firmly tucked into the fork of the tree trunk. Though he'd seen eagles' aeries before, they never failed to astound. Enormous in size, chaotic in appearance, a tangle of sticks and branches going every which way. By contrast, the interior would be as soft as velvet, lined with grass and moss and lichen.

"In use?" he asked Micah. The exterior was whitewashed, a genteel way of saying it was covered with excrement, a sure sign of an active nest.

Micah grunted, which Ben was learning to take as his version of a yes. No's came with a shake of his head. "There."

Ben looked up and saw the male eagle fly toward the nest with a fish in its talons. A white head popped up. The female. They both disappeared into the nest, and not much later, the male appeared again, perched on the rim of the nest, standing guard while his beloved ate her breakfast.

"How big do you think it is? Six feet across? Seven?"

Micah shrugged. "Yesterday, the m-male brought in s-sticks and the f-female would wait until he left, then put the sticks in a d-different s-spot."

A laugh burst out of Ben. "Just like a typical married couple."

"Penny r-remembers that n-nest when she was a g-girl."

"Hold on. Penny was here as a girl?"

Another grunt. "V-visiting our g-grandmother."

"Think it's the same pair?"

"D-doubt it. M-maybe its offspring."

Ben handed him back his binoculars. "I heard once of an eagle in captivity that lived to be seventy years old."

Micah tucked his head through the binoculars' neck strap and rose to his feet. "But what k-kind of life would that b-be for an eagle?" He started off through the brush and Ben hurried to catch up.

Micah Weaver lived up to his reputation. He had a remarkable ear. As they trooped through the woods, every half mile or so, he would stop at a sound and cock his head. "Hear that?"

Ben would listen with all his might, every muscle in his body tense. The woods trilled with all kinds of birdsong. "What exactly am I listening for?" It was only after Micah pointed out a specific call or song that Ben heard it. He went back and forth with his optics, sometimes looking through his binoculars and other times through his camera lens, and occasionally he'd get tired of squinting and he would just look with his eyes.

The morning was a near triumph. Ben saw more migrants in a few hours with Micah than he normally saw in full days with other birders and guides. Even with lifers, who aggressively pursued as many bird species as possible, just ticking off their list.

Following behind Micah, Ben felt like he was a guest in the woods, taking great delight in all the different birds they encountered. To his surprise, slowing down the pace allowed him to see birds that he might have missed.

Ben and Micah returned to Lost Creek Farm around noon after seeing vagrant heron and egrets: the Snowy Egret, the Little Blue Heron, the Tricolored Heron, the Cattle Egret. Micah showed him the secretive American Bittern, hiding in a sheltered marshy area of Wonder Lake. Virginia Rail and Sora were among the cattails.

But no White-winged Tern. Not yet, anyway.

Ben walked into the guesthouse, dropped his equipment bag by the door, collapsed on the green couch, and fell asleep without even removing his shoes. He woke five hours later, disoriented, stomach rumbling—but for food, not for upset. As he stumbled to the bathroom to wash his face, he cheered himself with the thought that if he was hungry, then he was on the mend.

Boyd Baldwin had kept calling until Natalie finally answered her phone. He asked her to come back to Stoney Ridge, that there was a place he wanted to take her, and to wear casual clothing.

Natalie's casual clothing consisted of a pressed, crisp white blouse with sleeves rolled up a precise two and a half folds, black skinny jeans, black leather flats, and a Kate Spade oversized black cobbled leather purse. She was a city girl, through and through.

Yet he kept persisting and she finally ran out of excuses and said yes. She packed a small bag and started out for Stoney Ridge.

This was ludicrous, crazy. She had nothing in common with a country vet. Yet there was something about the way he pursued her that made her knees feel wobbly.

When had a man ever treated her that way? Looked at her the way he looked at her? As if she were a prize to be won, a pearl of great price.

It was evening as she drove up the driveway to Lost Creek Farm.

Ben came out of the guesthouse to greet her. Smiling, he said, "I didn't expect you today."

"I, well, I thought I'd come and see how you're doing. Feeling better?" He sure looked better. The blue shadows under his eyes were gone, that perpetually fatigued look. In fact, his eyes held a brightness to them she hadn't seen in quite a while.

"Much. I'm glad you're here. I was going to call you later today. I'll pack up and we can head out."

"Nope. We're staying put."

"What?"

"Can't leave. I have a date."

He looked at her like she might be crazy.

Maybe she was.

～

Micah Weaver was turning out to be a real surprise. Some of the information that boy knew! Ben found himself learning all kinds of things from the boy. A few times out in the field with Micah, and he was properly humbled.

This morning took the cake. They were hiking the perimeter of a reservoir, slogging through its soggy border, eyes and ears peeled for the White-winged Tern. Micah assured him that if it was still here, he'd find it, and Ben trusted him.

Micah stopped so suddenly that Ben nearly walked right into him.

"There." Micah lifted his chin and tipped his head, a behavior Ben had come to recognize that meant he'd heard something out of the ordinary.

"The tern?" Ben craned to hear. "Oh. Now I hear it. A Carolina Wren."

Micah shook his head. "A Sedge Wren."

The elusive, endangered Sedge Wren? Ben set up his scope, listening for the Sedge Wren's characteristic song: two or three sharp notes followed by a rapid, chattering series of trill notes.

Sure enough, something moved in the tree.

And suddenly he saw it, hiding on a branch. A small bird with a streaked crown and back, faint buff-colored eye stripes, and a short upright tail. So small, it would be easy to overlook.

Ben was astounded with Micah's discerning ear. What kind of birder could pick out birdsong that was just slightly different from its common cousin, the Carolina Wren?

Mornings out in the field with Micah—each one better than the last.

Micah had been born quite late to parents already weary from raising eight children, and then he made nine. He never had to talk much at home because his much older siblings did so much of the talking. When the time came for Micah to go to school, he was as small then as he was tall now, so puny you almost didn't know he was there. But one boy noticed. The school bully, ten-year-old Roland Miller. Roland took an instant dislike to Micah and made his school days painful ones. He encouraged the other children to treat Micah like an oddity—a gawky, silent, kindhearted boy who liked birds. Roland would burst out in harsh laughter whenever Micah had to recite in school or answer the teacher's question.

One afternoon, when Micah was seven, he was walking home alone from school and stopped to watch an Osprey in flight over his head. What must it be like to be a raptor, the top of the predator chain? Nothing to fear.

Suddenly Roland jumped out from behind a tree and shoved him to the ground. When Micah tried to get up, Roland strutted over and kicked him. He stood next to Micah with widespread feet, firmly planted, his beefy fists akimbo. "Hey, fellas, look who I stumbled on." He lifted his head and let his gaze sweep his buddies to make sure none of them missed this. "I think we got ourselves a bird boy," he said, loud enough so all the others could hear.

Again Micah tried to get up, but Roland planted a heavy boot on his crotch and pushed. Hard. A shot of pain flattened Micah.

Roland pushed back his hat. "What's that, Bird Boy? You got something to say? Speak up."

A cold sweat broke out over Micah. He thought he was going to throw up.

"Just admit that you're a pansy bird lover and I'll let you go." Roland smiled, a cold hard look.

Micah felt a strangling sense of humiliation. He could see words in his head, white on black, like chalk on a slate board. He could feel them form in his throat and curl around his tongue. He could see them and feel them, but he couldn't get them out. They clogged in his throat. He made some sounds that came out as grunts, which only fired up Roland.

Just at that moment, his sister Penny appeared out of nowhere, clamped a hand on Roland's ankle to force the dusty boot off Micah. She stared Roland down until he backed away, sheepishly, waving his hands in the air like a surrender. "We was just funning him, Penny."

Penny kept her eyes fixed on Roland, like a raptor on its prey. "Your dad will be interested in hearing about your funning."

Roland shook his head like a dog after a swim. "Don't tell him." Everyone knew about his father's harsh temper.

Penny took a step closer to Roland. They were about the same height, but she had an authority that made Roland shrink. "You touch my brother again and I'll have the deacon at your door."

Roland took off running. His friends had already vanished.

Micah rolled on his side to rise, still hurting.

"I know you could have handled this yourself, Micah."

No, he couldn't. He really couldn't.

It was embarrassing to have a sister come to his rescue, but he was grateful for it. Penny, his favorite sister, had a knack for showing up at all the right times, and knew how to handle sticky situations. She said just enough and not too much.

His stammer, appearing only when he was nervous (which was most of the time), settled in for a permanent stay on that day. Roland never physically harmed Micah again, but that didn't stop his big mouth from running him down every chance he got.

The only place Micah knew true freedom was out in the woods and fields, so he started to play hooky and spend time outside. Penny had sparked his passion for birding. She'd taught him how to identify birds, how to understand what they were trying to communicate. Mostly, how to listen.

After he graduated from grade 8, he worked for his older brothers in the family dairy. He participated in the Cornell Lab's Great Backyard Bird Counts, and then the Audubon Society's Christmas Bird Counts. Birders started to notice his trained ear. Some sought him out, hiring him as a field guide. That's when the church leaders decided that being a part of the birding community with outsiders would lead Micah away from the straight and narrow path. No more field guiding, they told him. No more bird counts.

For the first time in his life, Micah stood up for himself. He flat-out disagreed with the leaders. You just didn't do that, not in his church. Micah was put under the Bann until he repented. He found himself between a rock and a hard place, and he didn't know what to do. He couldn't give up his love for birding, but living under the Bann was worse than he had expected it to be. Eating alone at a set-apart table, treated like a leper wherever he went. Being separate, that was what he couldn't bear.

And then, in a miraculous turn of events, his parents offered him and Penny the chance to go live at their late grandmother's farm in Stoney Ridge—someone Micah had barely known. In one fell swoop, Micah had a chance to keep chasing birds and keep being Amish. Two birds, one stone.

He felt like he'd been set free from a cage.

Micah Weaver, Bird-Watching Log

Name of Bird: Osprey

Scientific Name: *Pandion haliaetus*

Status: Low concern (a comeback story after being an endangered species)

Date: November 3

Location: Blue Lake Pond

Description: Juvenile, with white spots on its brown back. Distinctive white chest. Black sharply hooked beak, white head with a broad brown line through the eyes, like a bandit's mask. With a wingspan of five to six feet, the Osprey isn't as large as a Bald Eagle (their wingspan is up to seven and a half feet) but it's bigger than a Red-tailed Hawk. Distinctive shape—slim body, long legs, M-shaped kink in its wings.

Bird Action: Juvenile hunting for fish. Circled high in the sky, hovered briefly before diving, feet first, to grab a fish.

Notes: Unlike other raptors, the Osprey eats only live fish. (Probably why some call it the River Hawk, Sea Hawk, or Fish Hawk.) They're able to spot a fish 200 feet away and catch it with their talons.

What's most amazing about Ospreys is their migration story. During spring migration, they'll travel nearly nonstop from South America, flying two weeks or longer to reach breeding grounds in North America. That's over 5,000 miles! They're in a hurry, and for good reason. Timing is everything if you're hunting for a good woman and a place to call home.

9

Natalie slept late the next day after a better night's sleep than she'd had in a while. She went to the kitchen expecting to find Ben pecking away at his computer, but the room was empty. The door to his bedroom was open, his optical equipment bag was gone. Birding, no doubt.

Out of her suitcase she pulled a package of freshly roasted coffee beans. In the mini-kitchen, she found a coffeepot and filter but no coffee grinder. Drat! She should've thought to bring one.

She dressed and went to the big house to see if Penny might have a coffee grinder, though she doubted it. No one answered her knock at the kitchen door, so she tried the door and found it unlocked. She opened it to call Penny's name once, twice, then thrice. No response.

She smelled the coffee before she saw the pot. If nobody was home, no one would ever know that she trespassed, right? Longing for a hot cup of coffee, she could convince herself of almost anything.

Hoping Penny wouldn't mind if she helped herself, she found a mug, filled it, then leaned against the counter for a moment, sipping the dark brew, sweeping the room with her gaze. Someone, long ago, had planned well. The morning sun streamed through the bay window, illuminating the entire kitchen in a soft and cheery glow.

She called Penny's name again. No answer. No sounds of anyone in the house. She took a few steps around. The kitchen, she realized, served as an everything room—living room, dining room, and kitchen. It felt like a throwback to the old-timey times, when a well-loved cast-iron woodstove held the prominent place in the room. A peg wall carried a random collection of battered tin pots and pans.

Emboldened, she nosed around a little further, venturing around the room.

No mirrors! There were no mirrors in this house. At least, none hanging prominently on the walls like in most homes. What must it be like to not be distracted by your own reflection? Natalie couldn't pass a mirror without running a hand through her carefully styled hair, or stopping to fix her lipstick, or . . . well, frankly, to catalog one disappointing feature or another. That was the problem with mirrors. Constant reminders of one's shortcomings. She turned in a circle, letting her imagination run.

There was a sweet spirit in this home. Almost palpable.

But it lacked so much. It lacked all the decorative touches that Natalie excelled at providing—rugs, lighting fixtures, art on the walls, pillows on the chairs and sofa, paint on the walls that wasn't a pale green. This house, this room, was calling to her, begging for her attention. The mismatched furniture felt like it was one stop away from the city dump.

Hmm. It wouldn't take much money to bring this house into the twenty-first century. It already had the popular "open concept" in the kitchen/family room area.

Scratch that thought. She smiled at her foolishness. She'd forgotten where she was for a moment. The entire house would need to be wired for electricity; a heating and cooling HVAC system would need to be installed. It would cost a small fortune to update.

She pivoted and turned back to head into the kitchen. Lying on top of the table was a sketch pad. Ever nosy, Natalie walked to the table to lift the cover of the pad. On the first page was a pen-and-ink drawing of a red-breasted robin, painted with watercolors, so life-like, so specific in its detailing, that it could have been framed. Should have been framed. Was this Penny's? Or Micah's? It was unsigned.

Curiosity pressed her to peek under the first illustration. Page after page were watercolors of birds, each one more exquisite than the one before. She could not believe her eyes as she lifted the pages quickly, as if the drawings might disappear. She sat in the chair to go through the sketch pad again—and then three more times, each time more slowly than before.

Out the window, she saw Penny coming from the horse barn to cross the yard and head to the house. Quickly, Natalie closed the cover of the sketch pad and put it back, exactly as she'd found it. She felt a tinge of guilt for snooping in this woman's house. Embarrassed too. What excuse could she give, other than desperately wanting coffee? Which was the truth, actually.

Penny was halfway to the house when a truck rumbled up the driveway and she paused, then veered away to greet the driver. Boyd! He'd come. Like he said he would.

Natalie slipped out of the house, unnoticed, and hurried down the path to meet them.

~

Ben tried not to roll his eyes when Natalie handed him a glass of water and his antimalarial meds and ordered him to take them. "Just because you're feeling better doesn't mean you stop taking them."

"Thank you, Dr. Natalie."

She curled up in a chair across from him. "Ben, someone in that house is an incredible artist. Incredible."

Mid-sip of water, Ben stilled. Had she seen in the night what he'd seen? "What makes you say that?"

"I saw the illustrations. They were on the kitchen table."

"Were you snooping?"

"No! Maybe. I needed a cup of coffee this morning, and no one answered the door, and so I popped in to get the coffee—"

"You were snooping."

"As I said, they were right there, on the kitchen table." She leaned forward. "They're stunning. Truly impressive. The detail, the coloring. Almost like a photograph . . . yet the Amish don't use cameras, do they?" She clasped her hands together. "Ben . . . they should be shown to the world."

Ben laughed. "There's so much wrong with that thinking, I don't know where to begin."

"Why?"

"The Amish . . . they don't want to draw attention to themselves. They might draw something on a calendar or to decorate a Bible verse, but never—or rarely ever—would art be created just for art's sake. The Amish upbringing doesn't encourage artistic creativity. They think it could lead someone down a prideful path."

"The drawings had no signature. Who do you think drew them? Micah? Or Penny?"

Ben lifted his shoulders in a shrug, as if to say he had no idea. But he knew.

"Could you at least ask Penny about the drawings?"

"And tell them you've been snooping in their house?"

She frowned. "Not snooping. Just . . . getting coffee."

He lifted an eyebrow.

"Just . . . keep it in mind, in case one or the other mentions their hidden talent."

"Well, that's it right there. To consider themselves talented would mean they're prideful. And that would mean they'd have to be brought under church discipline."

"Maybe it's changed since you were young. This bishop, David Stoltzfus, he's the very one who suggested that Penny open the guesthouse to you. He's encouraged Micah to be a field guide to you. Isn't it possible the Amish are changing? Opening up to new possibilities as farmland shrinks?"

"Even if they can consider new ways to support their families, what you're asking is something else entirely. To be recognized for a specific skill like artistry, it's not the same as feeding your family."

"How is it different from building a piece of furniture or quilting a beautiful quilt? They do all kinds of crafts. I've seen Amish furniture shops."

"Not the same at all. Furniture has a function. Quilts have a function. But an individual artist, that's something else entirely. Natalie, these people think differently about life than anyone you've ever met. Especially Americans, who pride themselves on being different. Independent."

"That's it!" She clapped her hands together. "That's the way to approach it with Penny, or Micah, or the bishop. Those pictures . . . they don't make you think about the artist who drew the birds. They make you think about the Artist that created the birds. Capital *A*." She lifted her head, as if considering something, then dropped her chin to look right at him. "I'm not kidding, Ben. The world needs to see those watercolors."

"Why? Why should it matter to you? If someone is drawing watercolors of birds for their own pleasure, why can't you just leave it at that?"

She didn't answer for a long time. "There's just something about them. Like . . . they were calling to me."

Ben grinned. "Sounds like a convert is in the making. I'd recommend attending a Sunday church service, first."

Natalie lifted her eyebrows. "Maybe I will."

Good luck with that, Ben thought.

⌢

Yesterday afternoon, Penny had taken a meal over to Zeke Zook and discovered something she'd never known about him—he'd been skilled as a cobbler and could repair shoes. She was dishing up her casserole for Zeke when Hank Lapp blew through the door, like an unexpected rainstorm.

"I NEED a SOLE FIXED." Hank set a filthy boot right on the kitchen table.

Zeke, who had been sitting silently at the table with his chin tucked low, his customary posture, came to life. He picked up the boot and examined it, then slowly rose to head out the door. Hank followed, and Penny, now curious, did too. They trotted behind Zeke like ducklings, into the barn, absent of animals, for Zeke no longer farmed his land.

Zeke kept going. In the back of the barn was a small room, lit by one western-facing window. He stared at the peg wall, full of small tools that were carefully organized. He reached out for a few tools, set Hank's boot on the worktable, eased onto the stool, and got to work.

Leaning on the doorjamb, Penny watched, amazed. She had no comparison to what Zeke used to be like, so she took him as he was. But seeing him work so diligently over Hank's dirty boot gave her a hint of the man he once was. Determined, precise, skilled.

Hank kept getting in the way, peering over his shoulder, picking up tools, dropping them, asking him questions.

Finally, exasperated, Zeke pointed to the door. "Out." He said it as clear as a bell.

That, too, was a shock to Penny. Zeke was a man of few words, most of them robbed by dementia, and when he did speak, he often didn't make sense. She had to work hard to figure out what he wanted.

Surprisingly, Hank took the hint. "PENNY, we'd better LEAVE the MASTER to his WORK."

Penny and Hank walked down the aisle of the barn. "I didn't know Zeke could mend shoes."

"He's the BEST COBBLER in the COUNTY. We ALL COUNT on him. We DID, anyhows, BEFORE he got so ADDLE-MINDED."

Out of the barn, they walked to Hank's buggy. "I thought I saw MICAH marching across a FIELD with your HOUSEGUEST."

"Yes. They're birding along Lost Creek today."

Hank leaned forward. "PENNY, TOP SECRET NEWS." He put a finger to his lips. "THAT houseguest of yours . . . he's . . . well, he's . . ."

"Zeke's son."

"YES!" His bushy brows furrowed together. "DID ZEKE say something? He DON'T TALK much about BEN."

Penny swallowed. "Zeke doesn't know he's here."

"EDDY and ME . . . we WANT to get them TOGETHER before Ben FLIES OFF AGAIN. It's our DUTY."

"No, Hank." She shook her head firmly. "It's the Lord's work."

Hank stroked his thin beard. "SOMETIMES, the LORD needs a little HELP." He leaned forward. "SO I'M PLANNING to go out BIRDING with BEN and MICAH. Have a little TALK."

Penny shook her head. "Hank, that's not a good idea. Not at all. It's a really bad idea." Ben was like a Belted Kingfisher, solitary and skittish. Hank was a noisy, ever-present crow.

"IT'S a FINE IDEA. THOUGHT of it MYSELF." He gave her a thumbs-up and hopped in his buggy. "Tell ZEKE I'll be BACK for my BOOT."

Penny watched Hank's mule head to the road, praying he would go right, head straight home. Alas, he turned left, toward Lost Creek.

Ben slept most of the afternoon after returning from today's morning outing with Micah. After he woke, he showered and shaved, changed, and wondered where Natalie had gone. He went outside to see if her car was still there. Penny was crossing the lawn, and his steps faltered as he forgot about his cousin. Sometimes when Ben saw Penny, he'd think to himself, *What makes you so happy?* Or *You look especially pretty today, Penny.* But he would never say such thoughts aloud, because he didn't want her to think he was after something more than a bird.

Truth to tell, always in the back of his mind lingered the reason he'd left the Plain people, and why. Because of it, he kept a careful distance.

Penny stood in front of a rhododendron bush, admiring one last pink flower, as big as a dinner plate. He came across the grass and stopped, putting six feet between them before he said something. "It's big, I'll grant you that."

She startled at his voice and spun around. "The hummingbird?"

"Oh no. I didn't see a hummingbird. I thought you were looking at the flower."

"Both, actually. I was watching the hummingbird drink from the flower."

Now he saw it zipping around the bush's flowers, drawn to nectar. "Rufous Hummingbird?"

"Yes. A male, with that glossy orange throat." She turned to the buzzing sounds of its wings.

He came closer to watch. Running through his mind was his checklist: It was a Rufous Hummingbird, common to Pennsylvania. Fearless, aggressive. Excellent memories for location. Notoriously territorial. Known for chasing away other hummingbirds and even large birds and rodents from a good food resource. Able to tolerate more extreme temperatures than other hummingbirds.

"Each one," she said, "a miracle."

"A miracle in how it can hover up and down like a helicopter?"

"Their migration is the miracle. To think of how far that tiny bird has to go soon. Central America, or Mexico. Over large bodies of seawater." She let out a happy sigh. "All of migration is a miracle, but somehow a hummingbird seems like one of the biggest miracles of all. It's amazing they exist at all."

"I agree with you about the mystery of migration. It's one of the greatest natural forces in the world." The Rufous Hummingbird had the longest migration route of any hummingbird—over four thousand miles. Talk about the marvel of migration. Staggering.

Everything was silent for a moment, then the tiny bird flew off, and suddenly it seemed very awkward between them.

They exchanged a nervous glance, and then she dropped her head, turning on her heels.

His hand shot out, grabbing her arm. "Penny, wait."

She stopped so abruptly that he dropped his hold on her.

"I just wanted to say . . . Micah's living up to his reputation."

She smiled, relaxed. "He has a gift."

"Yes, he's a very unusual young man. If Micah weren't Plain, he could make quite a successful name for himself as a field guide." The words barely left his mouth when he wished them back. Had he forgotten what it was like to be Plain?

A soft pity filled her eyes, stinging Ben's pride. "Thank heavens that he is Plain, then."

Ben cleared his throat, hoping to clear away that comment. "Somehow I need to keep Hank Lapp from joining us. He makes an infernal noise wherever he goes. Scared the birds right out of the trees." A little bit of Hank went a long way. He was just too much for Ben. Too loud. Too talkative. Too everything.

Penny cringed. "I'm the one to blame for that. He saw the two of you head out this morning and I mentioned you were going to Lost Creek. So I apologize." She paused, as if waiting to hear more, then started on her way to the kitchen door and he hurried to catch up.

"Penny, the way you were watching the hummingbird . . . it was as if your mind was photographing it."

She cocked her head to look around her shoulder at him. "Photographing?"

"Like you were trying to memorize the location of every feather."

She stopped, pivoted to face him. "But isn't that how you observe birds?"

120

No. It was once, but not with the pressure of publishing. He relied heavily on taking photographs with the intention of studying the birds later. "Once or twice, I thought I saw you drawing at night. I wasn't spying on you," he hurried to say when he noticed she stiffened. "Nothing weird like that. I just couldn't sleep, and I saw the lantern on in the kitchen. That big bay window is . . . well, it's big. I just wondered if you might be drawing birds." Flustered, he jerked his gaze away from her steady one.

"Would you like to see what I draw?"

He snapped his head to face her. "Indeed I would."

He stepped into the house behind her and stopped abruptly. Penny had been baking. The delicious smell of warm chocolate hit his senses full on, the table had a cheerful tablecloth covering it, with a mason jar full of amethyst beautyberries. A wave of nostalgia washed over him. He could smell his childhood—all the good parts.

"Wait here," she said, pointing to a chair at the kitchen table before she disappeared into the pantry. Lowering himself into a chair, he heard sounds of rummaging, and something that sounded like a book dropped on the floor. Gazing around the kitchen, he spotted a tray cooling on the stove top and smiled. *Ah, brownies.* Suddenly she reappeared, closing the door carefully behind her. She held a large sketch pad in two hands, and set it gently on the table, as if the pad were made of thinly blown glass.

He hesitated, resting his hands on his thighs, nearly afraid to touch it. "May I?"

When she nodded, he lifted the pad's cardboard cover to reveal a red male cardinal on the branch of a birch tree in a snowy winter scene. He stared at it, half expecting it to take flight. Natalie's assessment was spot-on. Ben had seen many illustrations of birds, but there was something special about this. Something real. Touching. As if inviting the spectator into the scene. "No formal training? You're entirely self-taught."

She nodded.

He lifted another page to find a Great Horned Owl taking off from its perch. On the next page, an Osprey lifting upward toward the sky with an unlucky fish in its talons. "Why do you sketch, Penny?"

"I suppose . . . because I want to remember."

"Tell me more."

"Drawing makes me a better observer of the natural world. It's the best way to learn birds because you have to stop and really think about what you're seeing."

"Field marks stick."

"Yes."

Some pages were filled with practice sketches—tails, eyes, wings, feet. "You sketch in every season?"

"Oh yes. Year-round offers different approaches to finding the birds. It's easiest in summer, of course. And fall brings the waterfowl. In the winter months, I mostly sketch what I see at the feeder, or remember what I've seen in the summer. But spring . . . it has a special joy. I especially love to observe the chicks and fledglings."

"Penny, you do this all from memory? You have no images you're copying from? No camera?"

"I'll consult certain books and field guides. But the finished sketches are moments I've observed in nature. I'll go out with a pad and pencil and watch. There's nothing like time in nature. Things like noticing the size of a bird compared to its environment. You can't always get those from a picture."

"Not just watching. You're paying attention. Patient, keen observation." Page after page, the avian world unfolded in front of him. "This one. This Gray Catbird. You've caught its personality."

In a voice so soft it was like velvet to Ben, she explained her methods. "I like to see what keeps a bird busy, and how it interacts with other birds. And its idiosyncrasies. Sometimes, like that Gray Catbird, I'll compile many birds into one. Sketching, I suppose, is my form of keeping a diary. Of taking notes. I start with line drawings. Later, I'll add watercolor."

"What's your favorite bird to draw?" Ben said. "And the most difficult?"

"Oh, picking favorites. That's always hard." Penny shifted in her chair. "I suppose it's the same answer for both questions. I love drawing owls. They make such good subjects. If you see an owl in the daytime, they'll sit still for hours. They're very different from other birds, like a robin or a chickadee or a warbler. Their facial structure, their posture. That's what makes it so difficult."

"So then . . . what's your best advice to someone who wants to draw birds?"

"A novice? I suppose I would say . . . pay close attention to the common birds that are right in your backyard. Watch them, notice them, study them. Ask questions of other birders. That's how I've learned so much about birds. It's the foundation of anything, I suppose."

"Curiosity."

"Yes. Yes, that's exactly it." Penny paused. "Birding takes patience."

"Indeed it does." He came to the last page and, reluctantly, closed the sketch pad. "No White-winged Tern."

"I'm afraid not. I haven't seen it. Only Micah and Trudy have spotted it."

"Trudy?"

"Trudy Yoder. She's a young girl who loves birding. Micah, who has a big and gentle heart, finds her annoying. I find her to be charming." Or maybe Penny enjoyed Trudy so much because the girl was so fond of birds and equally fond of Micah.

Ben grinned, tapping the sketch pad with the tips of his fingers. "Penny, by all counts, you've an impressive body of work here."

She picked it up from him and held it against her. "Not so. Lots of amateur errors." She smiled. "But every birder knows that not all sticks in the nest are straight."

He stilled. "What did you say?"

"Every birder knows that not all sticks in the nest are straight.

It's just a way of saying that we all make mistakes. Human beings, each one, have foibles and flaws."

She wasn't looking at him anymore, and he couldn't really tell what she was thinking, if she had meant that saying for him. "I think my cousin Natalie would like to see these. More than like it. She'd love it."

She hesitated. "Someday, perhaps." She glanced out the window. "It's such a pleasant day that I thought Micah and I would light a fire in the pit tonight. I made some rocky road brownies."

"They smell delicious."

"You and your cousin would be welcome to join us."

"Count on it."

Then Penny squared her chin and looked him dead in the eye. "Natalie wants to come to church with us."

A shaft of dread speared through Ben. He looked down, visibly stiffened, waiting for her to extend an invitation to him, but none came. But when he finally glanced up, he saw only compassion in her gray eyes. She gave him a little nod and took her sketch pad into the pantry to put it away.

He left the kitchen before she reemerged from the pantry, unsettled by this Plain woman. These conversations they'd been having this last week, they alternated between leaving him calm and at peace . . . or fraught and unsettled. This time, the latter.

Micah Weaver, Bird-Watching Log

Name of Bird: Belted Kingfisher

Scientific Name: Megaceryle alcyon

Status: Low concern

Date: April 27

Location: Hank and Edith Lapp's goldfish pond

Description: Female, robin-sized, blue-gray with white collar and chestnut belly band. Impressive mohawk hairdo.

Bird Action: Female perched on high branch before plunging headfirst into the small backyard pond, coming up with a small goldfish. Edith ran out of the house screeching and off it flew.

Notes: Solitary, active bird. A sit-and-wait predator that mostly hunts from a tree branch to have a clear view over feeding territory. One of few birds where the female is more brightly colored than the male. Females have a chestnut belly band and flanks. A nesting pair will work together to dig a tunnel for an underground burrow near water (their nest).

To avoid getting eaten by hawks, the Belted Kingfisher will dive into the water. Clever.

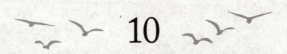

10

Boyd Baldwin stood on the doorstep of the guesthouse. His sandy-blond hair still wore comb marks from dampness, fresh from a shower. He held up a wicker picnic hamper, his eyes warming as he looked at Natalie. "You promised."

And so she had. He had been talking about going on a picnic to Blue Lake Pond since she'd arrived at Lost Creek Farm and had even bought her a pair of Wellington boots. So far, she'd begged off. She finally agreed to go as long as the temperature cooperated and didn't dip below sixty degrees.

Today was a gorgeous day, sunny and warm. A perfect autumn day for a picnic at the lake . . . but they'd also gone out for dinner two nights in a row. When he called her this morning to set up a time for the picnic, it occurred to her that it was probably not very smart to see him again so soon. Mostly, it was probably not very smart to look forward to being with him as much as she did.

On the bumpy ride in his truck out to Blue Lake Pond, she reviewed all the reasons this relationship made no sense. He was a country boy, she was a city girl. He was planted in Stoney Ridge like a tree with deep roots. She felt the same way about her little home in Philadelphia. He spent his days at farms and, to quote him, "carried the barnyard on his boots." She was slightly neurotic about cleanliness. She and Boyd . . . they made no sense together.

And yet . . . she couldn't help herself. He dazzled her. It wasn't just his appearance, which she found very attractive, but it was his kindness, his thoughtfulness. His unfeigned openness to her. There was nothing hidden or secretive in Boyd. He said what he thought, he shared what he felt. He was a wonderfully refreshing man to be around.

She tried to keep her focus affixed to the scenery around her—the trees that still had colorful leaves on them, the sun streaming through branches, the still water of the large pond—because each time she looked at Boyd, she started to feel dizzy . . . as if everything was slightly out of focus.

They settled on the sand, a thin ribbon of beach that lined the pond. Boyd spread out an enormous red-and-black buffalo plaid blanket. Ridiculously large. "I'm not entirely opposed to nature," she said.

"As long as it doesn't include mosquitos," Boyd said.

She knit her forehead, brushing off her jeans. "And ants."

Out of the hamper he took a waxed bag and handed it to her. It was a chocolate chip cookie he'd picked up at the Sweet Tooth Bakery. "First things first." Somehow, he intuitively knew that she would prefer to start with dessert. This man thought of *everything*. She took a bite, closing her eyes in delight as the chocolate melted in her mouth.

Boyd settled back on an elbow, crossing one ankle over the other. His gaze swept the pond in a way that reminded her a little of her cousin Ben. Constantly scanning for creatures.

Natalie shifted so she could look at the pond. "I'm pretty sure those are geese and not ducks, but I can never remember what kind."

"Canada Geese," he said, "who don't really live in Canada."

Natalie reached into the hamper and took out two deli sandwiches, handing him one. Then she took out two water bottles and passed him one. He lifted the wrapped sandwich and the water bottle slightly in the air, offering a short prayer: "Thank you, Lord, for all this." He smiled at her. "For all this and more."

So simple. So natural. So like Boyd.

As they ate, she found herself enjoying the feeling of being surrounded by such peace and quiet. The sandwich, the cookie, even the bottled water—all tasted fresher outdoors. As if each sense was fully participating—smell, sight, taste, feel, even hearing. So many birds! They were everywhere. As she finished up her sandwich, she balled up the paper and tossed it in the hamper. "So, you're always asking me questions. What about you? What's your story?"

His eyebrows wiggled in that funny way he had. "Nothing too exciting. Grew up not too far from here. I'm the son of a vet who was the son of a vet. When my grandfather retired, my father took over his practice. When my father retired, I took over the practice."

"But you love it here? You love what you do?" She wondered if he'd had a choice in the matter.

He had been watching the flock of Canada Geese that were swimming smoothly along the surface, barely making a ripple. He turned his head toward her. "Absolutely. To the very marrow of my bones, Natalie."

She smiled, loving the sound of her name rolling off his tongue. "It's good to have a life you love."

"It *is* good to have a life you love," he repeated, then gave her a sideways glance. "Even better . . . to create a life you love."

Now there was something to ponder. How to create a life you love? Especially after the life you thought was yours had been ripped out from under you.

"People need to be brave enough to go after what they really want." Something beeped and he glanced at his smartphone. "Time to go. I'm expected at the Yoders'. They have a sick pig that needs worming."

"Now there's a way to kill the moment," Natalie said, and he laughed, as if she'd made a great joke. She'd been entirely serious. He started to pack up their picnic, so she followed suit, a little disappointed. The time had gone too quickly. It always did with Boyd, she realized.

As she rose, she noticed there was an odd-looking goose swimming along with the Canada Geese, trying to be a part of the flock. *Funny*, she thought. *That's exactly how I feel here.*

~

Late in the afternoon, Micah stopped by the Yoder farm to ask Trudy if she'd seen any sign of the White-winged Tern, but in truth he had high hopes that Shelley would answer the door. Unfortunately, Trudy recognized Junco pulling the buggy and burst out of the house like a bat out of a cave.

"You won't believe what I saw today, Micah! A Pink-footed Goose."

He stopped short. "Where?"

"Over at Blue Lake Pond. It's mingling with some Canada Geese."

"T-Trudy," he said with a warning tone.

"I just saw it this morning at Blue Lake Pond. I was gonna come tell you about it, soon as I finished up feeding the animals."

No way. No possible way. A Pink-footed Goose was a native of Europe, an incredibly rare species to spot in North America.

She tipped forward and backward on her toes. "If you helped me, I could take you to see it. Guessing it's still there, looking for supper."

He glanced at the cows coming slowly over the hill toward the barn from the field. "You have to m-milk 'em all?"

"No. Just get them into their stanchions and give them feed."

Micah glanced at the house. He thought of Shelley, most likely in the house, possibly watching him from the window. Then he thought about the Pink-footed Goose. He'd never seen one. "I'll help."

Micah followed Trudy into the barn and was immediately enveloped by the warmth and aroma of animals and silage. It wasn't an unpleasant combination, but it did take Micah right back to his childhood in Big Valley, to the daily monotony of dairy farming.

129

Micah, along with his brothers, had spent their childhood rising early to milk cows. There was much to appreciate in the farmer's life, but Micah was grateful that his older brothers wanted to take over the farm for his father. He had no problem leaving it.

The Yoder farm was a dairy farm, which meant that Trudy's father, like Micah's own father had been, was wholly occupied with growing silage to feed his livestock. The Yoder barn was enormous, larger than most. The horses demanded the first attention, stomping and snorting and carrying on until supper arrived. Then the cows started to gather in the yard. The smaller calves in their stalls began to clamor for their meal while their gentle mothers patiently waited. He knew the drill without being told and waited until Trudy gave him the signal to let the mamas in, one by one. Each one knew where it belonged, went right to its stanchion, a frame to hold the cow's head in place during milking.

As soon as the last one was in and settled, Trudy appeared at his side, her freckled face full of eagerness. "How's your list coming?" She started talking even before she climbed into Micah's buggy. "Mine's up to ninety-two this year, after those six Tundra Swans came through in August's big rainstorm. I'd never seen a swan here before. Bet your list is a lot more. Still, I'm already way ahead of last year."

She never stopped yakking, all the way out toward Blue Lake Pond. Junco went right to his favorite tree, where there was grass to nibble. Micah wrapped the reins around the tree, took out his binoculars and scope from the buggy, and followed Trudy down to the water. She didn't stop yakking away until she reached the beach, then she seemed to know it was time for silence. Birds, everywhere, were feeding. The sun would be setting soon and a sliver of moon was peeking from behind the tree line across the pond. Near the water's edge, they stopped.

"There," she whispered. "Didn't I tell you? There it is."

So Trudy's ID was spot-on. The Pink-footed Goose was swimming in the water alongside eight Canada Geese. Micah set up his scope and peered through it. He saw its pink feet as it nosedived into the water. Wow, wow, wow. "G-good find."

"I wonder if it got lost or if it thinks it's a Canada Goose."

He watched it for a while until it popped up. "Trudy, you're p-positively sure about the White-winged T-tern?"

She was looking up at him, her face serious. "I'm sure."

"B-but you haven't s-seen it recently?"

"Not since that second time at the lake. Have you?"

He shook his head. His stomach shook a little too. He felt like such a liar.

"But I'm keeping an eye out for it, Micah. I'll find it. Don't you worry. And when I do, I'll come and get you."

It was growing dark, but they stayed there for a while, watching the geese swim and dive for food, noticing other birds coming in to feed.

The arrival of a couple of cars disturbed the peace of the moment. Suddenly down the beach came a group of teenagers, laughing like hyenas, flushing the geese right out of the pond. Tommy Fisher and Nate Glick. And there was Shelley Yoder, coming right along behind them, dressed not in her Plain garb but in Englisch clothing. Wearing tight jeans and a jacket that showed her belly, and her hair was loose and flowing. And her face! Even in the twilight, Micah could see her painted eyes, her bright red lips, as red as berries. She stopped in her tracks when she recognized Micah and Trudy.

So did Tommy Fisher. "Well, lookie who's here. It's Shelley's little sister hanging out with the rare Blue-footed Booby bird!" He waved his arms in the air like a bird flying. "Caw, caw!"

Nate Glick joined him. "Hey, Shelley, does your dad know that Trudy's hanging out with the b-b-b-b-bird p-p-p-peeper! Who're you really watching through those binoculars?" He cupped his eyes like binoculars and turned around in an exaggerated circle, then zeroed in on Shelley.

"Cut it out," Shelley said, which only egged Tommy and Nate

on. They circled Micah and Trudy, flapping their arms, screeching like angry crows.

Micah's jaw tightened. It was Roland Miller and school days all over again.

"Just t-t-t-tell us to g-g-g-go!" Tommy jeered. He knocked Micah's hat on the ground, and as he bent to get it, Tommy snatched the binoculars hanging off his scope and tossed them to Nate. "Here you go! See if you can find the rare Blue-footed Booby in it!"

Micah was furious, but he knew to keep his mouth shut. He had no hope of getting any of his own ordinary words out from around his twisted-up tongue, so instead, he took great care to keep all expression from his face. When he straightened up from fetching his hat, he kept his eyes on Nate Glick's. Tommy was the true bully. Nate was just going along for the ride.

Without removing his eyes from Nate, he whacked his hat on his thigh to shake off the sand and settled the brim low over his eyes.

It was Shelley who intervened to grab the neck strand of the binoculars from Nate and returned them to Micah. "I'm sorry."

That only added to his humiliation. He felt a searing heat of mortification rise all the way from his toes to the tips of his ears. He picked up his scope and started up the beach.

"Wait, Micah," Shelley said, running to catch him. "Don't pay any attention to them."

Trudy followed behind both of them. "They flushed out the geese we were trying to watch."

"Come back. Join us. We're having a barbecue. Kumme esse!" *Come eat!*

But Micah kept marching up the beach. It wasn't the insult from those two idiots that made him refuse Shelley's invitation, it was that he couldn't get the words in his head out the way he saw them, and heard them, and knew them to be.

"Trudy!" Shelley's voice rang out sharply. "You can stay too!"

Trudy whirled around. "Don't worry. I won't tell Mom and

Dad on you, Shelley." Then she pivoted and broke into an all-out run to get to the buggy.

Slipping Junco's reins from the tree, Micah glanced back at Shelley. She stood where they'd left her on the beach, staring at them, arms at her side. She looked forlorn, abandoned. He wondered if he should go and get her, take her home where she belonged.

"You can't expect her to be someone she's not, Micah."

He shot a startled look at Trudy. She was in the buggy, leaning out the window, a sad look on her face. When he turned his head in Shelley's direction, he saw that she had walked back to join the two buffoons.

Neither Trudy nor Micah said a word on the ride home.

Penny brushed leaves off the Adirondack chairs while Micah trooped off to get wood and kindling from the woodpile on the side of the house. Surrounded by silence, she realized that sitting around the firepit had become a cherished time for the two of them, a favorite pastime. This was what refreshed Penny after a long day, the complete quiet, the sense of living within a hushed world. Gradually, her mind stilled, her breathing slowed, and she relaxed. Above her, the Big Dipper twinkled against the vast black sky. Something rustled in a bush—an animal? No, it was only Micah, returning with an armload of wood.

She watched her brother stack the wood in the large, round pit. He was bothered about something, but she didn't know what it was, and she knew that it was always better to wait until he was ready to talk. She did hope that Ben and Natalie would join them tonight . . . otherwise, with Micah in a sullen mood, it would be a very quiet evening. And this early December night sky, a dome full of sparkling stars, a sliver of a new moon, was just waiting to be shared, to be appreciated.

"'When I consider thy heavens,'" she said, "'the work of thy fingers, the moon and the stars, which thou hast ordained, what is man, that thou art mindful of him? And the son of man, that thou visitest him?'"

Micah glanced over at her as she recited the verses from Psalms, then up at the sky, before turning back to stoking the fire.

She let out a sigh. Yes, it would be a very quiet evening tonight if Ben and Natalie didn't join them.

And not a moment later she heard the door to the guesthouse open and shut, and saw them approach. Natalie was wrapped up in a thick coat, a hat, a scarf, and gloves, as if she were heading into a blizzard. Ben just had a coat on. Penny smiled, wondering what conversation had gone on between them just now. She handed them both knitted afghans to drape over their laps, though the temperature was in the fifties, unusually warm for this time of year. And Micah, anticipating Natalie's need for comfort, had doubled the size of the fire. The firepit radiated heat. By the time Penny served up brownies and hot cocoa, Natalie had started to shed her winter clothing.

It was private here. The firelight cast a soft glow, and the world seemed to disappear into the darkness. Natalie asked endless questions, as she was prone to do, and Penny didn't mind at all because she aimed many questions at Ben. Even Micah's spirits seemed to lift as Ben shared a few recent adventures while in South America. Micah even chimed in a few times with questions. Then Ben brought up his wonder at sighting the Blue-footed Booby in the Galapagos, and Micah went gloomy again.

⌣

Trudy Yoder was dead wrong. Her sister Shelley was everything Micah hoped she was—even more. Even in Englisch clothing. Even in the company of the two morons.

Micah had first met Shelley Yoder last summer, soon after moving to Stoney Ridge, when he came across her buggy on the side of the road. A wheel had come loose and Micah had stopped to help. Micah pulled off his hat, staring at Shelley, mesmerized. He'd never seen such a breathtakingly beautiful girl. She had wide cheekbones and a dainty, pointed chin that gave her face a heart shape. Her lips, full and ripe, were as red as if she'd been eating berries. Her skin was pale, like freshly skimmed cream, and her hair was the color of wheat just starting to ripen. He squatted in front of the wheel to see what was wrong with it, though his whole awareness was held captive by the nearness of this stunning girl.

A cool wind blew around them, and he saw her shivering, arms tightly wrapped around her middle. He came to himself with a start. Cold. She was cold! He practically tore his coat in his haste to get it off and wrap it around her shoulders.

It turned out the buggy wheel just needed some bolts tightened, an easy fix, but Shelley acted as if he'd performed a miracle for her. "I can't thank you enough. Micah, that's your name, isn't it? Micah Weaver? My sister Trudy talks about your vast knowledge of the aviary world. A walking encyclopedia of birds, she calls you."

He swallowed hard, making an odd clicking sound. Then he winced, because it seemed as if he was agreeing with Trudy's assessment of him, which Shelley might interpret as thinking he thought he was something special, full of pride. He hoped not. He wasn't.

He'd come across Trudy a number of times, out birding, and never would've put those two together as sisters. It wasn't just their age difference. Shelley was a graceful swan; Trudy was an awkward duckling. "M-Micah. That's m-my name." Criminy, he was stammering worse than ever.

"Well, if you can spot a rare bird as quickly as you fixed the problem with my buggy, I can certainly see why Trudy enthuses over you."

What he wanted to say was that Shelley was a rare bird, a beautiful, exotic one, but his mouth had gone dry, and his stomach felt as if he'd just swallowed bees.

Above them, a racket of cawing crows started up, and they both looked in the sky at the same moment to a black cloud of flapping wings and angry caws. "What's wrong with them?" Shelley said.

"M-mobbing," Micah said.

"What's mobbing?"

"C-crows protecting their t-territory from a hawk." He pointed to the sky. "See?"

She shielded her eyes to peer at the crows chasing away the hawk. "I don't like crows much. They're nothing but a nuisance."

He grinned. "They have a b-bad r-reputation. B-but they c-can surprise you. They're v-very intelligent."

She dropped her hand and slanted a look at him, and the sun seemed to catch at something in her brown eyes, making them sparkle. "You should join our youth group. On Wednesday nights, we play volleyball, and have a barbecue afterwards. Sometimes a singing too. This week, it'll be at our farm. Come, why don't you?"

He felt like a fool to just stand there bouncing his head like a bobblehead toy, rocking from one foot to another. As he dusted off his pants from sitting on the ground, he tried out what he wanted to say to her in his head, but everything he came up with sounded too complicated for him to say. Or too stupid.

She tilted her head back to look up at him and she smiled again, and his heart did a flip-flop in his chest. "You have nice eyes. Has anyone ever told you that? Smoky gray. No, better than that. Foggy gray, like a day at the seashore."

He wanted to return the compliment, to describe her eyes the way he would describe a bird's plumage in his bird-watching log. Brown like the back of a robin. No, a robin was too common, too ordinary for a girl as pretty as Shelley. Brown like a sparrow, brown like a . . .

She didn't seem to expect him to say anything. "I haven't been to the ocean, but I want to, someday. I want to see lots of places, don't you?" Her horse let out a whinnying sound and she turned to it. "It's getting late. I'd better get home. Thank you again, Micah Weaver, for coming to my rescue."

Before he could say anything, she handed him back his coat and moved off to climb into her buggy. Too late, he realized he should have stepped up to help her. He could have touched her hand. His heart sank. A missed opportunity.

She gathered up the reins and looked down at him, smiling again in a way that made him feel taller and bigger than he was. "Wednesday night. The Yoder farm. Don't forget." She lifted one hand to give him a wave of her fingers, then gave the reins a little shake to get the horse started. Micah watched the back of the buggy sway and dip along the road until it disappeared.

Wednesday. Micah inflated his cheeks and blew the air out in a gusty sigh. He wouldn't forget. He couldn't. He held his coat against his face, breathing deeply of the lavender soap that he now recognized as Shelley's scent. He'd never let Penny wash this coat again.

He went to the youth gathering at the Yoder farm that Wednesday, and every Wednesday after that, but other than a quick, passing moment when Shelley would make a point to say hello to him, he stood alone, on the edges of the group, watching her from afar.

Micah Weaver, Bird-Watching Log

Name of Bird: *American Crow*

Scientific Name: *Corvus brachyrhynchos*

Status: *Low concern*

Date: *March 15*

Location: *Along road with Shelley Yoder*

Description: *Large, all black, even its legs and bill. Slight gloss to its plumage. Long and thick bill. Makes full-throated cawing calls.*

Bird Action: *Mobbing and harassing a Red-tailed Hawk to drive it from their territory.*

Notes: *To be honest, crows are annoying. But they're also intelligent, inquisitive, mischievous problem-solvers. In fact, they're a lot smarter than most people might think. They can make and use tools, like fashioning a stick into a spear that they use to eat grubs. Handy.*

They have a variety of sounds, from caws to clicking. Their flight style is unique, a patient, methodical flapping, like rowing a boat, rarely broken up with glides. I wouldn't expect that from such a raucous bird.

Very social, sometimes forming flocks in the thousands. They warn each other of danger.

Here's what most people don't know: An American Crow leads a double life. It might spend part of the day at home with its ex-

tended family in a roost and the rest of the day with a flock feeding at the town dump or gleaning from country fields.

And be warned: Crows hold grudges. The flocks, curiously, are called murders. Unsettling.

11

Sunday morning started out cool with light rain. Ben felt well enough to head out on a bird hunt, though he knew Micah wouldn't be available. Not today. He dressed and left his room to organize his optical equipment bag. This heavy, cumbersome bag full of expensive equipment. He was rarely without it, as conscious of it as the whereabouts of his wallet.

He paused. How was Penny able to capture a bird in her mind to later draw it from memory? As detailed and accurate as if she were copying it from a photograph. Yes, she said she used field guides, and no doubt that helped, but there was something about her drawing that was so lifelike. As if the bird had been caught unawares. As if she were part of its world.

He thought he smelled coffee. Curious, he opened the door to find a carafe on a tray, with sliced pumpkin bread and a ramekin of butter. When had Penny brought it? She must have wanted to get breakfast to them early so she and Micah could head off to church. He set the tray on the kitchen table and went back to check his camera, to make sure the battery had fully charged.

The door to Natalie's room opened and she emerged, fully dressed. "Morning." She sniffed the air and smiled. "Coffee?"

He pointed to the carafe on the small table. "Where are you going?"

"Church. With Penny and Micah."

Kneeling on the floor by his bag, Ben leaned back on his heels. "You're kidding. You're really going?"

"Not kidding. I want to go." Natalie poured a mug of coffee and walked to the window to look out over the hill to the road. "Being here, something about this whole place, it just keeps calling to me." She turned back to face him. "Do you ever miss being here?"

He started to say *No way, not a chance*, but then he thought of having breakfast with Penny, and traipsing behind Micah along trails, and the objection stuck in his throat. Instead of answering her, he changed the subject. "Natalie, if you really want to go to an Amish church this morning, eat a big breakfast now because you'll be sitting for three hours on a backless bench." Her eyes went wide. "And wear clothing that covers up your limbs."

She looked down at her bare calves. "Oh."

"And no makeup."

She gasped.

He grinned. His cousin loved her makeup. "And wear something on your head." He heard the sound of a barn door opening. "And you'd better hurry."

Natalie acted like he'd set off a firecracker. She bolted to her room and returned a few minutes later wearing a maxi dress and a fully buttoned sweater, with a white handkerchief pinned to her hair. "Better?"

Ben had to bite back a grin. "Better." He still thought she would regret going. "Tell me again, why do you want to go?"

"I guess it has something to do with Penny. She's so . . . content. She seems like a cork bobbing about in the ocean, just riding along the currents. She says that she believes everything happens for a reason. Do you think that could be true? That there's a master plan? A sovereign God? That's what Penny calls it. A sovereign God."

Ben had no answer for her. It's not that he didn't believe in

God. He did. More often than not, he would find a church on his travels and attend services.

"Well, I don't think I've ever known someone who is so content with her life. I want to know why."

"You think you'll find out by attending an Amish church service?"

"Maybe. If Penny and Micah are any indication, then maybe I will. It just seems like the Plain people have something for the rest of us. Like . . . they seem to have such a gentle faith."

"Gentle and severe," he said, thinking of his father.

A disturbing consideration struck Ben. Would Natalie see his father at church? Would he recognize her? Probably not. She looked considerably different from the last time he'd seen her. Levi's funeral.

She was searching through drawers for something. "Aha!" She spun around, lifting a butter knife as if she'd made a great discovery.

"Is the vet going with you to church?"

In the middle of buttering a slice of pumpkin bread, she glanced up. "His name is Boyd Baldwin and he goes to his own church."

"He seems rather smitten with you." This Boyd Baldwin had stopped by the guesthouse at least twice each day since Natalie had returned.

"I know, right?" She took a few bites of bread. "Doesn't that seem a little . . . suspect?"

"How do you mean?"

"Like . . ." She chewed thoughtfully, then swallowed. "Like there must be something wrong with him."

Ben burst out with a laugh, then grew solemn when he realized she was serious. "Natalie, Boyd likes you. Don't overthink everything."

She wolfed down her last bite. "It's just that Joel—"

He lifted a hand. "Nat, Joel is gone."

"Exactly." She brushed the crumbs off her sweater, gave him a quick wave at the door, grabbed an umbrella, and darted out to meet Micah at the buggy.

Apart from Natalie's bottom going numb from sitting still for three hours on a hard bench, and not understanding the sermons because they were in Penn Dutch and she had only studied Spanish in high school, and being shocked at the slow crawling pace of the hymns—one lasted twenty minutes!—she actually loved attending an Amish church service. She even loved the modest fellowship meal afterward, despite being appalled that the men ate first, served by the women, and after they left the tables, only then did the women eat. Seriously?

"You *loved* it?" Ben asked, astounded, when she returned to the guesthouse past one o'clock in the afternoon.

"Maybe love is too strong, but I truly enjoyed the experience." She pulled bobby pins out of her hair and the white handkerchief dropped in her lap. "I couldn't understand a word, but I felt God's presence." She couldn't even describe how she felt it. She just knew she had a wonderful sense of well-being and was pretty sure that came from God's presence in that barn.

Ben didn't respond. He turned his attention back to uploading bird pictures from his camera onto his computer.

"And the children . . . how are they able to sit quietly for so long?"

Ben glanced up. "From a culture that appreciates children but also strongly encourages them to know their place."

"I can't imagine a typical American child to be able to hold still so long . . . without an electronic screen in their face."

"I agree with you there."

"Penny says it even surprises her when she's in town, to see how children talk back to their parents." She leaned back and crossed her arms. "Makes you wonder, doesn't it?"

"About what?"

"If for all the conveniences of modern life, society has lost something."

He shrugged. "Maybe society never had it in the first place."

"All the more reason to show the world the best side of the Amish. The way they revere nature, for example."

"Natalie, not all Amish are like Penny and Micah. There's plenty of stories of Amish children who use birds for slingshot practice." He shot a look at her. "I suppose Roy King was there?"

"That big guy? Oh yeah. He couldn't keep his eyes off of Penny." Natalie knew, because she stayed glued to Penny's side.

"So I've noticed."

When she raised her eyebrow, she could tell he regretted his words.

"He comes around a lot, that's all I'm saying."

Was it? she wondered.

Last night at the firepit, Ben seemed a different person. He had insisted Natalie come with him, which she thought was a crazy idea. It was December, for heaven's sake! But afterward, she was glad he had insisted. They'd had a lovely evening, though Micah got sulky and slipped away at one point. Penny, Ben, and Natalie remained until the fire died down to embers. Ben and Penny compared bird notes and Natalie noticed how animated Ben seemed. He told stories she'd never heard from him, funny ones that made Penny and Natalie laugh.

This was a side of Ben she had rarely seen before, if at all. Natalie knew she drove Ben crazy. To be honest, he drove her a little cuckoo too. First of all, he was hard to find. Always flitting around the world. And when she did track him down, he wasn't always easy to talk to. He could be reluctant to share his thoughts and was prone to brooding. Natalie liked to think of herself as an open book, unafraid to speak from her heart, to share her feelings. He called her a drama queen, which was patently ridiculous. He should spend some time with some of her former clients and then he'd see how a drama queen *really* acted. Sophia Parker, she was dramatic. Natalie was mild compared to *that* eccentric woman.

Well, she'd have to ponder the Ben-acting-animated-around-Penny topic another time. For now, she needed his help. "This whole experience here, it's got me thinking. The world needs some of what the Amish have figured out. I mean, we're all Americans. Why can't we get in on the secret? Borrow some of what they have?" She overlapped her hands together in her lap, as if in prayer. "Ben, would you ask Penny if I can have one of her watercolors to frame? Just one? I have someone in mind who I'm confident—absolutely confident—would like to buy it."

"Why not ask her yourself?"

"I think it would be better if it came from you."

He let out a sigh. "We did talk about it."

"When?"

"Yesterday. She let me see them."

"She let you see them? That's great!"

"And I told her that you'd probably like to see her work."

"You didn't tell her I snooped through them, did you?"

"No. I should've, but I didn't."

"Please?" Her tone took on a pleading sound. "Just ask her."

"Why?" He leaned back in the chair and stretched. "Why is it so important to you?"

Natalie took a moment to gather her thoughts. How to explain this in a way that Ben would understand? "On the way to church this morning, Micah pointed out a bird. He said that some bird species are complementary to each other."

Ben nodded. "What kind of bird did he point out?"

"A bird is a bird." She lifted her shoulders in a small shrug. "They sing. They fly. They lay pretty eggs."

He rolled his eyes. "It was probably a Red-tailed Hawk."

"No . . . no, I think he said it was an owl. I feel as if . . ." She glanced away, reluctant to complete the thought, after all.

"You feel what?" he encouraged.

"It occurred to me that's exactly what being here feels like to me. Complementary species. Micah's helping you find your bird, you're helping Micah get his career up and going." She bent over to slip off her shoes, thinking, *I could be the complementary bird to Penny's watercolors, the go-between. Sell them to the outside world that longs for the peace and serenity Penny's artwork evokes. A win-win.*

When she popped back up, she realized Ben had been watching her, almost as if he knew what she was running through her mind.

"Birds only help each other for selfish reasons. They're creatures of instinct and are motivated by just two things—to eat and to mate."

"Oh, come on. There's got to be some birds that help each other. They live in flocks. And what about those geese that fly in a V?"

Ben lifted one finger. "Just one. The African Gray Parrot. A study found it to be the only nonmammal who seemed to willingly help others. But that was a captive bird. Not sure it would be true in the wild." He shrugged. "Birds are prickly creatures."

"Speaking of prickly creatures . . . I think I saw your father."

Ben's eyes narrowed.

"I don't think he recognized me." She let out an intentionally lighthearted sigh, hoping to break the sudden tension in the room. "I haven't changed that much, have I?"

He didn't answer her question. "So you didn't talk to him."

She shook her head. "I haven't seen him in a long time and, I gotta be honest, there's not a lot of fashion diversity to identify one man with a long beard in a black coat from another. But I'm pretty sure I saw him." When Ben looked up at her, she added, "He looks really, really old."

He gave her a warning look. "Don't."

She lifted her hands. "I'm not pushing you to see him. That's your call. I just wanted you to know." She went to her bedroom door. She wanted to change and get some makeup on. "But a lot of time has passed since Levi died. And . . ."

"And what?"

"And time might be running out."

Ben closed his computer. "The rain has let up. I think I'll head out for a while. Get some fresh air." He grabbed his precious equipment bag and dashed out the door.

In other words, Natalie had pushed him too far.

~

By the time Ben made it to the road, the skies had cleared, leaving bright sunshine. His mood, though, remained damp and gray. It started when Natalie told him she was going to church, and grew worse when she returned so pleased. So at peace. And his mood took a worse nosedive when she mentioned Levi.

Sometimes he forgot how much Natalie knew about him—forgot how long she had known the real him, the person he now only remembered himself to be.

What was wrong with him? Why couldn't he be glad that Natalie was finding some happiness, even in such an unlikely place as an Amish farm? He knew how sad this year had been for her, after Joel the jerk left her for another woman, after her business imploded. He knew because she emailed him practically every day, filling him in on every sordid, tragic detail. She finally seemed like she was turning the corner. Good grief, she even had a beau in that veterinarian. He hadn't seen her smile and laugh so much in a long time. Natalie's lighthearted nature was always a delight, but it had gone missing this last year. Being here was obviously good for her. A healing thing.

But he couldn't ignore that being here was getting increasingly uncomfortable for him. Too many memories kept bubbling up. Too much distress had come back. Why must the past always intrude on the present? Too much time in the past hobbled a person—and that's just what was happening here to him.

He'd made a mistake by coming back, even if Natalie did have a boyfriend in the making. Tomorrow morning, he wanted to head back to Philadelphia, back to civilization with its stable Wi-Fi connectivity, and send in the manuscript, even without a picture and story of the elusive White-winged Tern.

A buggy came down the road and stopped in front of Ben. A black hat popped out of the window. "BEN ZOOK!"

Hank Lapp. With him came all the booming voice that one human body could possibly contain without imploding. "JUST the MAN I was coming to SEE. The TERN! I SAW IT!"

"You what? Where? When? How long ago?" Ben's heart started to pound.

"BEHIND the HARDWARE STORE. YESTERDAY after-noon."

Yesterday? Ben's heart returned to its normal pace. "Right."

"I did!" Hank drew himself up like an injured rooster. "I saw your BIRD!"

Ben set his equipment bag on the ground beside him. Normally, he thought Hank Lapp was always looking for a reaction, for shock value. This time, he seemed sincere. Frankly, it was nice that he even cared about the tern. "Okay, Hank . . . what did it look like?" He didn't have much confidence that Hank would know enough to identify it. Mainly, he didn't have much confidence in Hank. Period. *Er verschteht ken Buhn davun. He didn't know a cow from a haystack.* Ben squeezed his eyes shut. It had happened again! Penn Dutch kept popping into his head.

Hank's hands hovered in the air, trying to estimate the size of an invisible bird. "BIGGER than a SONGBIRD. SMALLER than a SEAGULL. Nine, ten inches or so." He flung his arms open. "Wingspan was more around two feet wide."

He had just described thousands of bird species. "The plum-age, Hank."

"BLACK body, BLACK head, BLACK chest, white wings above and dark below. Very EYE-CATCHING."

One of Ben's eyebrows lifted. "Go on."

"I THINK it likes the HARDWARE STORE because there's a POND behind it, FULL OF MOSQUITOS. It was CAPTURING those annoying critters in the AIR."

"Go on."

"HAD a short, harsh 'kek' call."

Hank then tried to imitate the sound and Ben wanted to cover his ears. Despite the fact that this was Hank Lapp, Ben had to admit that the bird he described resembled the White-winged Tern. Its foraging was done while in flight as it captured insects in midair. "Hank, did anyone else verify the sighting?"

Hank seemed puzzled by the question, as if to wonder why anyone would doubt him. "Well, no. But TAKE HEART. The BIRD hasn't flown the COOP. The FROST ain't on the PUMPKIN quite yet." He grinned as he clapped Ben on the shoulder. "Your LITTLE bird is STILL HERE."

Ben blew out a puff of air. "Okay, okay. I'll go see if I can find it."

"HOLD IT!"

Ben stopped, pivoted. "What?"

"HAVE YOU given some THOUGHT about SEEING your POOR OLD DAD?"

Ben wheeled around and lifted his free hand in a salute. "So long, Hank." He wasn't going to bite that bait. He checked behind the hardware store, walked slowly through the mud around the pond, checked roosts in the nearby woods. He even used his cell phone app to call it out, something he frowned on as amateurish. No bird.

Trudging back to the road through the muddy woods, his shoes soaked, he thought of Cody Burkett's First Law of Birding: The greater the time spent searching for a rarity, the greater the chances it will be sitting on your car when you return to the parking lot.

He sighed. If only.

Micah Weaver, Bird-Watching Log

Name of Bird: *Great Horned Owl*

Scientific Name: *Bubo virginianus*

Status: *Low concern*

Date: *April 30*

Location: *On a high branch in a clump of cottonwood trees near Windmill Farm.*

Description: *Female, larger, long earlike feathered tufts on head. Mottled gray-brown, with reddish-brown round head, yellow eyes, short bill, white patch on throat. Slightly larger than a Red-tailed Hawk. Call is a deep, stuttering series of four to five hoots.*

Bird Action: *Malevolent yellow-eyed stare. Stared at me like I murdered his whole family.*

Notes: *Contrary to popular opinion, owls aren't the brightest of birds. But they sure do look wise, with that piercing intimidating glare. A bit ironic, because although they have excellent night vision, all owls are very farsighted and can't focus on objects in close range. Instead, they use their moustache of whisker-like bristles around their beaks to help them figure out what's nearby.*

Typically, an owl doesn't build a nest but adopts (as in, helps itself to) a nest built by another species. In this part of the country,

Great Horned Owls take over old Red-tailed Hawk nests.

Owls and hawks feed on similar prey (rodents), but somehow they've figured out how to coexist and share the same habitat. Owls hunt only at night, avoiding direct competition with day-hunting hawks. Pretty smart.

Mated pairs are monogamous and stay within territory during breeding, but then they roost separately. I can think of a few married couples who might like that idea.

12

On most Sunday afternoons, the youth group would gather at a house for a time of singing. Today, it was held at the Yoder home, and Micah wouldn't miss it for the world. Not even for a rare bird. Weather permitting, the Yoders provided a picnic for die Yugend, the teenagers, and then the singing would start.

The hymns weren't like the old and slow ones used in church. They were German religious songs but with faster tunes and, also unlike during church, they included harmonies. Now and then, they'd even finish with some Englisch gospel songs. Singings could last three to four hours, though to Micah it felt like minutes, because Shelley was there. Shelley with her nightingale's voice.

Micah fell a little more in love with Shelley during each singing.

Afterward, die Yugend lingered outside, reluctant to leave and break up their precious time of socialness. Tommy Fisher had beer in his buggy, drawing the boys like bears to honey. Micah stood alone, near the house, trying to work up his courage to talk to Shelley, practicing the words in his head, waiting for a moment when she was alone. He watched as she came out of the house, carrying something in her hands, and made his move. He bolted across the yard in a fast stride.

"Micah!" Trudy called out, hurrying to his side.

Ignoring her, he kept going.

She grabbed his arm. "I saw it! I saw the bird!"

He shook her off and spun around to face her. "Not now!" The look of hurt in her eyes stung him. Just because he was anxious not to miss his chance to talk to Shelley, he had no call to hurt Trudy's feelings. He softened his tone. "S-saw what b-bird?"

"The White-winged Tern," she said, her expression a mix of hurt and annoyance. "I'm sure of it."

He opened his mouth but nothing came out.

"It was hovering around the sheep dipping pond at Windmill Farm."

He shook his head. "Couldn't be."

"They like to eat insects, don't they?"

"Yeah, but they prefer l-larger b-bodies of water."

"Sometimes"—Trudy stuck her hands on her hips—"things can happen that you don't expect. You don't know everything, Micah Weaver, even though you think you do." She dropped her hands to her sides and left him.

When he turned around, Shelley was gone.

Penny worried about Micah. He'd always had a hard time making friends and he had yet to find any here. Not one. She'd hoped that leaving Big Valley to come to Stoney Ridge would give him a fresh start. She'd hoped that his field work would build his confidence. But she hadn't expected him to fall so head over heels in love with Shelley Yoder, the most popular girl among die Yugend. Micah didn't give his heart easily, but when he did, he was loyal to a fault. From what Penny could gather, Shelley had no interest in Micah, though that didn't stop him from hoping he had a chance.

And there were other things troubling Micah, Penny thought, though he'd never said so. She couldn't find a way to get him to talk to her, as much as she tried. She wondered if Ben Zook had much success talking to Micah while they traipsed around, searching for this hard-to-find bird.

Maybe Penny was the one who was troubled. Ben had been here two weeks now, and Penny had been almost thankful for his illness, because it kept him grounded at Lost Creek Farm. But he was feeling much better, and though the weather hadn't turned bitter cold yet, not like it normally was in December, the bird had most likely moved on to winter grounds. She fully expected Ben to move on soon too. Without seeing poor Zeke. She sighed. Without remembering poor Penny.

Those were all the bothersome thoughts that ran through her mind as she refilled Junco's water bucket. The sweet horse bumped her hip with his nose, and in spite of her worries, she laughed at him. He nuzzled her hand with his nose, hoping for something sweet, and she wished she had thought to bring a carrot or apple.

"What's so funny?"

She whirled around to find Ben, standing outside the open stall door. "Junco. Giving me a love pat."

"It's a horse's way of exchanging hellos, I suppose." The smile lines around Ben's mouth deepened for a moment.

Penny straightened, glad Ben kept his eyes on Junco and not on her, for it gave her a chance to study him. How handsome Ben was up close, with his eyes the color of cornflowers, with his thick dark hair the color of mahogany. Some of it had to do with the way he carried himself, not cocky but sure.

"You just have the one horse?"

"That's right. Micah uses him, mostly."

"I've noticed. I see you out walking everywhere."

It pleased her that he'd noticed her habits. "I don't mind walking. Micah goes farther afield than I do. We're able to make do with one buggy horse. It helps to keep our costs low." She turned off the hose. "Were you looking for Micah?"

He held up a boot. "Actually, I was looking for some tools. And small nails."

She looked at him curiously. "That's Micah's boot."

"The heel broke off while we were coming down from the ridge yesterday. I told him I'd fix it for him."

"You know how to repair shoes?" *Interesting.*

"I, well, yes. A handy skill when you're out in the field."

"If you go down the aisle, there's a workroom. Some tools are in there, but not many. My grandmother had a hired hand to help her manage Lost Creek Farm."

He looked up and down the aisle and she knew what he was thinking. There wasn't much to this farm, set on the steep hillside as it was. "What exactly got managed here?"

"Goats." She smiled. "That's why there's hardly anything left growing on the hillside. My grandmother had to give it up after they started eating the fences."

Ben didn't seem in a hurry to fix the broken heel. "It's not typical for an Amish widow to live alone."

"My mother pleaded with her to come live with us in Big Valley, but the church there is much . . ."

"Stricter."

More than you can imagine. "Yes. I think my grandmother felt as if she'd done enough adjusting in life. She was happy here. She was, well, probably more independent-minded than most Amish women."

"You take after her." It wasn't really a question.

Penny felt her cheeks grow warm due to the way he was looking at her and was grateful for the dim lighting in the barn. "She had a strong influence on me. Once, I spent an entire summer with her." A hint at their past. Her first.

"That was the summer you fell in love with birds."

Her eyes darted to his, wondering if he might be starting to remember her, at long last. He remained by the door, leaning against it, a look on his face that she couldn't read. But then, she had yet to figure out what he was thinking. It never ended up being what she expected.

"I happened to tell my cousin Natalie about your drawings, and she"—he paused, rubbing his forehead—"she keeps badgering me to ask you if she can see them."

Ah. A timely example. That was the last thing she thought he was going to say. As Penny passed by him, she waited until he stepped into the aisle, then slid the stall door closed. "Natalie doesn't strike me as a birder."

"I don't disagree," Ben said, "but then she's been surprising me lately. You see, this last year, she's had to endure some hard things."

She watched him for a while, wondering if he was going to say more. "I guess," she said at last, "you're talking about her husband leaving for a younger woman."

Ben's head jerked up. "She told you?"

Penny nodded. "On the way home from church the other day. She told me more about her divorce, and about her business going belly-up. And feeling so depressed she can't leave the house. Until now. Until you made her come with you, and she's feeling better than she has in a long time." She smiled. "Your cousin is quite . . . open. Rather forthcoming."

He coughed a laugh. "Yes, I suppose that's one way of saying it. She's a very open book."

Unlike you. "So, if she wants to see those drawings . . . maybe she should ask me herself."

He regarded her with inquiring eyes, his head slightly tilted to one side. He stared at her for what seemed like forever. He took a step toward her, one, then another, until he was close to her, so close that for a moment she thought he was going to reach out and touch her. "You know, you're not exactly like most Plain women."

Her eyebrows lifted. "I don't recall you ever mentioning knowing any Plain people."

"Penny, by now you must know . . ." He opened his mouth to speak, then snapped it shut.

She waited to see if he would say more. She thought he probably hadn't meant to reveal even that much about himself. "Know what?" *Know that you were raised Plain, just a mile down the road?*

He shifted self-consciously from one foot to the other. "Know . . . that I'm familiar with Plain ways." There was a strange roughness to his voice and a sadness in his eyes. The note of weariness in his voice pinched her heart with pity.

She wanted to reach out, lay her hand against his cheek, and tell him everything would be all right. That if he would just let the Lord into those broken places, he would find healing, he would be whole again. What stayed hidden couldn't be healed. But she didn't touch him nor say those things. Instead, she laced her fingers behind her back. "Familiar?" she said in a gentle voice, the way she spoke around Junco when she needed to give him a dose of medicine.

"That first day, when I passed out, I came to and spoke to you in Penn Dutch. I guess . . . I thought you might have wondered why."

"I didn't think twice about it," she said in all truthfulness. She didn't have to; she knew why. His heart was still Plain.

Boyd Baldwin was the first man to make Natalie wake up and smell the coffee since her life had collapsed. Friends had tried to set her up on dates this last year, but she had little enthusiasm for it and trouble hiding her feelings. Boyd was different. His energy, his charisma, his enthusiasm. He was fun, enjoyable, easygoing, nice-looking. He seemed thoroughly content with his bachelor life in the small house behind his vet clinic.

Content. That was it. Boyd was content with himself and his lot in life, and it puzzled Natalie.

That evening, they were making dinner together in his kitchen. He had a killer risotto dish that he said he wanted to make for her. It was touching, to be cooked for by a man.

This little house, though, desperately needed a woman's touch.

It was over one hundred years old, full of character. Full of potential.

"I drove by this house every day," Boyd said, "and always noticed it. One day, I saw the for sale sign out front and I knew I had to have it. I probably paid way too much for it." He gave her a tour of each room, which only took a few minutes. "It had been a rental," he said, a little apologetically.

Boyd told her that parts of the house had been badly remodeled and other parts hadn't been touched. When he pushed open the door to the kitchen, she gasped. "Oh no. Someone's DIY project has gone terribly wrong." Doors were missing off cabinets painted pink (*pink!*), the floor had a visible seam running down it—separating two entirely different patterns of the linoleum vinyl flooring. It looked as if someone had run out of one flooring and hoped no one would notice if he used another pattern. The countertop was even more offensive—a bright orange laminate minus a backsplash.

"Actually, I remodeled this room myself."

Oops.

Then he burst out laughing and she realized he was pulling her leg. Thank goodness! It was a truly horrendous kitchen . . . which only made Natalie's brain spin with ideas.

Walking around, she imagined new cabinetry, navy blue below for a masculine look. Above would be white floating shelves. Countertops of marbled white quartz, with a gray hand-molded tile backsplash. She even knew the grout color she would add to the tile, a darker gray than the tile so it wouldn't show stains. And along the island, she would add vintage metal stools.

Stop it, she told herself. *Stop trying to change what doesn't need to be changed. The man has not asked you for any advice. He is content! Leave him alone.*

But it was so hard not to think it, not to improve it, when that was what she was experienced at doing. Helping people make a house a home was what she did best.

A Blue Jay flew to the kitchen window feeder and peered in the window, as if curious what was going on inside the house. Boyd noticed. "Did you know that seeing a Blue Jay is supposed to be a warning? It means you're in the company of tricksters and mischief-makers."

"Who says?"

"Old folklore. Personally, I think the trickster is the Blue Jay. They're the mischief-makers. Last year, on a cold, snowy morning—February second, to be exact. I remember because it was Groundhog Day—I went outside to get the newspaper and was sure I heard a robin's song. I followed the sound down, down, down the road—in my robe and slippers—thinking I'd found an early sign of spring. Turns out I was being fooled by a Blue Jay that could mimic other birds." He stuck his head in the fridge to look for something.

Birds, birds, birds. "Did everybody around here grow up loving birds?"

He popped his head out of the fridge and handed her a head of lettuce. "There's two camps on the topic. Loving them or hunting them."

Thoughtful, she started to tear lettuce leaves for a salad while he patiently stirred risotto at the stove.

They worked silently and companionably for several long moments. "What was it like," she asked him, "to grow up here?"

"What was it like?" He looked up from the stove. "Like you'd expect from a life in the country."

"I mean . . . being around the Amish."

He poured a small amount of broth into the risotto, while continuing that patient stirring motion. Natalie had never made risotto for that very reason. She never had enough patience for it.

"Growing up, we lived pretty separate lives from the Amish. Separate schools and such. But I remember my dad taking us kids to a Family Farm Field Day that the Amish put on each fall to raise money for charities. It was like a county fair without competition. No contests, no ribbons, no trophies."

"What was its purpose?"

"Exhibits, mostly. Amish-style, that is. Abandoned bird nests. Gigantic, run-amok pumpkins. Curious-looking bugs in shadow boxes. Quilt displays. And homemade ice cream under a big tent. The best in the world." He added more broth while stirring. "At first, we kids thought the whole thing seemed odd. But the older we got, the more it seemed right. The way it should be. Like, everyone won." He scooped a spoonful of the risotto, blew on it, tasted it, added more broth, and kept on stirring.

"So tell me this. Why do birds love Amish farms? I feel as if I've seen more birds in the last week than I have in my entire life in Philadelphia. And it's December! They should be sunbathing in Mexico by now."

He grinned. "Migration goes in stages as birds head to winter grounds. Lots of stopovers to rest and fatten up before they head south. The mild temperatures are making them linger here. I'm hoping the weather will hold for Micah's CBC."

"Micah's what?"

"The Christmas Bird Count. From dawn to dusk on a specific day, birders count birds in their locale—even their own backyard—and report the numbers. It helps to see how birds are faring. They're the . . . well, the canary down the coal mine." He tasted the risotto again and added still more broth.

This was why Natalie didn't make risotto. An endless process.

"The CBC has an interesting history. In the late 1900s, hunters would head off on a holiday tradition known as the Christmas Side Hunt. Whoever shot the most feathered quarry won."

"Hold on. You mean it's a killing game? Of dead birds?"

"Well, it was. Probably had to do with bringing home food for a Christmas feast."

She leaned against the hideous orange countertop. "Then what?"

"As you can imagine, there was a rapid decline in bird populations. So an ornithologist came up with the idea of counting birds rather than hunting them. A census. Thus began the Christmas Bird Count." He added more broth. "This year will be the first CBC for Stoney Ridge. All because of Micah."

"Micah and his weirdly good ears."

He laughed. "All great birders bird by ear. But Micah, he has supersonic hearing." He wiggled the end of the spoon at her. "I think you're onto something about birds loving Amish farms."

She found a carrot peeler in a drawer and used it to grate a carrot. "But why?"

"Some say the Amish have a back-to-nature approach to farming, but I think it's more of a never-left-nature approach. Their farming practices haven't changed much over the centuries, nothing like a commercial farm with pesticides and herbicides and no-till farming. Modern farming leaves very little behind for critters. But the Amish and their corn shocks, left in the field to overwinter, provide shelter for wildlife. Birds, especially. Mice."

Natalie gave an involuntary shudder at that, and he noticed. "Don't knock mice. They're food for raptors. And raptors are a farmer's friend. It's all a circle of life." He took another bite of risotto and this time his eyebrows wiggled in delight. "Ready in just a few more minutes."

"I'll set the table." Natalie took two dishes from his cupboard, rummaged through a few drawers to find silverware, another to find napkins. She set the salad bowl in the center of his little round table, and looked around the wood-paneled room. Oh, what she could do with this room!

First thing, paint the paneling to lighten up the dark room while still providing texture.

Second, rip up the vinyl flooring. She wondered about the age of this old house. There might be wooden floors under the vinyl.

Would Boyd mind if she suggested it? On the other hand, she didn't want him to get the wrong idea. She wouldn't be staying in Stoney Ridge much longer; she could tell Ben was antsy to leave. She ended up swallowing her wonderful design advice.

He brought the pan of risotto to the table. As he sat down, he took her hand in his. "Mind if I offer thanks?" He bowed his head before she could respond. "Lord, thank you for this day, for providing this food set before us, for the company of this lovely woman beside me. Amen." Then, matter-of-factly, he picked up her plate and dished a spoonful of saffron-infused risotto for her. "What?" He set her plate in front of her. "Is something wrong?"

Natalie had been watching him the whole time, taken aback by his . . . what was it? His ease with the Almighty. It wasn't that she was unfamiliar with the act of saying grace. Ben dropped his chin before every meal. But he did it silently. Boyd spoke of God often, as if he were talking with a friend. And to think he gave thanks for *her*. It was almost too much to bear. Tears pricked her eyes, so she looked down at the risotto and picked up her fork. "It looks delicious." She took a bite. "And it tastes even better."

His face relaxed in a smile. "Good. It's my best company recipe." He clinked his wine glass with hers. "Sadly enough, my only one. Next time, you're on chef duty."

Natalie slowed her chewing. "Next time?"

"Lots of next times, I hope."

Then came one of those unexpected and dazzling smiles, and she felt a tingle run all the way down her legs. She could feel the heat of his gaze on her, as real as a sunbeam.

"I've never met anyone like you, Natalie. I'd given up hoping to, in fact. In case you haven't noticed, I'm growing rather besotted with you." He leaned over and kissed her, just a graze on her lips. Just a simple kiss, yet it didn't evoke a simple response in her. Just the opposite.

She couldn't breathe.

She didn't know what to say.

Fortunately, he didn't seem to expect any profession of the heart in return, nor appear to feel let down when one didn't come. Instead, he jumped up to get the salad dressing and finished telling her a story he had started before dinner—about a stray dog that kept turning up at Amish funerals. "It wasn't just the funerals this dog seemed to like, he made a point to come show his respects at the burial too. When the first shovel of dirt went down on the casket, he'd let out a mournful sound." Boyd cupped his mouth and let out a woeful howl until she laughed out loud. "An Amish family adopted him and named him Funeral Fred."

It was clear that Boyd loved what he did. He'd made a fine life for himself.

Besotted. Why in the world would someone as remarkable as him . . . be besotted with someone like her?

There was something wrong, her gut feelings told her. There must be something seriously wrong if someone like him wanted someone like her.

Micah Weaver, Bird-Watching Log

Name of Bird: *Blue Jay*

Scientific Name: *Cyanocitta cristata*

Status: *(Very) Low concern*

Date: *November 20 (though most every day Blue Jays appear)*

Location: *Pretty much everywhere, as evidenced by relentless noisy squawking calls*

Description: *Smaller than crows, larger than robins. Blue, white, and black plumage; broad, rounded tail. Black bridge across face, nape, and throat. Beak is straight and sharp, suited for a variety of tasks—hammering, probing, seizing, and carrying.*

Bird Action: *Circled, inched closer, eyes locked on my lunch. Made off with my cookie.*

Notes: *Social bird, lives in flocks when not nesting. Strong family bonds; mates for life. I find that to be curious, because Blue Jays seem to be constantly fighting with each other.*

Migration remains a mystery. Some remain throughout winter, some migrate south one year, stay north the next winter, then migrate south again. No one knows why.

Fondness for acorns is credited with spread of oak trees.

Intelligent. Notoriously aggressive. Steals

and eats other birds' eggs and nestlings. Bold
enough to steal food from humans, like me.
Blue Jays are a big fat pain in the neck.
Do not trust them.

13

On Wednesday afternoon, Micah stood inside the Bent N' Dent, near the door, thumbtacking a flyer on a big community bulletin board. Penny had made the flyers with her fine and measured handwriting, inviting everyone to volunteer to help count birds in their farms and neighborhoods on the Christmas Bird Count.

He wondered if Shelley might consider being on his team for the CBC. He pondered how to ask her. And when.

"What's that you're posting?"

He wheeled around and there was Shelley Yoder. *Shelley!* Looking gorgeous, beautiful, with wisps of buttery-colored curls poking out under her prayer cap. He hadn't even heard the door open. He tried to speak, but the words got lodged in his throat and all that came out was a squeaky noise. Stupid, stupid, stupid.

Shelley read the flyer out loud, with her lovely, lilting voice. Standing close, he noticed small things about her. Her posture, for one. She stood with her slender back straight, her shoulders flat and square. One capstring was caught in the collar of her coat, and he nearly reached out to untangle it, but at the last second, he held himself back. He felt so hulking and clumsy around her, too big for his own skin.

Shelley didn't seem to notice Micah's acute awkwardness. She had a serious look in her eyes as she read aloud the details Penny had written: *Start early, stay late. Every bird counts!*

She turned to him and he quickly looked away. "Micah, why do birds sing?"

He fixed his eyes on the top of his boots. "T-two reasons, actually. Attract a m-mate. And . . . uh . . . w-warn of p-predators."

"Not just for fancy, then. God gave them those sweet voices for a special purpose, don't you think?"

He nodded, not entirely sure what she meant. Taking in a big gulp of air, and mustering his courage, he said, "Would you l-like to g-go on the Christmas B-bird C-count?"

Shelley tilted her head and smiled. "Maybe."

It wasn't a full yes, but it was some comfort to know that she hadn't said no, either.

Ben felt good, really good. Better than he had in weeks. He stopped in at Dok Stoltzfus's for a blood smear to be sure the parasite was gone. And it was! The smear was clean. The treatment had worked. Pleased, she gave him strict warnings about the possibility of a relapse. "Any chills or fatigue, any fever . . . you call me right away."

He promised that he would.

"Malaria is nothing to mess around with," Dok continued. "It can take a long time for someone who's had malaria to get back on his feet. You're very fortunate that you were diagnosed quickly."

"That, I am well aware of." Fortunate to have landed at Lost Creek Farm. Fortunate to have been the recipient of Penny's kindness.

The White-winged Tern was not as kind to him. Despite a few sightings of it reported by others, it remained elusive to Micah and to Ben. In fact, Ben wondered if the whole thing had been made in error. Not a ruse, not exactly. But a mistaken sighting that grew bigger with each telling. The more he thought about it—as well as the recently reported sightings had been by Hank Lapp and a fifteen-year-old girl—the more he felt convinced it had been nothing more than a wild-goose chase.

On the way back to Lost Creek Farm, he stopped at the phone shanty to call his publisher, Charlie Snyder, because his own cell phone had such spotty service in this rural area. "It's time to wrap things up, Charlie. The book already has plenty of unusual birds in it."

"None as rare as the White-winged Tern in Pennsylvania. This bird is a win in the bird world. No, Ben. You promised me that tern and I'm holding you to it."

"I think I've been dipped, Charlie. I was thinking that I could even add an epilogue about nemesis birds. I think it would make other birders feel less defeated by their own experience getting dipped."

"No such thing for you. Not Ben Zook. You've never missed a bird yet."

"But—"

"No buts. Imagine how embarrassing it would be to have Ben Zook miss his chance for *that* bird."

Yes, Ben was quite cognizant of his reputation. He'd made his mark at an unheard-of clip, spurred on by his discovery of a New Zealand bird considered extinct, and the *Rare Bird* book that followed. He'd always suspected he could lose his reputation just as fast. "Charlie, even if it had been here, chances are pretty good that it's had its stopover and now it's gone."

"When was the last sighting?"

Ben swallowed. "Just a few days ago." But it was by Hank Lapp, whose judgment in all things was suspect.

"Just a few days ago? And the weather's still holding, right? Well, that settles it. You stay put and get me a picture of it. Then you can leave, turn in your manuscript, and take a long vacation." Charlie hung up.

Ben replaced the receiver and walked out of the phone shanty, annoyed, irritated, trapped. It was true that he had never yet missed a bird he was chasing. This was the first. He always knew this day would come, someday.

Penny was halfway down the driveway holding a pot with oven mitts. He picked up his pace to meet her and reached his hands out. "Need any help?"

She shook her head. "It's not heavy. I'm just going down the road a bit."

"You sure? I've noticed that when Micah says 'a bit,' it can mean anywhere from a mile to the next town over." Man, whatever was in that pot, it smelled good. Really good. Ben was hungrier than he'd realized. Funny, he'd never had much of an appetite, not until being at Lost Creek Farm. He used to go for hours and hours without thinking of food. Now, by the time he finished breakfast, he wondered what Penny was making for lunch. And dinner.

She smiled. "Micah's got the buggy this afternoon. He's putting flyers around town for the Christmas Bird Count."

"Yes, he's been talking about it." In fact, the coming Christmas Bird Count was the very reason Ben thought it was time to give up on the tern. If there was any chance of it still being here, which he doubted, all those amateur birders working the same territory would only drive the skittish bird away.

Ben's gaze went beyond her, to a falcon circling in the sky. "Is that what I think it is?"

"A Peregrine Falcon. It nests over at Windmill Farm."

He shielded his eyes to watch the falcon, the fastest bird on earth, circle and swoop until it disappeared behind the ridge.

"You don't have your equipment bag. I've hardly seen you without it."

Evidently, Penny could read his mind. Just now, he'd been wishing for his camera. It dawned on him that she might think he was too dependent on his expensive optical equipment. Lost his basic instincts. Lately, watching Micah while birding, he'd wondered.

Micah didn't use a cell phone app to call in birds. No recordings, no speakers, no nothing. He didn't call the birds in, he let them call to him, as if to follow them. To Micah, calling out birds was interfering with them, teasing and confusing them for selfish reasons. Stressing them, baiting them. When Ben asked him why he didn't call them out, he said he felt concerned that it might put a bird in danger by changing its behavior. If a bird didn't want to reveal itself, Micah said, then why force it?

So unlike most birders, who wanted to bird-watch on their terms, not the bird's. The interesting thing was that Ben had enjoyed birding with Micah more than any other guide he'd ever gone out in the field with. Micah was relaxed. The birds were relaxed. Micah went at a slow pace. Everything about it felt very natural. It felt right.

"I guess," he said, "the falcon will just have to remain seared in my memory." The way Penny observed birds to later draw them.

A concerned look filled her gray eyes. "You'll stay for it, won't you? To help Micah count birds on the Christmas Bird Count? He could really use your help, if you're feeling up for it."

The CBC was scheduled for Saturday. He didn't want to be here that long. "Don't you have other bookings for the guesthouse? We certainly don't want to hold it up from any other guests."

"No," Penny said, eyes wide. "You're our first guests. So far, our only guests. We're planning for birders to come regularly to the guesthouse, hiring Micah out as a field guide. There's a hope . . ." She paused, then started again. "I suppose I'm hopeful that after you find the White-winged Tern, well, then Micah's field guiding will really take off."

Ben hadn't realized that there was so much riding on him. He felt a little squeezed in—first by his publisher and now by Penny. Ben could feel her gray eyes upon him, making him unusually uncomfortable. How could he turn her down, after all she'd done for him? "Well, then. Yes, I'll be here for the Christmas Bird Count." He sighed. He knew when he was beat.

Penny left Ben and hurried down the driveway with the cooling casserole in her hands. As she reached the road, she pondered some theories as to why Ben had no memory of her. Perhaps he was suffering from dementia just like his father. Or perhaps the malaria had affected his brain.

It didn't seem likely, though. Ben's short-term memory seemed to be just fine. She'd forgotten to bring him a jar of cherry jam like she'd promised and he reminded her. Twice.

Last night, he joined them at the firepit again and told stories about unusual birds he'd seen in other continents. He described a bird with a silly name that he found in Australia, the Williewagtail, that would land on his shoulder like it was a perch. He described it with very specific detail, even trying to imitate it—chatting, wagging, bobbing its tail. It was so amusing that they all doubled over in laughter. That didn't sound like someone whose mind was slipping.

His father, though, seemed to be slipping a little more with every passing week. Birdy Stoltzfus, the bishop's wife, had dropped by Zeke's place the other day to check in on him, and she noticed the same decline. She told Penny that he was turning into a shell of his former self.

"What was his former self like?" Penny said.

"Don't ask," Birdy said.

Penny had watched Zeke during last Sunday's church service and noticed that he had stared at the floor for most of the service, all but the hymn singing. The moment the Vorsinger opened his mouth to release the first note, Zeke woke from his torpor. He lifted up his gray-bearded chin and belted out the words. His mind came back, if only for a short time. Music . . . *such* a wonder. How did a damaged brain retain words to sing, but not to speak?

There were only two other times when Penny saw a glimpse of the former self of Zeke—as he cobbled Hank Lapp's broken boot, and when a red cardinal came to the bird feeder near his kitchen window. He spent most of his time sitting at the kitchen table, just waiting.

Penny wondered. What was Zeke waiting for? Or maybe . . .

Who was he waiting for?

Ben.

There was another problem for the Lord to solve: how to get Ben to go see his father before he left Lost Creek Farm. She knew he was getting itchy to leave. When she prayed about it, she sensed a strong warning from the Lord to wait, to not interfere. All she knew to do, for now, was to keep quiet and, in the silence, let the Holy Spirit do the talking to Ben.

But oh . . . how she wanted to!

As she walked down the road, she wondered why she'd blurted out to Ben that she hoped his time at Lost Creek Farm would help Micah's field work get off the ground. It was the truth, but it ended up sounding like he owed them something, and he didn't. Micah had yet to deliver the bird for him, though it wasn't for lack of trying.

She supposed she told Ben too much because she was feeling wobbly and anxious today after receiving the tax bill for Lost Creek Farm, adjusted by the county for the transfer of title from her grandmother. It was three times what she'd expected it to be. Three times! She wasn't sure how that bill was going to get paid. And she had just barely been able to pay the school tax bill in July. Even though the Plain people didn't use the public schools, they still paid tax for them.

She'd thought it would be easier to sustain Lost Creek Farm because there was no mortgage on it, thanks to her grandmother. But the costs of maintaining it were shocking.

She had no idea where the money would come from to pay those bills. She couldn't ask her parents or siblings for the money. That could get them into difficulties with their own church leaders in Big Valley.

Somehow, this venture of Micah's had to work. They couldn't go back. *She* couldn't go back. Not after attending church in Stoney Ridge. David Stoltzfus led the church in a way that spoke to her heart. He was a true Spirit-led leader. Just the right combination of depending on the word of God in Scripture, and the word of God in hearts.

She just couldn't return to a spiritually dry church, led by a bishop who elevated his own thinking to a place not far under God's Book. Who discouraged his flock from reading Scripture on their own, but told them to wait until the ministers interpreted it for them. She'd tried to convince her family to come here, to Stoney Ridge, but their roots went deep in Big Valley. They didn't seem to feel the same stifling spiritual effect from the bishop as Penny did—and that worried her too. Why didn't they sense the quenching of God's Spirit? Why couldn't they see how the church lacked joy, lacked fellowship? Instead, it focused on rules, obedience, and shame. Lots and lots of shame. It was a very effective tool to control a church community that was sensitive to pleasing God.

A gentle breeze lifted her capstrings, pushing away her gloomy thoughts. She was measuring her worries against her own feeble strength, forgetting the Lord's infinite abilities to solve problems.

Leave those worries in the future, she sensed the Lord telling her. *Come home to the present.*

Be more like the birds, she reminded herself, as chickadees darted through tree branches. Among all God's creatures, only humans could anticipate future events. And worry about them.

Behind her, she heard a buggy rumbling up the road, so she moved to the side to get out of its way. "PENNY WEAVER." Hank Lapp stuck his head out the window, reminding Penny of a Pileated Woodpecker with its tuft of shocking hair on its thickly buttressed head, topping its thin neck. "HOP IN. I'll take you where you NEED to GO."

Oh dear. Spending time with Hank left Penny with ringing ears. "I'm nearly at Zeke's, Hank. I'll just go up by myself."

"NONSENSE. I need to HEAD THERE myself. Need my BOOT back!" And he lifted his leg and swung it through the open window to show his shoeless foot.

Penny tried not to let out a sigh and climbed into the passenger side of the buggy, as soon as Hank pulled his foot off the open window.

"I had ME a FINE IDEA. How about THIS? Get MICAH to learn how to cobble SHOES from ZEKE."

Penny turned to him. "Why?"

"Zeke's got all this KNOW-HOW stuck somewhere in his HEAD. But you KNOW as well as I KNOW that poor ol' ZEKE is MISSING a few CUPS in his CUPBOARD." He tapped his head with his finger. "He OUGHT to be PASSING the CRAFT along before it's GONE."

The more Hank talked, the more Penny thought that a woodpecker described him to a T. His loud voice reminded her of the constant drumming, brash and rapid, peck, peck, peck, followed by the shrill sound of a woodpecker looking for food. "But Micah is trying to be a field guide. He doesn't want to cobble shoes."

"Doesn't HAVE to be ONE or the OTHER. He can do BOTH. Once he gets LEARNED, he could HUNT birds by day, COBBLE shoes by night."

Penny didn't answer, but it wasn't because she dismissed the idea. She was actually thinking it over. She had been worrying about how seasonal field guiding could be, drying up when the weather turned cold and the birds headed south. Even if Micah could find rare birds in any season, birders weren't as hardy. Most likely, the guesthouse would be empty during winter months.

Hank Lapp, strangely enough, might have given her a good idea. It might be wise for Micah to have a trade, something flexible, something to fill in during those quiet stretches in the year.

Soon enough, they were at Zeke's house. Penny knocked on the door and went right in, like she usually did. Zeke was sitting at the kitchen table, in the dim light of the fading afternoon sun. Just sitting. Just waiting. Next to him on the tabletop was Hank's mended boot.

Maybe, just maybe, teaching Micah to cobble might be as good for Zeke as it would be for her brother.

Micah Weaver, Bird-Watching Log

Name of Bird: *Pileated Woodpecker*

Scientific Name: *Dryocopus pileatus*

Status: *Low concern*

Date: *April 15*

Location: *Fallen tree along the ridge behind Lost Creek Farm*

Description: *Female, about the size of a crow, black with white stripe down neck, bright red crest, powerful grayish-black bill as long as its head.*

Bird Action: *Whacking away at a snag for over an hour. That's a lot of head smacks.*

Notes: *Solitary nature. Shy. Monogamous. Male parent does most of necessary incubation for eggs, especially at night. Favorite food is carpenter ants and beetles. Pileated Woodpeckers will excavate a cavity 10–24 inches deep in a dead tree to create a nesting burrow. Most woodpeckers use their nesting burrows only one season (with the exception of the Common Flicker). Cavity-nesting birds will reuse nests of Pileated Woodpeckers the following year— owls, swifts, ducks, songbirds like chickadees, titmice, bluebirds, House Wrens, nuthatches, Great Crested Flycatchers, starlings, and House Sparrows.*

Doesn't sing. Gives a loud, rapid drumming "kuk-kuk-kuk-kuk-kuk-kuk" call that can be ear piercing.

Noticed one nesting burrow made in a telephone pole that caused the pole to snap and break in two. Telephone company sent a truck out; repairmen were flabbergasted when I pointed out the woodpecker burrow. They called the woodpecker an unrepeatable name.

14

The firepit had been Micah's idea. Sometime last summer, while out birding, he'd found a large cast-iron pot that had been abandoned in a creek and dragged it home. He set it up in the yard and Penny added lawn chairs around it that she bought at a tag sale and painted a bright lime green. Ever since, it had become a once-or-twice-a-week event at Lost Creek Farm to sit around the firepit after supper. Once Ben and Natalie started joining them, they had a fire nearly every evening, weather permitting. It was just an assumed thing.

Around seven o'clock, Micah and Ben would gather some wood from the woodpile and Penny would bring out mugs of hot cider and Natalie would pass out blankets or throws. This week, twice, Boyd Baldwin had driven up in his big truck to join them. All kinds of topics were batted about, but the best ones were about birds.

Penny noticed how, around the firepit, Micah talked more, stuttered less. She thought it had something to do with the darkness that surrounded them, attention mesmerized by the flickering flames. He was at ease, and the words flowed more easily when he was relaxed. Those moments brought Penny such a deep satisfaction. Whenever she saw him fighting to form words, it never failed to pierce her heart. Coming here, to Stoney Ridge, had been the right decision for Micah's sake, of that she had little doubt.

Add Ben to that mix, the confidence he had in Micah's abilities, and any lingering doubt was wiped out.

And Penny shouldn't neglect giving some credit to Natalie. Quirky Natalie, who jumped like a cricket with quick, jerky movements. She took an interest in everything, asking questions, offering comments. She would coax Ben to tell some stories about his travels, or ask Micah about his favorite bird, or quiz Penny on the Plain life. Tonight, she asked what the word for *loneliness* was in Penn Dutch. Penny exchanged a knowing look with Micah. "I don't think there is a word for it."

"Then what do you call it?" Natalie said.

"There's not a word for it," Penny said, "because it's not part of our culture."

"How can that be?" Natalie asked. "How is that even possible? How can the Amish be immune?"

"But we're not immune," Penny said. "We have sorrow and grief and suffering and pain and broken hearts. We just don't have loneliness."

Natalie seemed absolutely astounded at that thought. Ben remained quiet.

~

Someday. What was up with that? That's how Penny responded when Natalie finally asked her if she could see those secretive bird drawings. "Maybe someday."

Why in the world wouldn't Penny want Natalie to see them? For goodness' sake, she had volunteered to show them to Ben. Why him and not her? It was so disappointing.

Natalie had thought she and Penny were starting to be friends. They talked together each day. Natalie made a point to watch the window to see when Penny might be hanging laundry and she'd dart outside to help. Natalie would pepper her with all kinds of questions about the Plain life, right down to the underwear they wore. Penny didn't seem to mind Natalie's presence, nor her questions, though she had a strange habit of flipping the questions around whenever she could, which was often.

"If you think there's something peaceful in the Plain life, have you considered how to bring more peace into your own life?"

Or . . .

"What do *you* think it looks like to have a life that pleases God?"

Or . . .

"You can always pray, Natalie. God always hears our prayers when we seek him."

Those about-face questions startled Natalie. She knew what Penny was trying to do—get her to see past the lifestyle, to not assume life was easier on the Plain side of the fence.

Natalie thought Penny was wrong about that. She was confident that life was easier for those who were born Plain. Simpler, less complicated. Take Joel, for example. Imagine being a part of a community that highly valued marriage, that would frown on his infidelity rather than ignore it or justify it.

Imagine being part of a marriage where children were longed for, rather than postponed indefinitely. The way Joel did. *Someday,* he would tell her, whenever she had brought the subject up.

The next morning, over a cinnamon roll and coffee at the Sweet Tooth Bakery, she asked Boyd about whether he could've been Amish. "I just find them fascinating. The life seems so orderly, so peaceful, so safe and predictable—but not in a boring way." Not the way she had assumed it to be.

"You're wondering if I would have stayed in the church if I'd been born Amish? Probably so. Most of the lifestyle is pretty appealing. Not all of it, though." He tipped his head. "More importantly, I think God plunks us down right where we're supposed to be."

"So a person has no choice in the matter?"

"Plenty of choice. It's the inside that I'm talking about." Gently, he thumped his chest with his fist. "Wherever God puts us, he wants us in relationship with him. That's for everyone, wherever they are. Amish or Englisch or any other label."

The waitress brought coffee mugs to them, giving Natalie a moment to reflect on Boyd's remarks. He was much more spiritually attuned than she was. He'd grown up with a comfortable trust in religion. The church was a safe place.

Natalie had grown up with the opposite view—with her grandmother's hurt from being excluded, her anger toward the Amish church, toward being judged so severely.

They were an odd pair, she and Boyd. It made no sense to invest in this relationship, no sense at all. Yet she knew he was very interested in her—he spoke often of places he wanted to take her, of things he wanted them to do together. As if she didn't live in Philadelphia but here, on an Amish farm. As if she were staying here, past the migration of Ben's little bird.

It made no sense. Yet . . . Boyd Baldwin, vet to the Amish, was hard to dismiss. There was something about him that she found so terribly attractive.

He pushed the creamer toward her. "Why do you ask?"

"My grandmother was raised Amish, but she left when she met and married my grandfather. Most of the people she knew from church would have nothing to do with her."

"Strict shunning. That's when a person has been baptized and chooses to leave. That's one of those pieces of the Amish life that I have a hard time understanding. I know the rationale behind it, the theology, but it still seems really harsh."

"It was brutal on my grandmother. All of her extended family was kind of ripped away. My own folks were older when they married, and older still when I was born. They've both passed away. Ben and I, we're all that's left." She hadn't told Boyd that Ben had been raised here, that his father was less than a mile down the road. Ben continued to make it very clear that he didn't want others to know. Not Boyd, and definitely not Penny, he'd told her. She gave him her word, because she knew his reluctance had everything to do with Levi.

After the waitress brought their cinnamon roll to their table and they'd oohed and aahed over the size of it, the sweet spicy scent, the icing dripping down the sides, and debated whether they could replicate this in Boyd's kitchen, Natalie steered the conversation back to the Amish. "You know Penny better than I do. Why wouldn't she want to show her artwork to me?"

Boyd had no answer. "Probably has something to do with how the Amish view art." He cut the cinnamon roll in half and put it on a second plate. "Don't take it so personally, Natalie. Besides, I thought you'd seen the drawings."

"Accidentally."

He glanced up at her, eyebrows lifted.

Natalie's fork stopped in midair. "Don't give me that look. I was getting a cup of coffee in the kitchen. She'd left them on the kitchen table and I happened upon them. Entirely accidental."

"Well, why do you need to see them a second time?"

Natalie chewed slowly, taking time to form her response. "To take a closer look. They're very impressive. All kinds of birds."

"Don't tell me you're getting bit by the bird bug?"

"Maybe." Not bird-watching, though. Too slow. Too dull.

Boyd polished off the last bite. "I was hoping we could partner on Saturday for the Christmas Bird Count. Unfortunately, I'll be castrating some bulls over at the Miller farm."

Midbite, Natalie's appetite vanished.

～

It wasn't often that Penny made people upset, but now there were three. Natalie and Micah and Roy.

Natalie wanted to see the bird drawings in the worst way, which only made Penny all the more determined to keep them from her. She wasn't trying to be obstinate. There was something about

Natalie that caused Penny to have a check in her spirit, a warning to keep her at arm's distance. She wasn't quite sure why she had such a feeling, but she knew not to ignore it.

Natalie was warm and charming and amusing and terribly interested in all things Plain.

That, Penny realized just now, was what troubled her. Natalie was like so many tourists and gawkers who, often enough, descended on the Amish with unbridled curiosity, eager to see something, longing to find that life here was just like they imagined it to be. As if the Plain life held the elixir to cure all the troubles in the world. Penny wanted no part of such foolishness. Life had plenty of troubles, no matter what bonnet you wore.

Micah's upset was another story. He was downright mad at Penny. He wouldn't say so directly, but he refused to look her in the eyes. Over supper last evening, she had told him about the idea of apprenticing under Zeke Zook. "Consider it as a hobby that you could do during the winter. And it pays well." Maybe she shouldn't have added that part. She didn't really know. Hank Lapp was the one who told her Zeke had made a lot of money. She knew better than to take Hank Lapp's word for anything.

Eyes cast down, Micah focused on eating. "I w-wanted to be a field g-guide. And I am."

"I know. And I'm completely supportive, Micah. But field guiding is seasonal work. It wouldn't be a bad idea to learn a skill like shoe repair."

He shook his head. "I l-like to be outdoors. With the birds."

"But you keep saying you don't want to hire out as a farmhand. Your choices are rather limited."

He went back to eating.

"I was thinking you could do the shoe repair work around the field guiding. Work at night, for example." When he still didn't answer, she added, "Zeke is willing to teach you all he knows."

He snorted. "That won't t-take long."

She frowned at him. It wasn't like Micah to be sarcastic. "You'd be surprised. There's still a lot of Zeke left inside. Especially when he gets his hands on those tools. It's like he comes alive again. It's . . . instinctive. The way you are with birds."

She noticed that he slowed down for a moment at that, but just for a moment.

"Micah, we need a steady income."

Micah frowned and reached out to refill his plate, and she knew that was his way of saying the conversation was over.

And finally, there was Roy. It was becoming a rare day when he didn't stop by Lost Creek Farm for one reason or another—offers to help get the farm ready for winter (there wasn't much to do) or chop wood (Micah chopped plenty of wood) or make shy requests to take Penny out on a date. She always said no, and it pained her. She knew Roy had his heart set on her. If only she felt the same way about him, things would be so much nicer and simpler. Instead, she was waiting for the man in the guesthouse.

～

Ben looked out the window at the setting sun, and at Roy standing near the bird feeder with Penny. By Roy's side was a basket.

Ben was starting to notice how Roy always came to Lost Creek Farm bearing gifts. He looked so right standing there, in his Plain clothes and wide-brimmed felt hat, with his face framed by his black shaggy hair and full beard. He saw the farmer reach down into the basket and gently pick up something furry to place in Penny's arms. Ben got out his binoculars and focused them on the gift, aware he was in full whacko-neighbor mode. The gift was a kitten. He saw the way Penny's face lit with delight over the tiny animal, watched her stroke the taffy-colored coat, nestle it in her arms like a newborn baby. Then Roy gave the kitten a little pat and turned to leave, a hop in his step, looking pleased. Very pleased.

Ben lowered his binoculars, feeling a sting of shame for spying on them. What was happening to him? He was turning into a nutjob.

But what exactly did Penny feel for Roy? She'd never said. Then again, why should it matter to Ben? It shouldn't.

But it did.

Natalie had a great day.

The other night, Penny casually mentioned that she would be hosting a quilting for some women in the church on Thursday, so Natalie invited herself. Penny stared at her like she'd suggested swimming with polar bears. It was a look on her face that Natalie was now familiar with. As if Penny wondered why Natalie seemed so interested in the Plain people. Finally she said yes, rather half-heartedly, and Natalie grabbed it.

She was so excited. What an opportunity to observe generations of women gathered around a woodstove, sewing something by hand. It was a peek into history, a bygone tradition. Natalie's friends gathered in homes mostly to play Bunco and drink wine.

And then there were the actual quilts . . . works of *art*. She wanted to see how a group of Amish women, all dressed alike, worked together to create such unique quilts, full of startling beauty and color out of solid patches of fabric.

Years ago, Sophia Parker, her first design client, had Natalie search high and low for an antique Amish quilt to hang on her master bedroom wall. In the process, she'd learned a lot about antique Amish quilts. She knew they had patterns, and she even knew there were patterns specific to Lancaster County that were more buttoned up than Indiana or Ohio patterns. Less influenced by the big bad world, was how she came to think of Lancaster patterns.

The quilts she had searched out for Sophia used dark and muted colors, leftover from clothing. Not to mention they were tattered and worn and threadbare, though Sophia paid a small fortune for the one she hung in her bedroom. That quilt looked nothing like the vibrant colors that hung on Penny's clothesline. She couldn't wait to see how the women chose to fit the pieces of fabric into place like puzzle pieces.

Thursday was a cool autumn morning, the threat of rain heavy. Buggies started arriving at Lost Creek Farm at ten in the morning, each one bringing a covered dish in one arm and a sewing bag in the other. They set right to work, stopping only for lunch—and what a lunch! A Thanksgiving feast had less food. Ham, green beans, bread rolls, deviled eggs, sweet potatoes gratin, multiple pound cakes, and something beige that Natalie couldn't identify.

The Amish women treated her as something of a curiosity, but one let her hold her baby and a few spoke to her in English. One kind, big-boned woman named Birdy asked her a few questions about her life in Philadelphia. Then she asked if Natalie liked to go birding with her cousin Ben.

"Oh, goodness no. To me, one bird is the same as another." The moment the words left Natalie's mouth, she knew she'd said the wrong thing. Birdy's jaw dropped open. She stared at Natalie as if she just didn't know how to respond to such a comment. As if she'd suggested they should all go skinny-dipping at Blue Lake Pond after lunch.

Overall, Natalie thoroughly enjoyed the entire experience of watching the women, all different ages, all as purposeful and efficient as bees making honey in a beehive. They seemed to arrive at Penny's knowing the part they played in making the day of quilting, and perhaps even more so a day of all female companionship, into a complete success. Natalie especially enjoyed the food. It might not be considered fine dining, but it was absolutely delicious. Even that mysterious beige something-or-other.

This was the life her grandmother had lived, and her great-grandmother, and every grandmother before her. This would have been the life of Natalie, had her grandmother not fallen in love with a non-Amish man and chosen him over the church. One decision altered the course of life for generations to come.

These Plain people fascinated her. Now she understood why Sophia Parker had been so enamored with the Amish. She'd been noodling an idea to present to Sophia, something she was sure would appeal to her. Something that might help resurrect Natalie's career. It was no accident she was here, right now. Someone up there was looking out for her.

Later that afternoon, Natalie slipped on her jacket and joined Ben on the porch to watch the sunset. As she settled in the rocker, she said, "It's getting cold, isn't it?"

"Uh-huh."

He didn't sound happy about it. "Did you hear those quacking ducks in the night?"

"Canada Geese. What you heard were nocturnal flight calls."

"What?"

"Nocturnal migrants. Most birds migrate at night, as much as eighty percent. And most migrate in flocks. The peak of migration in this area is in September, but with the mild weather this fall, birds have been lingering. I've heard a lot of nighttime activity."

She rocked back and forth. "You've got me curious. Why don't birds just fly during the day?"

"It's an efficient way to use time. They use days for stopovers, to rest and forage. Somehow, they don't get lost at night. Or eaten. At night, there's fewer predators, they're much safer."

"I'd think they'd get lost at night." Natalie shrugged. "I sure would."

"Birds have so many cues at night. Stars, for one. And the weather's nicer. Winds are calmer. Some scientists think they follow polarized light that wafts from the sun in the night sky."

She hoped he wasn't going to start getting all technical on her. He could do that sometimes. Ask him for the time and he'd tell her how to build a watch.

"There's all kinds of theories about night migration, but no one really knows. I think I'm most amazed at migrating birds that wing it alone. Hummingbirds, owls, some hawks, most herons."

"That's kind of sad. Going it alone. Such a lonely journey."

"Flocks are pretty conspicuous. Going solo might be safer." Ben leaned back in the rocking chair, folding his hands behind his neck. "Birding never fails to astonish."

"No luck yet with finding your little bird?"

He released a strained sigh. "Not with that bird, but plenty others. My life list has grown markedly since I've been here. Micah . . . he truly has an extraordinary gift."

"Too bad he's Amish. It's a pity."

He looked at her. "A pity?"

"Couldn't he make quite a name for himself"—she pointed down the road—"in the big bad world?"

"Well, yeah, I suppose so. But then again, people do come to him. Like I did." He rocked back and forth. "I don't think I would use the word 'pity' to describe Micah Weaver. I think he's happy here. He has sort of a settled soul."

"Like Penny. She has a settled soul."

"Like Penny," he agreed.

"I shouldn't have used the word 'pity.' I just meant that he could be chasing birds all around the world. Like you do."

"He's in a church where the bishop will let him chase birds. He just can't use an airplane to go after them."

"It just seems like a restricted life. Isn't that how you'd describe your childhood?"

"Restrictive? I suppose it might seem that way if you grew up outside the Amish, but I never thought of it that way."

She scoffed. "I spent my teens hanging out at shopping malls with my friends. Or glued to a chair in a movie theater."

"Well, that's true enough. My friends and I wouldn't have been at a shopping mall. Or at a movie theater. But we also had all the freedom we wanted to roam the countryside. When Levi and I were boys, we would head out the door with our fishing rods on a summer day and not be back until milking time, and no one thought twice. No danger. No worries. Just freedom to be children."

Natalie tilted her head. "That's the first time you've mentioned Levi since you've been here."

Ben's gaze flicked to the sunset.

Softly, she added, "Being here . . . it must bring up a lot of memories for you."

He nodded, but just barely.

"Good ones, not just the hard ones, I hope."

"Yes," he said, without meeting her eyes. "Good ones too."

"So does that mean we can stay on a while longer?"

"At least through the Christmas Bird Count on Saturday." He leaned back in the rocker, studying her with interest. "You really like this veterinarian, don't you?"

She took her time answering, rocking back and forth, hands on her knees, which bounced worriedly. "I do." She really did.

Admitting that out loud, not just to Ben but to herself, surprised her.

Ben woke in a cold sweat, and for the first time it wasn't a lingering effect of malaria. It was well after midnight, and he could hear the wind outside. But it wasn't the wind that woke him. It was his dream. Sparked by that comment Natalie had made, that solitary migrating birds have such a lonely journey.

He had dreamt of his brother, Levi, being boys together, fishing on a summer day at Blue Lake Pond. Levi had just reeled in a big trout, the biggest he'd ever caught. He held it high in the sky, and shouted, "Wait'll Dad sees this!"

In the dream, Levi started walking up the beach with his trout. Ben called to him to come back, over and over, begged him to return, but Levi paid him no mind. Just before reaching the bend, he turned and lifted the trout up high, waving to Ben with his other hand. And then he disappeared. It was the same Levi, but he'd gone to a place where Ben couldn't follow.

He looked so happy, so full of joy, so at peace. So different from the last time Ben had seen him. He squeezed his eyes shut, trying to rid his mind of the memory of his brother's body hanging lifeless in the barn, the squeak of the rope as it swayed.

Micah Weaver, Bird-Watching Log

Name of Bird: *Canada Goose (or Honker)*

Scientific Name: *Branta canadensis*

Status: *Low concern*

Date: *December 8*

Location: *Stoney Ridge High School baseball field (lots of grass)*

Description: *Females and males resemble each other, large with a long black neck and white cheek patch. Body brown with pale chest and white undertail. Bill, legs, feet are black.*

Bird Action: *As if someone set off a firecracker, the flock took off from the grass baseball field at dusk, instantly falling into a V formation.*

Notes: *In the V formation, the lead goose (point man) uses all its wing power. Experienced geese take turns leading the flock and the lead goose flies lower than the rest of the gaggle. Each goose behind is slightly higher than the one in front, all the way to the last goose, which is flying the highest and benefiting the most from the air turbulence (draft) of the other geese. Ben Zook said that flying in formation adds 71% more distance that geese can fly than if they were flying alone.*

191

Canada Geese mate for life with very low divorce rate (like the Amish). But these geese are tough! Hank Lapp is trying to train one to act as a watchdog.

15

All afternoon, Micah practiced his best ask-Shelley-out lines on Junco in the barn. The patient horse listened, rarely commenting. Micah wanted to ask Shelley to join his team for the Christmas Bird Count on Saturday. His team of two, though he didn't plan to reveal that part.

When he finally felt as if he had memorized the lines down pat, he drove Junco over to the Yoder farmhouse and knocked on the door. To his delight and relief, Shelley answered right away, as if she'd seen him coming and hurried to greet him. His confidence bloomed.

He figured she must have been baking, because her sleeves were rolled up and she had a dusting of flour on her cheek, and some on her black apron. Slowly, taking great care, his voice smooth as silk, he said, "Care to come bird counting on Saturday?" Consonants were easier than vowels.

"With you? On that Christmas bird thingy?"

He nodded. So far, so good. No stutters, no stammers, no weird sounds as he froze up.

She closed the door behind her and joined him on the porch. "Just about everyone will be out counting birds on Saturday, won't they? Trudy sure will. She won't rest until the whole family is outside with binoculars and a pad and pencil."

Again, he nodded.

"Why do you like birds so much, Micah?"

Why? How to sum up his vast, deep appreciation for birds? Their freedom, their beauty, their variety, their resiliency. How to gather those big thoughts into a concise answer so that he didn't stammer his way through it? "They're . . . everywhere."

And they were.

She gave a thoughtful nod. "You know, Micah, you're right. I never thought of it that way, but I see them when I get the mail, or walk down the road, or drive the buggy someplace. They're a part of daily life, aren't they?"

Yes, daily life, but he was thinking on a much bigger scale. There were even records of the South Polar Skua in the South Pole.

Say it, Micah. Say it.

He tapped the flyer he'd brought to her house. "So . . . p-partner with me?" A little stutter, but not too bad. He hadn't planned on having to ask her twice.

Her eyebrows lifted in surprise. "You mean, count birds with you on Saturday?"

He nodded, breath held. *Please say yes, Shelley. Say yes. Give me a chance.*

She tightened her lips, pursing them together, and he couldn't take his eyes off them. What would it take to persuade her to kiss him with those soft-looking lips? What would it feel like to have that sweet mouth beneath his—

Stop it, Micah.

Man o' man, his mind was getting hard to control where Shelley Yoder was concerned.

She looked at the flyer again. A long moment passed. Then she looked at Micah. "I think that's a real good idea, Micah. Let's meet at the Bent N' Dent. Seven o'clock on Saturday morning."

"S-six."

She glanced behind Micah, and when he turned, he saw that her mother was peeking out the window at them. "Six? Even better."

194

She handed him the flyer. "You take it, Micah. You can probably use it for others. I won't forget." She gave him a smile right before she closed the door, though it didn't quite reach to her eyes.

It was little wonder that Ben's appetite had blossomed while staying at Lost Creek Farm. Penny's cooking was stellar. Restaurant quality. Tonight Natalie had sampled a bite of lemon cake, with lemon zest blended in the batter and the buttercream icing. She pointed her fork at her plate. "The calories in this? Totally worth it."

Ben forked off another appreciative bite before lifting his hand in a thumbs-up. This cake might be his favorite of Penny's desserts: moist, sweet, and tangy. Undeniably delicious.

Natalie licked a crumb off her fork. "I'm going to gain twenty pounds before we leave here."

He shot a glance at her. He hoped she wasn't going to ask him to stay on. He had promised Penny he'd support Micah with the Christmas Bird Count, and he had every intention to keep his promise. It helped that Trudy Yoder—someone Ben had yet to lay eyes on—had seen the tern twice this week, even though the night temperatures were dropping. Not freezing yet, though. If the tern had found a place to stay warm—a barn rafter, for example—it might not feel an urgency to leave quite yet. His determination fired up to bag that wily bird.

And it also helped that he hadn't bumped into Hank or Edith Lapp, hadn't had to swallow a dose of heavy guilt for not seeing his father.

Being here at Lost Creek Farm, staying on the fringes, it was pleasant. Peaceful. This must be how Natalie perceived the Amish. Naive, but from this detached angle, he understood why she found it appealing.

Boyd's attention, Ben thought, seemed to be inspiring a positive change in Natalie. She seemed less restless, less prone to those erratic waves of depression. He hoped she might start to see herself in a new light, the way Ben saw her: her kindness, her generosity, her creative flair, her intelligence and humor. Boyd seemed to get a kick out of Natalie's quirkiness, which came as a relief to Ben. Joel had often criticized Natalie as a flaky artist.

Ben wasn't blind to Natalie's shortcomings. He knew the breakup wasn't entirely Joel's fault. Natalie and Joel had a shared love of ambition that used to nettle Ben whenever he visited them. He tried to ignore it, assuming he was just sensitive to it because of his Amish upbringing. He wasn't raised to be a money-hungry man.

Maybe Boyd might help Natalie face that demon once and for all. She commented often on how satisfied he was with his life. His contentment seemed to astound her, as if it wasn't normal.

A stab of jealousy pierced Ben. He didn't begrudge his cousin any happiness, but he wouldn't mind a little bit of that happiness in his own life. One day, it might be nice to have someone special in his life. And that thought startled him. Where did it come from? He'd always prized his independence. A rolling stone gathers no moss. No baggage.

"Can I ask you a personal question?"

"No." He wasn't in a smiling mood, but he tried to offer up a small smile to Natalie to soften his blunt answer.

"In that case, I won't ask if you've ever considered asking Penny out on a date."

"Thanks for not asking."

"In so many ways, she's perfect for you."

"Except for that minor issue of being Amish."

"Right. Except for that. But, Ben, you're not such an unlikely pair. I think she might be good for you. She doesn't take life too seriously, and she's an incredible cook, and she has the *most* endearing face . . ."

Ben let Natalie prattle on for a while, thinking of Penny's face.

Endearing was just the right word for it. Her delicate features made her seem almost fragile, impossibly fine, fair and gentle. Yet the more he knew her, the more he realized how strong she was, how sturdy and secure. She seemed unshakable. Or maybe it was her faith that made her so steadfast. When she smiled or laughed, which she did often, it felt as if the whole world were set right again.

He refocused his attention just in time to hear Natalie say, "—and she loves birds. I mean, how can you resist that package?"

How was he supposed to resist the hold that Penny had on him, one that kept growing in strength with every minute that he spent in her nearness? He wished he knew.

~

This week, Natalie had spent some part of every day or evening with Boyd, often both. At first she thought it was just a little flirtation, then a crush, and now she found herself wondering if she might be falling in love. She wondered who had first come up with the phrase "falling in love," because that's exactly what it felt like. A free-fall jump out of an airplane. Terrifying and exhilarating and very dangerous.

Not that Boyd was dangerous. He was the kindest, gentlest, most thoughtful man she'd ever known. Tonight he'd even remembered that she liked a dollop of cream and a teaspoonful of sugar in her coffee. For all the years she'd been married to Joel, he'd never remembered. Since he drank his coffee black, he assumed everyone did.

It was love that worried Natalie. Love could be dangerous. A heart could be shattered into a million pieces. Mending was hard, lonely work.

Whenever she thought she might be falling in love with Boyd, she found it best to just shrug it off as a fleeting feeling. She still couldn't believe she could attract a man like Boyd, so she assumed he was only having fun with her. And that was just fine. She could do the same. This was *not* a relationship. It was just fun.

Tonight, she and Boyd were nestled on the couch in his house, watching the flames in the fireplace. Pretending to watch the flames. Her mind was busy updating his living room.

"Natalie, stop thinking about what paint color you'd use in here and tell me if Micah talked you into being on a team for the CBC." They'd only known each other a few weeks, but he "got" her. He said it was because her face revealed everything she was thinking.

"What's CBC mean again?"

"Christmas Bird Count. Micah has me passing flyers out to all my clients."

"When did you get so interested in birds?"

"As a boy. I had a teacher who was really into birds. In fact, she's probably the one I credit with giving me an appreciation for animals."

Natalie looked up at him. "How'd she do that?"

"I'll never forget the day when a small bird flew into our classroom. Everything stopped. The teacher told all the kids to sit quietly so we didn't scare the bird. We watched that poor little panicked bird circle the room, bonking into the windows. The teacher caught it in her hands, and lo and behold, there was a band on its leg. She told me to write down the numbers on the band, and later I wrote a letter to the US Department of Wildlife. About a month after that, we got a letter back with all the information about that little bird."

"What kind of bird?"

"A male Ruby-crowned Kinglet. Banded the previous May in Meredith, New Hampshire. And we were thanked for our cooperation."

"You remember all that?"

"Vividly."

"So how did that experience trigger a love of all animals?"

"Something about that experience, that connection—to the

bird, to the original bander, to the government—it gave me a sudden sense of importance. Of what it might look like to be a good steward of this earth. Including birds and animals."

Boyd Baldwin was a lovely man, Natalie thought. A kind and gentle and good man.

"I thought we could go on the Christmas Bird Count together, assuming I can switch the Millers' bull castrations to another day."

She pulled back and looked him straight in the eye. "You think I would spend a day counting birds?" She slapped a hand over her heart. "Me? I don't even know the first thing about bird-watching."

"Want to find out?"

"I don't have the right equipment." She'd tried to carry Ben's oh-so-precious optical equipment bag once and nearly dropped it, staggering under its weight. After that incident, he didn't let her touch his bag. How many times did he give her a look and say, "600mm camera lens, Natalie"? Like she had any idea what *that* meant.

"You don't need much. Only things you really need are a field guide, a pair of binoculars, and some enthusiasm."

"Ah, you see? Enthusiasm. *That's* what's missing." But she did feel badly when she saw the disappointment in his eyes. As much as she would like to spend a full day with Boyd, it wouldn't be spent trudging through Amish fields, cold and wet, stepping in who-knew-what. To count birds for who-knew-why.

⌣

Ever since Shelley had agreed to partner with Micah for the Christmas Bird Count, he had barely been able to concentrate on the search for the White-winged Tern. Ben kept asking him if he thought the bird was gone.

"S-still here," Micah reassured him, only because Trudy said she'd seen it twice this week. Man o' man, he hoped that girl knew what she was talking about.

He also hoped Ben Zook wasn't counting on him as a partner for the CBC. He thought Penny might be willing to team up with Ben, but he hesitated to ask for a favor. He was still upset with her for bringing up the ridiculous notion of him becoming a shoe repair man.

Micah had a lower than low interest in learning how to repair shoes, but he knew that to hold on to Lost Creek Farm, they needed a steady income and field guiding was anything but steady. Too seasonal.

Penny pointed out one thing that was hard to dismiss. Having a trade would only lift his reputation in the eyes of any future father-in-law. Penny didn't say which father-in-law—she didn't say the name Dave Yoder—but Micah knew she knew how he felt about Shelley. Penny was like that. She might be right. If he did have a steady income, maybe it would be a way to prove to Shelley's father that he could support a wife someday.

Not too soon, of course. But someday.

Micah Weaver, Bird-Watching Log

Name of Bird: Wild Turkey

Scientific Name: Meleagris gallopavo

Status: (Extremely) Low concern

Date: December 3

Location: Parking lot of Bent N' Dent (they're pretty much everywhere this time of year)

Description: Male, as big as a goose. Large, plump bird with long legs, wide, rounded tails, small head on long, slim neck. Rump and tail feathers are broadly tipped with chestnut tail tips. Bare skin on neck and neck looked blue-ish.

Bird Action: Male was performing courtship display. Puffed-up body feathers, flared tail, swelled-up face wattles, drooped wings, strutted while making a gobbling call. For some reason the females find this ritual particularly attractive.

Notes: Travel in flocks, roost in trees at night. One male will mate with several females. Nest sites are shallow depressions, usually on ground, lined with grasses, leaves. Females tend the young.

Later that day, Wild Turkey male was circling Hank Lapp's mule and buggy, determined to not let him out. Kept running at and pecking at Hank's legs each time he tried to leave buggy.

"Turkeys," Hank yelled in his everyday voice, "are a foul fowl."

201

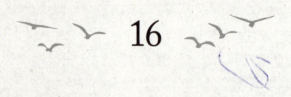

16

The day had come. Through the kitchen window, Penny could see the sun casting its first long red light onto the land. She was up earlier than usual to help Micah prepare for the Christmas Bird Count. He'd been working so hard, persuading as many volunteers as he could to participate in the bird count, giving them a circle of territory to cover and long lists of common birds to watch for, teaching them how to keep track of the birds they saw, and then delivering the information to Micah as soon as the sun went down so he could compile it and provide it to the local chapter of the Audubon Society.

Penny was so proud of Micah. He'd done all that volunteer work as the count compiler while continuing to take Ben Zook out on a bird hunt each morning and evening. All but today. She had a pretty strong hunch that a girl was involved in Micah's bird-counting team. He took such a long shower that he ran out of hot water. Freshly shaved and scrubbed, smelling of pine soap, wearing clean and ironed clothes—when had Micah ever cared about the condition of his clothes? Oh yes, there was definitely a girl involved. And Penny had little doubt the girl was Shelley Yoder. She had noticed how particularly nervous Micah acted whenever Shelley was near, how solicitous he could be to her, how attentive.

It wasn't hard to see why Micah fancied Shelley—the prettiest girl in Stoney Ridge. She had a touch of mystery about her, like she was always preoccupied with something else, or somebody else. Or maybe . . . Penny wondered, preoccupied with herself.

A few months ago, Penny had been in town to mail a package. Just as she came out of the post office, Shelley passed by. She was with a group of Youngies, ones Penny didn't recognize. They were all dressed in Englisch clothing. Standing at the door of the post office, Penny watched them climb into a beat-up car. All of them, jammed in like sardines. At the last minute, just before getting into the car, Shelley turned. Her eyes met Penny's. She knew exactly what the girl was thinking: Would Penny tell her parents?

Of course she wouldn't. Of course not. Penny didn't judge Shelley for being tempted by the outside world. It *was* tempting. The conveniences, the choices. But it worried her that Shelley might influence Micah to consider worldly temptations.

Mostly, she worried Shelley Yoder would break Micah's heart.

She heard a knock on the kitchen door. Through the window she saw Ben standing there, the morning sun catching him full on the face. Such a beautiful face, Penny thought, and her breath caught with pleasure at the sight of him. Unconsciously, she smoothed out her apron before opening the door. "I'm afraid Micah's long gone."

"Micah told me he had an obligation to someone else today. I'm guessing it's got to do with a cute girl." He gave her a crooked grin.

"I had the same thought." She swung the door open for him. "Come in quickly. Don't let the kitten out. She goes right to the bird feeder. Yesterday she brought me a little brown sparrow and I nearly cried."

He stepped into the kitchen, shutting the door behind him with a soft click just before the kitten tried to slip out. "What's its name?" The little kitten sat on her haunches, glaring at him accusingly.

"I haven't come up with one yet."

"I thought you'd be out counting by now. Hasn't your brother given you a territory assignment, like everyone else in this town?"

"Yes. I'm heading up the ridge to count."

The kitten curled against Ben's ankle and he bent to scratch her. As he straightened, he said, "With Roy?"

"Roy? Oh goodness no. He shoots birds."

Ben's face swung toward her, his dark brows drawn down as though he'd never heard of such an outlandish activity. "He shoots them?" A corner of his mouth quirked, a grin started, then spread. "Shoots them?"

"Roy is a good man," she added, feeling guilty. He *was* a good man.

"You need at least two to count, don't you? To confirm the sightings?"

"Trudy was supposed to join me, but she's over an hour late. I must have misunderstood. My guess is she's with Micah and the other volunteers."

"I told Micah that Natalie and I would cover the ridge, but she has no interest in joining me." He rubbed his forehead. "Since there can't be single count observers . . ."

Penny held her breath.

Ben glanced away. "Maybe . . . if you don't mind, you and I should join forces and tackle the ridge."

Would she mind? Mind?! She would *love* it. There was so much she wanted to talk to him about, to learn about. She drew out the words with the slow easing of her pent-up breath. "I wouldn't mind. If you feel up to it."

"I know it's a long day, but I'm up for it. Actually, I've been feeling pretty good. And I've been up to the ridge with Micah a number of times. I know what to expect."

The ridge. Maybe being there together, sitting on the resting rock, gazing at the eagles' nest, surely then he would remember. Slowly, she nodded.

"When do you want to leave?"

"I just have to hang some laundry on the line so it'll dry while I'm gone. And I need to pack up some food for us." And take a moment to pray, to settle her pounding heart.

An entire day alone with Ben Zook? A gift of time sent straight from Heaven.

But she also knew the word God had given to her on this: to rest patiently and wait on the Lord. So easy to say, so hard to do. The more familiar she became with Ben, the more difficult it was getting to hold her tongue. She wanted to tell Ben she'd been waiting for a day like this since she was twelve years old. She asked God to guard her mouth, to let Ben reveal himself in his own time.

"I think we'll make a good team for Micah." He put his hand on the kitchen door handle.

Oh we do! Penny thought. *We make a good team. A* wonder- ful *team.*

Ben couldn't be more pleased at how this day was unfolding. He'd been sure Penny would be off counting birds with Roy today. He hoped he didn't sound too pleased when she said Roy would sooner shoot a bird than count it. The way she looked at him, her gaze tracing over his face just the way she observed birds—as if trying to memorize him—had sent a spiral of heat down his spine to his toes, as hot as a comet.

Pull it together, Zook, he warned himself as he gathered his optical equipment bag and slung it over his shoulder. *This day is meant for birds.*

Natalie had gotten the message enough times from Ben about how she truly didn't understand the Amish life. Try it out, he told her, and so she thought she would. Penny had been kind enough to wash their clothes, and when she saw her hanging them out to dry, Natalie grabbed a sweater and hurried outside to take over the task.

"You're sure?" Penny said. "It won't take me more than a moment."

"Ben already has his gear packed up for the day. He wants to get started on this bird-counting project. Go ahead. I'll handle it." To Natalie, Ben seemed excited about the day, not that it was easy to tell.

Penny's gray gaze turned to the guesthouse. "It's all yours, then." She hurried back to the kitchen.

Natalie made a discovery about the Amish life: hanging clothes on a laundry line, especially in the chill of early morning, was not as easy as it looked. The wet clothes fought to be untangled, and the sleeves and pant legs kept slapping her in the face when a gust of wind swept through, and her fingers got stiff. She watched Ben and Penny head up the path that led to the ridge behind Lost Creek Farm and nearly called Penny back.

But she didn't. She could see they were laughing and talking to each other as they walked, and she didn't want to ruin the moment. There was something about Penny and Ben together, some kind of suppressed energy that was always simmering below the surface.

They'd be gone for the better part of the day. Micah had left early and wouldn't return until late. Boyd was doing something awful to bulls. Natalie was alone. All alone on the farm. All day long.

She finished hanging another pair of Ben's pants and stepped back. Penny's laundry line always looked so neat and orderly. Natalie's was a jumble, a cockeyed mess. She took the rest of the basket to the guesthouse and draped the leftovers—her damp lingerie—over the backs of chairs and tables. Her underwear had a better chance of drying here than outside, for all the world to see.

She refilled her coffee cup and walked outside, looking up at the big house. She went back inside. Sat down. Natalie bowed her head and whacked her palm on the table, as she did when she was excited. When she lifted her head, the coffee cup was still quivering in its saucer. A smile curled her lips. She jumped up to look out the window at the big house. Pulled to it like a magnet. To the kitchen. To the pantry. To Penny's hidden bird drawings.

Like a moth to a flame, she couldn't resist.

Micah had risen long before dawn. He left the house early to meet Shelley in front of the Bent N' Dent, which allowed him time to listen for birds as he waited for her. Watched for her. Half past six came and went. Micah wasn't too worried, because he was fully occupied with organizing the volunteers into groups, giving them specific directions for their counting territory, reminding them of their mission, and sending them off. Birdy Stoltzfus, bless her, had brought along some bird-friendly volunteers. Trudy didn't show up, which really, really bothered him, especially because that meant he had to let Hank Lapp lead a group. He started with a loud joke. "THERE are TWO sides to a TREE. Which two?"

Everyone looked at him blankly.

"The SIDE FACING you and the SIDE WHERE the BIRD is!" He laughed so loud at his own joke that he flushed a crow from a tree. A crow!

Birdy, no doubt sensing his worry about Hank's loud voice frightening away the birds and about Hank just being Hank, stepped up to suggest Hank's group be sent off to the town dump, where Black Vultures were roosting and they didn't care who might be looking at them. Or shouting at them.

By seven o'clock, as sunlight began to fill the sky, the volunteers were sent to their tasks. Micah really should've taken a group to lead, but he didn't want to leave without Shelley. He told Birdy and Hank the truth, that he was waiting for one more counting group to arrive. They didn't question him.

By eight o'clock, Micah wandered down the road toward the Yoder home, still counting birds, with one eye watching for a sign of Shelley, hoping she was coming like she said she was.

Micah Weaver, Bird-Watching Log

Name of Bird: *Black Vultures*

Scientific Name: *Coragyps atratus*

Status: *Low concern*

Date: *November 8*

Location: *Flocks, rummaging through mounds of disgusting, smelly trash at the Stoney Ridge town dump.*

Description: *Sooty black plumage, bare black heads. Highly social birds. Fierce family loyalty. Poor sense of smell, so they hang out with Turkey Vultures, which have an excellent sense of smell.*

Bird Action: *Followed a Turkey Vulture to a deer carcass and bullied it away. Stuck its bald head inside the rotting flesh of a deer. Eyed me with a face I'll never forget.*

Notes: *Black Vultures are particularly weird, with an underworld-ish look to them. Not a pretty bird, but pretty amazing. They're found all over North and South America and are a natural wonder. They clean up dead animals from the habitat before the spread of disease. Nice. They must have a remarkable immune system.*

If you can stand the stink, dumps are an endless all-you-can-eat buffet for vultures. They're enthusiastic pirates, happy to rob other predators of their foods. Like Turkey Vultures, they lack a voice box so their vocal abilities end up as hisses and grunts, striking terror in their own distinctive way. This bird packs a mighty punch.

Just stay out of its way.

17

Songbirds flitted through the trees, filling the morning air. Penny and Ben would stop at different points along the climb to count, spots she knew to gain ideal vantage points. Ben peered through his binoculars to count, Penny acted as scribe, writing down the species and the count on the clipboard Micah had given to her. She was right—they were a good team. Both so familiar with bird species that they counted quickly, in tandem. Only once or twice did they disagree about the bird's identity—one time, he was right. Another time, she was.

At one point of the climb, they approached a small section, running behind the ridge that bordered Lost Creek Farm, that was oddly void of trees. He stopped to peer at it.

"Six months ago," Penny said, as if he had asked for an explanation, "the remnants of a hurricane blew through here. Lightning struck a snag and started a fire. Fortunately, rain put the fire out but not before it burnt through this section. The hillside will need time to recover, but it will. The Lord is always in the work of restoring."

Ben didn't respond, but she could tell he was listening. Penny never minded quiet, but she felt a need to fill moments of silence with Ben. To fill up his emptiness, perhaps. Oftentimes, she sensed a deep loneliness in him, a long-carried burden. She'd had the same sense when she had first met him, twenty-some years ago.

"Funny thing is that the hurricane," she went on, "brought us quite a few vagrants. Micah spotted a Roseate Spoonbill. Such a beautiful, elegant bird, yet ridiculous in its way too. I wonder at times if the Lord created such birds just for the delight they bring. Just to make us stop and praise God and thank him for giving us so much in nature to enjoy in this life."

As she spoke, she turned her head to look at him. He lifted his eyes quickly to the burned-out hill behind her, almost as if he didn't want to be caught looking at her. Truth be told, she was more than a little nervous to be this close to him, to spend this much time alone with him.

They started up the trail again, back to the task of bird count-ing. Ben cocked his ear, and Penny lifted her chin. The clear *Peter Peter* whistles of a flock of Tufted Titmice. Ben cut off from the trail to find the gray songbirds foraging a Pyracantha bush full of berries. They stilled, watching from a distance. Ben counted aloud and Penny scribbled down the final number.

Suddenly, Ben said, "So why *did* you come to Stoney Ridge?"

She looked up, surprised at the question. "I told you. Lost Creek Farm. My grandmother had passed and left the farm to my mother."

"It's not typical for a woman your age to leave her family to move to a different church, even if it's an Amish church. They're all different, all with their own rules." Almost as an afterthought, he added, "Isn't that so?"

"The church in Big Valley . . ." She drew out the words with the slow easing of pent-up thoughts and feelings. "It seemed to quench the very Spirit of God with its endless rules."

"Churches can be like that sometimes."

"Even birds were not to be admired."

"Birds?"

"Doing so turned one's heart and mind from the Creator to

the creation. I had trouble understanding that, especially . . ." She tightened her grip on the pencil in her hand. "Especially when Micah was put under the Bann."

Ben swung around at that. "Micah? Has he even been baptized?"

"He had. He was only sixteen when he was baptized, something he wanted to do. He's always had a spirit as strong as bedrock."

"Like you," Ben said. "Steady as a rock."

Penny felt a spiral of pleasure at Ben's comment. Tucking her chin so he wouldn't see her smile, she smoothed down her apron, pushed stray hairs beneath her prayer cap. They came to a lookout spot and Ben sat on a rock to rest, to drink from a water bottle. She was relieved to see he stopped now and then, pacing himself, though he did seem to be handling the rigorous hike without any trouble. She sat on a nearby rock.

"So, how did Micah get himself put under the Bann?"

"It came about not long after he was baptized. Not a month or so later, he was asked to be a field guide for some Englisch birders. His keen eye spotted a Snail Kite, a South American bird. First time ever that it was spotted in Pennsylvania."

"I remember," Ben said.

"That caused quite a stir. Then a photographer hired Micah to go out birding. He ended up receiving an Audubon award, and gave Micah credit for helping him get such a remarkable shot."

"A male Ruff, spotted in a mudflat. That was when I first heard Micah's name."

She nodded. "And *that* was when the deacon came calling. The deacon felt it wasn't right to interact with the Englisch in such worldly ways, that it would taint Micah, make him prideful. He told Micah to stop, and that brother of mine . . . who can seem so gentle, so quiet . . . he told the deacon no. He said he just couldn't stop seeking out birds that the Lord had created for his glory. So the deacon put him under the Bann. Some felt that the deacon had gone too far. Others thought differently. A division was starting to brew. As my father often said, 'A river absorbs some of whatever flows through it.'"

"My father said that too. He meant it as a warning."

His comment surprised her and she waited to see if he would say more, but typical of Ben, he didn't. So she went on. "Our family worried that Micah would feel the need to leave the church altogether. We had long talks, all of us, about what to do. My mother was the one who suggested Micah go live at Lost Creek Farm, to care for the property. Micah, being the absentminded boy that he is, needed someone to go along with him. I volunteered to go with him, to keep house." Her lips lifted at the corners. "To make sure he ate."

"There was no one you were reluctant to leave in Big Valley?"

"My family, of course." She wasn't quite sure what he meant, but then his meaning dawned on her. "Friends too. But no one particular friend."

Ben kept his gaze on the trees, as if out of habit. Scanning for birds. She wondered if he had stopped listening, but suddenly he turned to her. "So what happened next?"

She gripped her knees tighter. "My father made a phone call to Bishop David Stoltzfus, to tell him about our circumstances. We knew Micah wouldn't come if he had to give up birding. David said that the church here held a different view about birding, and hoped Micah might consider field guiding in Stoney Ridge. He said that rare birds always bring goodness along with them."

"Ah. Ecotourism. All those birders who come flocking in to sightsee can add real benefits to the local businesses."

"I suppose so, but now that I know David, I think he also meant that he was giving us his blessing to pursue the work that Micah loves. And that clinched it. We left that very week and haven't looked back. We both had no doubt that the Lord has brought us here. All part of his wondrous and mysterious sovereignty."

"Your former church—is Micah still under their Bann?"

Penny took in a deep breath. "He is. The Stoney Ridge church is considered too progressive."

"So Micah can't go back," Ben said, a harsh edge to his voice. "Not to his own family. Not to his parents, brothers, and sisters. Cousins. Nieces and nephews."

She looked at him. "He can't go back."

Ben searched her face. "Nor can you."

"That's right."

"What about your mother and father?"

"We were all in agreement. This was the best decision." She lifted her palms. "Though it doesn't stop me from trying to persuade them to join us. I do believe they would enjoy this church, very much. Everyone has been feeling the strain of Big Valley church's leadership. It was like spending the winter without ever lighting the fire in the stove. There it was, right in the main room for all to see, but no one thought to strike a match."

"So what, Penny Weaver, made you want to strike the match?"

"My grandmother. She's the one who opened my eyes. To so much." She saw a Red-tailed Hawk sail past and marked it on the clipboard. "We'd better keep counting."

About an hour and fourteen bird species later, they came to a vantage point that overlooked the entire Stoney Ridge valley. It was her favorite view. They stopped for a moment and she let her gaze roam over the rolling hills. "Seeing it like this always reminds me of a patchwork quilt." At this time of year, the farmland was mostly brown, freshly plowed, furrows straight and narrow. Come spring, it would be velvet-green with the start of young crops.

He passed her a water bottle. "Imagine it from the window of an airplane."

She lifted her chin. "No thank you. I have too great a respect for gravity."

A laugh burst out of him. "You are quite a puzzle to me."

"Am I so very different from whom you'd expect me to be?"

The remark blurted out, surprising her before she could stop it. It shamed her, how she'd sounded just now. Bold. Audacious.

But when he didn't respond, she chanced a glance at him. He'd seen something down in the valley, something that caused a cold shiver to pass across his face.

It was the Amish cemetery he was staring at.

She watched him for a while, noticing how his hands clenched tight, as if he were barely holding himself together.

She longed to know all that was running through his mind right now. What was he hiding? Or ignoring? She couldn't tell which. She only knew that it was a burden. Of sorrow, of anger, maybe both.

"Wouldn't it be nice if we could turn back the clock?" he said, a roughness to his voice, which she was coming to recognize as words that came directly from his heart. "Wouldn't it be nice to go back to a certain pivotal point and create a different ending."

There it was again. The burning emptiness radiated off Ben, as real as if it were something Penny could see. Almost like heat waves.

"But we can't," he said, as if they'd been having a back-and-forth conversation. "What's done is done. We just have to live with the choices that were made."

Seeing how hard it had been for him to admit such a thing, she wanted to reach out and touch his arm. Just touch him. "That's the mystery and wonder that God brings to us. Taking what's broken, what seems to be irreparable, and making it whole."

"Some things are beyond repair."

Oh no. That, he was wrong about.

He stiffened. "We'd best keep going. Lots of birds to count for Micah," he said, ending the moment of closeness on an abrupt note.

Just then a gust of wind kicked up hard, slapping her skirts, lifting capstrings off her shoulders.

Suddenly Ben shrugged his shoulders in a careless way, as if tossing off a weight. The face he turned to her wore a polite expression. He tucked the water bottle into his backpack and hoisted his optical equipment bag on his shoulder. "Coming?" He turned and started walking away from her.

She rose from the resting rock to follow behind him. The moment of closeness was over, but it had given her a glimpse into the burden that he kept so carefully guarded. He sounded as if it was over, done with. She knew otherwise. The Lord brought him back for a reason, to address whatever it was that troubled him so. Despite Ben's valiant efforts to ignore it. The body was designed to heal, and so was the heart.

Micah Weaver, Bird-Watching Log

Name of Bird: *Ruff*

Scientific Name: *Calidris pugnax*

Status: *Rare fall migrant*

Date: *October 15 (when I was sixteen)*

Location: *Big Valley, Mifflin County, mudflats*

Description: *Non-breeding male that must have wandered off course from its migration route. He has a fine neck collar, a magnificent thatch of puffy feathers. Looks like a neck brace on a car accident victim.*

Bird Action: *Walking, running, head up, wading up to its belly, picking food from the mudflats.*

Notes: *Long-distance migrants from northern Europe and winters in southern Europe and Africa. Breeding males perform bizarre courtship rituals, puffing out its distinctive mane of feathers around its neck. The females come to a lek of male breeders to watch them stomp their feet like they're putting out a fire. They shake their tail feathers and strut and spin in circles. They make weird sounds, like the sound you get when blowing into an empty plastic bottle of soda pop.*

    After choosing a mate, the female will

leave the lek to raise her clutch without any help from the male. A real women's libber.

Such a non-distinct little bird, passing through on its way to Africa. Yet it turned my life upside down.

18

In one shattering moment, Ben had nearly broken. Seeing Levi's grave outside of the cemetery almost caused his whole self to unravel. He'd taken such care to avoid going anywhere near it, yet somehow it found him.

Levi had died in the summer. He should've been doing something he loved on that warm and sunny day, like birding or fishing, instead of being laid to rest in a pine coffin. On the day he was buried, it was raining hard. To Ben, it seemed the angels were weeping along with him. He was completely and utterly heartbroken over losing his only sibling, his brother, for the way he died, for the reason he died.

He and Penny made their way to the top of the ridge that rimmed Wonder Lake, stopping at numerous points to count birds, but nothing more was said between them. Penny didn't even try to engage him in conversation. He was sure she wanted him to say more, to open up, but there was no way he would let that happen. He wasn't going to allow anyone to let loose that terrible darkness inside him. That hatred that he felt for his father.

When they reached the place where Micah liked to pause to watch the eagles' aerie, Ben stopped and set down his optical equipment bag. "This would be a good place to set up the scope." As he unfolded the legs of the scope, adjusted dials into focus, he thought he should try to get things back to a more comfortable place between them. Good grief, she must think he was prone to mood swings. "Here. Take a look. The female eagle's head keeps popping up, as if she's expecting lunch to arrive. Guessing the male will come in soon."

"The male's over there. I think he's fishing." She pointed to a snag across the lake.

Sure enough, there was the male on a leafless branch. Ben glanced at Penny. She hadn't even used binoculars. Just instinct. No wonder Micah had such a head start on birding. He'd been taught by this remarkable woman.

"I could watch them all day," he said. "Imagine what it must be like to fly wherever one chooses."

"Yet isn't that what you do?"

Interesting. He hadn't thought of his life like that. Maybe from Penny's point of view, that's exactly what it seemed like. "Micah told me that eagles' nest has been here for years and years."

She wheeled around and released a sharp bark of laughter. "Micah told you that? Micah?!"

He'd gone back to adjusting a dial on his scope but looked up in alarm at the sharp tone in her voice. "I'm pretty sure that's what he said." Was that wrong? He straightened, watching her. She looked like she was about to burst. Or shout. Or cry.

Penny gripped her elbows and turned in a circle. Then she faced him, gaping at him in disbelief. "Do you truly not remember?"

His jaw sagged open. "Remember?"

"That summer! Hiking nearly every day to Wonder Lake. Showing you the eagles' nest. You called it your spark bird."

Thoroughly confused, he stared at her. "Penny, I have absolutely no idea what you're talking about."

~

In a tangle of thickets that banked the ridge, two Blue Jays were having an argument. Penny had to take a deep breath to ease the pressure growing in her chest. Caution seemed to slow her thoughts. How could he not remember her? She had spent years thinking about him, following his career, wondering if she'd heard the Lord properly when he told her that Ben would be back. Trusting God with this strong feeling he'd given her for Ben. A feeling that had never left her.

And then Ben did come back into her life, in a most unexpected way. Trusting the Lord took another turn. She had tried so hard not to get ahead of the Lord, not to reveal anything until she sensed that inner prompting. But something at this moment snapped in her, and it all blurted out. "Ben, how can you not remember me?"

"Remember you? What do you mean?"

"I have tried everything I could think of to get you to remember me. Cherry jam, my drawings . . ."

"Wait. Slow down. I'm not following. When had we met?"

"That summer, when I took you here. To Wonder Lake."

"What? When? How long ago?"

"That summer I was staying with my grandmother. Twenty-three years ago. I used a shortcut whenever I would come down from Wonder Lake and it cut across a corner of your father's property. On the day we met, you were cutting down dead trees, chopping them into firewood. You asked me why I went up and down that ridge like a mountain goat. I told you about the eagles' nest, about how it was as big as a buggy and you didn't believe me. So we hiked up here and I showed you this eagles' nest." She pointed to it. "This very one! You were fascinated by it. Completely mesmerized. After that, we hiked up here nearly every day, all summer long. We sat right there on the resting rock." She pointed to the large flat rock. "Later you said the eagle was your spark bird. You'd said you'd hardly noticed birds before that summer. And look at you. Look at . . ." Her hands flew up. "Look at all you've done with your love of birds."

"Penny . . . my spark bird wasn't an eagle. It was a . . ." Again, he shook his head. "Tell me more."

"I had told you a story about the eagles' nest once. How there came a time when the parents decided the fledglings needed to go, so they made the nest uncomfortable. Something about that story seemed to touch you, because you brought it up often. You would say you understood how the nest didn't fit anymore."

He rubbed his forehead. "Just how old were you?"

"I was twelve. I loved birds, even back then. My grandmother taught me to draw them, and I showed my work to you." She stared at him, stunned. "So you truly don't remember me. You weren't just pretending."

He took a long time to respond. "I'm sorry, Penny. I don't."

She whirled around, holding her hands on her flushed cheeks. "I waited and waited . . ." She heard him take a step toward her. She stiffened, keeping her back to him.

"What do you mean?"

Tears threatened. She shook her head, taking a step away. "Nothing." He caught her wrist and she turned back to face him.

"Penny—"

Their gazes met momentarily. They searched for something to say, something to do. Everything had changed between them.

She pulled her wrist out of his grasp. Tears flooded her eyes. "Ben, don't say anything more, please. I must have been mistaken." So sorely mistaken. "Let's get back to counting birds and not speak of this again." She felt so foolish, so disillusioned. So sad.

⌣

By nine o'clock, Micah had run out of birds to count, and run out of patience. He went up the Yoder driveway and stopped abruptly when Trudy came flying out the door to meet him.

"Why aren't you c-counting b-birds?" He was angry. He'd been relying on Trudy's keen eyes and ears today.

Her face was bright, but as his gaze settled fully on her, he realized something was wrong.

223

"Oh, Micah, something terrible has happened," Trudy said, her voice breaking.

Behind her, her father stormed out of the house, bellowing, "Micah Weaver!" He charged at Micah, pulling back his hand as he approached. Micah flung his arms over his head, a reflex, preparing for a blow. Dave Yoder grabbed Micah's upper arms with his large farmer hands and practically lifted him off the ground. "Where is she? What have you done to her? Where's my little girl?"

Micah froze, eyes wide. "I . . . I . . ."

Dave Yoder glared at Micah, his voice biting and cold. "Where did you take her? Where is she?" He shook Micah hard and dropped him so that he fell backward, onto the ground. He pointed a shaking finger at Micah, nostrils flaring, breathing hard. "Where is she?" His wife appeared behind him. Her face was red, her eyes were swollen.

Panic rose in Micah, and his mouth opened, but nothing came out. He gaped at Dave Yoder like a gutted fish, his throat locked around the words. Where was Shelley? What had happened?

"Dad, listen to me," Trudy pleaded. "Shelley didn't go anywhere with Micah. She's never been out with Micah." She stood between her father and Micah. "Dad, Shelley lied to you. All this time, she's been lying. She's been sneaking out at night to sing at an Englisch bar in Lancaster. Micah doesn't know anything about it."

Dave Yoder's jaw tightened. He stared at Trudy, frowning. "No. No! She told us she was out with Micah. All fall, he's been courting her." His hands clenched in fists as he sucked in sharp breaths.

Confused, Micah shook his head hard.

"Shelley told us so herself. Our little girl would never lie . . . never lie to her mother . . . never to me . . ." Dave Yoder's voice shook and broke and then stopped. His arms dropped to his sides, as if he couldn't keep denying something he'd suspected all along.

His wife put her arm around him, turning him around to face the house. Slowly, they walked away, leaning on each other as if one might fall without the other's support.

Quiet descended. The only sound was the sough of the wind in the treetops. Slowly, Micah got himself up off the ground, brushing off his pants. He fixed his eyes on Trudy, waiting.

"Shelley's run off."

"Run off?"

"Left. For good."

Micah's head rocked back, and his whole body shuddered hard, as if he were trying to shake off the words.

"A few months back, she told Mem that you wanted to court her. Mem was pleased, because Shelley's been so moody lately. Mem didn't even stop her from going out late at night with you. But it wasn't you she was meeting."

Frustrated to the point of tears, he could only give a quick shake of his head.

"Last night, she told Mem that she was going bird counting with you, and needed to leave the house extra early. Was that a lie too, Micah?"

"She was s-supposed to m-meet me," he choked out.

"This morning Mem found a note on Shelley's bed. I heard Mem crying her eyes out upstairs." She covered her mouth with her fist, eyes squeezed shut. "She sounded like a wounded animal. Shelley's note said she's run off to Nashville to start a singing career. She wants to be a famous singer at the Bluebird Café."

Micah knew Trudy was speaking to him, but he couldn't hear her, couldn't understand what she was telling him. All he could think was that he would never see Shelley again. Never see her at a singing, or volleyball, or at a worship service. He would never hear her sing again. Never again would he go to the Yoder farm for a youth gathering and watch Shelley from a distance, pretending that she was his and his alone. An echo kept circling through his mind, like the mournful hoot of a Great Horned Owl: *She's gone, she's gone, she's gone.*

"Micah? I'm so sorry. I know you cared for Shelley. I know you're hurting too."

225

His mind spun as he tried desperately for the right words to say, but what he was feeling couldn't even be shaped into thoughts, let alone into words. He looked down at the road where Shelley had disappeared. He wondered where she was at this moment, maybe all the way to Nashville by now, and if she had any idea of all the heartache she'd left in her wake.

Micah turned slowly, allowing his gaze to settle at last on Trudy. Tears rolled down her cheeks, splashing onto her dress. She was suffering, maybe worse than he was, if that was possible, and he felt the stirring of pity for the girl. "G-get your b-binoculars. There's b-birds to count."

~

Later that evening, Penny kneaded cinnamon roll dough in the kitchen of Lost Creek Farm. The feel of it smooth beneath her hands, the familiar movements of push and pull, applying pressure with the palm of her hand, it helped to calm her. She willed the process to flush away her humiliation. She absolutely needed to settle her mind and nerves after this day.

She felt so foolish. She knew she'd said too much. It was a miracle that she'd managed to stop, to not say anything more that would've revealed far too much to Ben.

She'd been so sure that the Lord was doing a great thing when he brought Ben back to Stoney Ridge, back to his faith, back to her, all through the wandering of a little bird. For twenty-three years, she had waited patiently for the Lord's timing, never doubting his faithfulness.

Had she misheard? Perhaps she was only being prideful. Had she so wanted to believe that young man she'd come to know as a girl was the one intended for her that she put those words in God's mouth?

But then . . . why had such peace filled her, for so many years, despite Ben's on-going absence? Peace, lasting peace, could only come from the Lord.

Strands of her hair escaped her prayer cap and whisked against her neck and cheek. She pushed them away with the back of her hand.

She had to rest on what she knew to be true—that God was a good shepherd, who searched relentlessly for that one lost sheep. She believed Ben to be that lost sheep whom the Shepherd was seeking.

What she doubted now was whether that lost sheep had been meant for her, set aside for her. For the first time in twenty-three years, she doubted it. Long ago Ben had kindled a fire in her that couldn't be put out, at least on her side. She'd held on to the hope that he was the only one there ever was for her, confident that there'd never be another man for her.

She had to wonder, though, if God had brought him back so she would finally release him.

Ben was grateful when he found the note tacked on the table from Natalie, saying she was off to Philadelphia for a job interview and wouldn't be back for a few days. He felt exhausted, discouraged, and troubled—especially when he said goodbye to Penny and saw a wariness in her eyes.

He flopped backward on his bed and stared at the ceiling. It was difficult to relax and even more difficult to get Penny out of his head. Thoughts of her wouldn't go away. She had a way of rattling him, unsettling him, like a frustrating itch in the center of his back that he couldn't quite reach.

Always before, if a woman bothered him, he would just move on. This was different, Penny Weaver was different.

He shouldn't be here. It was too much. Things were getting too complicated. He should have listened to his gut instinct, when he found out the bird was on an Amish farm in Stoney Ridge. He knew it wouldn't be comfortable for him to be here, but he thought he would be able to stay so busy, like he always did, that regrets and sorrow wouldn't have a chance to catch up with him. Stay so busy that he could avoid questioning what the point of his life was all about. Convince himself that it was all about rare birds. That's all that mattered.

But it wasn't all that mattered.

Penny had seemed so upset about confusing him with someone else. But why? It was such a long time ago. She was only a girl, and she'd spent one summer here. It could have been anyone. Ben Zook was a common name, as common as John Smith. Why was she so sure it was him? She was so bothered, so disappointed.

Restless, he pushed himself to sit up, letting his feet dangle over the edge, and as he did, something occurred to him. It caught him like an uppercut on the chin, snapped him to stare through the window at the big house. Ben ran a hand through his hair, draped it around his neck, and smiled at the floor. After a moment, his chest lifted with a gasp. His brother's face suddenly swam into view.

Levi. It was Levi whom Penny had met so many years ago.

Micah Weaver, Bird-Watching Log

Name of Bird: Summer Tanager

Scientific Name: Piranga rubra

Status: Low concern

Date: May 22

Location: High in a pine tree on the edge of a farmer's wooded lot

Description: Adult male, brilliant red, full-bodied, chunky songbird with large head, thick blunt-tipped pale-colored bill for eating insects.

Bird Action: Male sat still as a stone, then suddenly would sally out to catch flying insects in midair.

Notes: Long-distance migrant, mostly at night (like most birds). Crosses Gulf of Mexico to reach wintering grounds.

Specializes in eating bees and wasps. Rubs the stinger against a branch until it falls off, then eats the bee.

Often mistaken for a male Cardinal, a Summer Tanager is the only completely bright-red-colored bird in North America. Was formerly placed in the Tanager family, but now its genus is classified in the Cardinal family. Confusing.

It's bothersome when you've thought one way for a long time and then it turns out to be different.

19

Gloom had hovered over Ben ever since yesterday's Christmas Bird Count with Penny. He was jogging along the path that led him up the ridge behind Lost Creek Farm. Breathing hard, he drew cold early-morning air into his chest. His running shoes hit the earth in a slow but measured cadence. Sweat stung his eyes.

The path tilted upward, then curled to the left, crossing Lost Creek as it flowed down the hill. He made himself keep going. It was one of the ways he felt he could mark his recovery. Daily exercise had always been a habit for him, wherever in the world he was, up until recently when he was struck by this bout of malaria. He'd told himself he would know he was fully recovered when he could jog all the way to the top without stopping. So far, he had to stop every five hundred yards and lean over, hands braced on his knees, sucking air.

Man. If this was how he felt after a mild case of malaria, imagine a severe one.

He rounded a corner and caught sight of the top of the ridge. With a huff of relief, he pressed on, nearly collapsing when he came to the spot that overlooked Wonder Lake, the same place he and Penny had been yesterday. He stayed there for several minutes, studying the trees and still pond, noticing birds that flitted through the trees, mindful of how the heavy gray sky overhead mirrored his mood. Loneliness squeezed in on him.

When did he become aware of such feelings as loneliness?

It started, he realized, when he came to Lost Creek Farm and met Penny Weaver. An unexpected ripple of disquiet swept through Ben at the thought. He worried about the wall that suddenly sprang up between them yesterday. She'd hardly said a word to him all afternoon. They continued to count birds until dusk, and once she even smiled briefly when Ben spotted a Baltimore Oriole's pendulous nest hanging in a tree. "It's as impossible to miss among the barren winter branches as it is impossible to spot during the breeding season when it's surrounded by leaves."

"Micah watched the oriole weave this nest. He called her the seamstress of the bird world. Orioles can fix and repair anything, he says."

For a moment, they stood together, observing the finesse of the abandoned nest. But then the moment was over and the wall between them remained. The pressure surrounding them did not lessen. On the contrary, it only intensified as they continued the count.

He knew she was upset. Dismayed. He knew her distress involved him. How did a man and woman learn to make up their differences? At thirty-seven years old, Ben didn't know, but it suddenly became vital that he learn.

If he told her about Levi, it would clear up the confusion. It might make things right between them again. He *wanted* to tell her. He wanted to trust her with the secrets that hurt most.

But it wasn't the kind of thing he did easily. He liked to keep all the messy parts of himself to himself.

Sitting there, overlooking the eagles' nest that had sparked this path of bird loving for Levi seemed like Paradise. Like the Garden of Eden.

Suddenly, he knew he wasn't alone. He sensed God's presence here, in this remote place.

He was behaving like Adam, hiding in the garden, as God came through to ask, "Where are you?"

Where was Ben? He was hiding.

But he had to stop hiding. Behind success, behind restlessness, behind even birds. Mostly, behind his anger at God. Angry, yes, but he'd never denied God.

Gradually the sun broke free of the mournful clouds and poured soft rays of light over the pond, and he understood that he wasn't alone. That he'd never been alone.

Turning his hands so that his palms faced up, Ben bent his head to pray. One word. *Help.*

~

When Penny opened the kitchen door for Ben, she said nothing. Nor did he. For a moment they studied each other. Numbly, almost detached, she thought he looked tired, as if he hadn't slept well. He must have recently showered because his hair was still a little wet. When he'd shaved his cheeks smooth, he missed a bit of shaving cream by his ear and she fought back an impulse to smooth it away. To smooth everything away.

The sound of the kettle whistling on the stove crashed into her thoughts, and self-consciousness struck them simultaneously. Ben ducked his head in a nod and took a few steps back. "Penny, I'd like to talk. About yesterday."

"There's nothing to talk about."

"Isn't there? I think there is. In fact, I'm sure of it."

"Ben, I appreciate it, but like I said yesterday, I'd rather not speak of this again." Not to him, not to anyone. She felt so bothered with herself—the Lord had warned her to hold back. And did she? No. She had trampled on whatever work the Lord was doing in Ben's life. She wished she could take back the day, redo it.

"Hold on a minute. Let me finish. You haven't heard it all." He drew a deep breath and plunged on. "Penny, I think I know what might have caused you some confusion. Please, let me come in and sit down."

She pushed the door open. As he passed by her, she felt acutely aware of his body, his clean soapy scent. She went around him to take the whistling kettle off the burner and turn off the stove, taking pains not to brush up against him. She filled two mugs with hot water and picked them up to take one to Ben, nearly forgetting the tea bags. She pivoted, set the mugs down again, plopped two tea bags in each mug, then crossed the room again to hand one to Ben.

He sat down at the table and stared into the mug, as if watching the tea start to infuse the hot water was the most fascinating thing in the world. He lifted his head and motioned toward a chair. "Penny, please. Sit down for a moment." After she settled into the chair, he took a deep breath and looked her right in the eyes. "The young man you met that summer wasn't me. I'm fairly confident that you met Levi, my older brother."

Her eyes narrowed. "He told me that his name was Ben." That didn't make any sense to Penny. "Why would he tell me such a thing if it weren't true?"

Ben paused, before saying, "I think he didn't want to be him."

She snapped her gaze back to him. "That summer, wouldn't I have seen you at church? I don't remember ever seeing you."

The corners of his lips turned up. "Well, if you were twelve, then I would have been fourteen. A gawky, gangly boy who spent his time in the pasture with the horses. Very easy not to notice."

Her mind traveled back to that summer. Whenever she went to church with her grandmother, she spent the entire three hours absorbed with casting furtive glances at Ben . . . or the young man she thought was Ben. The time flew by, she remembered that. And she remembered no one else.

"It was just the two of us boys. We were four years apart, but we stuck together. Our father was hard on Levi. Very hard. Levi could do nothing right in his eyes. He treated me well, but he had a hatred, a disgust for Levi, his own flesh and blood." Ben's eyes squeezed shut, as if he was trying not to shudder. Then he opened them. "The things he said to Levi . . ."

Overall, Ben was speaking calmly, but Penny could sense the tumult beneath the calm. The signs of pent-up emotions were subtle—in the flexing of his hands, the tic in his jaw, the furrowed lines between his brows. "But why?"

"Our father had a certain idea of what a man was, or should be. Especially an Amish man. And Levi was . . . well, he was gentle. Soft. Even as a boy, he was different. He stayed in the kitchen with Mem. He wouldn't hunt with Dad and me. He struggled with depression. No, not just struggled—he suffered greatly from it. There were days, weeks, when he wouldn't leave the house. When he couldn't get out of bed . . ." His voice broke.

Penny could sense the trembling going on inside him.

"Levi tried." He was talking in a raw, hoarse voice now. "He tried so hard to please Dad. To him, depression was a choice. Mind over matter. Our mother knew better. She did all she could to help. She wanted to get Levi to a doctor, but Dad wouldn't hear of it. He was convinced that if Levi just prayed harder, worked harder, believed harder, the depression would lift. She was terrified Levi would leave home, leave the church. One day, Dad went too far, said too much. The second-to-last memory I have of Levi is watching him walk slowly toward that ridge of yours, head dropped low. I remember thinking he looked like a horse that had its spirit broke." He rubbed his face with his hands, as if trying to wipe that image away.

After a moment or two had passed, she said quietly, "If that is the second-to-last memory you have of your brother . . . what is the last one?" Somehow, she knew the answer and she almost couldn't bear hearing it. But she knew he needed to tell the whole story.

"The next morning, I went out to the barn and . . ." His voice had gone flat and cold now, his eyes were fixed on the mug of tea held cupped in his hands. "And I found him. Sometime in the night, Levi had hung himself with a halter rope."

Penny hadn't even realized she'd been holding her breath. Tears welled in her eyes. One slipped down her cheek and fell onto the back of her hand in her lap.

"He wasn't buried in the graveyard where most everyone is laid to rest. He had to be buried elsewhere."

The Amish cemetery. Right outside it were a few small unmarked graves. Nameless, unrecognized by the church even in death. A single tear streaked along the edge of her cheek and slipped onto her shoulder.

"The night of the funeral, my father told us that we were never to mention Levi's name again. You know how Amish families have a chair for each member of the family? You sit in the same place, every day. Every meal. You know there's a place waiting for you. There's a place you belong. You know who's missing too. That night, Dad took Levi's chair away. I don't even know what he did with it. It was just gone." He let out a sigh. "That night, I left. I've never been back."

"Until now."

"Until now." He reached out to wipe a tear off her cheek with one finger. "Penny, it was Levi who taught me about birds. He loved the endless varieties. Once I asked him why he liked birds so much and he said it was because they were so free. They recognized no borders, no boundaries." He rubbed his face. "My brother couldn't see a way out. There was no end in sight to the dark tunnel he lived in. For a long time, I felt such overwhelming guilt about his suicide. That somehow, someway, I should have been able to prevent it."

"You were only a boy yourself. That's quite a load of responsibility for you to bear."

"I know that now. But it took a long time to get there."

She'd gone quiet beside him. Outside, the wind stirred the remaining leaves in the trees.

"Does knowing this . . . about Levi's death . . . taking his own life . . . does it bother you?" When she didn't answer right away, he pressed her. "I want to know, Penny."

She took a moment to gather her thoughts, knowing what he was really asking. Knowing how much rested on her response. "I think," she started slowly, "that God understands our weaknesses. I don't think he condemns us for them. In fact, I think he has far more compassion for us than we give to each other. And accepting God's unfailing love and compassion is part of the peace that Jesus promised. 'Peace I leave with you, my peace I give unto you, not as the world giveth, give I unto you. Let not your heart be troubled, neither let it be afraid.'"

Ben stared at her for a long time.

She wasn't finished. This part, this was going to be hard to say, but she felt she needed to say it. "Ben, I have wondered if *this* is why God brought you back when he did. Now. To finish this up before it's too late."

"Too late?"

"Your father."

His posture stiffened. "What about him?"

"Your father isn't at all well. I bring him meals three times a week."

"I thought . . . maybe it was Roy. I assumed you were taking meals to Roy."

Roy? "Goodness, no. It's your father who needs the help."

Ben kept his eyes fixed on his hands, gripped tightly on the tabletop. "Alde Fesser rinne gern." *Old vessels are prone to leak.*

She glanced at him, wondering if he'd meant to speak Penn Dutch or if it just slipped out. It was a common saying about the elderly, about how they were usually ailing. "Go to him. Tell him you forgive him."

Ben lurched back in his chair. "Oh no." He stared at her, as if he'd never seen her before. "You can't expect . . ." He held his hands up in the air. "Penny, you've been very kind to me these last few weeks. There's not much I wouldn't do to repay you in kind. But for that."

"It's not for me. It's for you. Forgiving your father will set you free as well."

236

He glared at her. "What makes you think I'm not free?"

"You live the life of a skipping stone."

"That sounds like freedom to me."

"If birds have taught me anything, it's that we're all connected. Everyone longs to belong, to be part of a loving, supportive community."

"Not all birds flock together. Maybe I'm a solitary bird. I don't need a community."

She gazed at him for a long while. "I don't believe you."

"And you don't know what hornet's nest you're stirring up." Stiffly, he rose and walked to the door and reached for the doorknob. "I can't." Then he added, "I won't."

"You should try to heal the rift while you can." She stood up and took a few steps toward him. "Ben, your father is all alone."

Coldly, he said to the wall, "There's a reason for that." Abruptly he turned to her and confronted her with fists balled and veins standing out sharply on his throat. "Penny, I lost my brother because of him. My *brother*. Dad could have helped Levi. He should have gotten him to a doctor. Should have shown him some mercy. But he refused. He even brought in the church ministers to shame Levi out of his depression. My father . . . *he's* the one who's responsible for Levi's death."

"You don't mean that," she said in a whisper.

"Don't I?" he shot back. "There are some things that can't be forgiven. My father broke my mother's heart. He broke my heart."

"There's no need to reciprocate." She leaned over and gently touched his arm, trying to calm him. "When you can, Ben, heal the rift."

He left her then. Penny watched him walk slowly across the yard as he made his way to the guesthouse. She thought that he moved like what he was, a man sorely hurting. A man who wandered the world, unable to just go home.

She had never seen Ben angry, and she wondered if he would pack up and leave her farm, giving up on his White-winged Tern.

She understood that was the risk in what she was asking him to do. She didn't regret it.

Despite the tension between them, Penny sensed the Lord had brought her needed reassurance through Ben's visit. God was still at work in this tangled, messy sorrow, and she could trust him to take care of them all.

Micah Weaver, Bird-Watching Log

Name of Bird: *Baltimore Oriole*

Scientific Name: *Icterus galbula*

Status: *Low concern*

Date: *May 1*

Location: *Elm tree near Wonder Lake*

Description: *Adult female, orange-yellow plumage (not as bright orange as male), sturdy-bodied, thick-necked, long pointed bill to eat fruit and insects.*

Bird Action: *Over a week's time, I watched female weave a pendulum nest, 3-4 inches deep, with a small opening and a bulging bottom. She anchored it high in the tree so that it dangled from a branch like a Christmas tree ornament. Unlike a bauble, it became nearly invisible.*

Notes: *Like Tailorbirds of Asia, Orioles are the seamstresses of the North American bird world. They use whatever material is available to stitch sock-like hanging nests: grasses, bark, horsehair, even stealing man-made materials like twine or string or fishing line. It's then lined with soft materials such as plant fibers, downy feathers, or even sheep wool. Amazing. Such unlikely things, woven together to create a bond.*

20

Natalie had spent the last couple of days in Philadelphia, returning with news. Big news. But she knew it had to be delivered carefully, and she spent most of the drive playing out different scenarios. She found Ben in his bedroom, changing the sheets on his bed.

"I thought Penny did this."

He stuffed a pillow in a pillowcase. "Penny has a life of her own to live. She doesn't need to clean up after us." He tossed the pillow near the headboard.

Hmm. He sounded a little prickly. Something seemed a little off here.

"How was Philadelphia?"

"Good. Really, really good."

"Get the job?"

"Well, not exactly. But . . ." She sat on the small wooden chair in the corner, watching him tuck in sheet corners. "Something even better. Guess what?" She knew this was a phrase that would make Ben stop and listen.

It worked. He glanced up after smoothing the bedspread on top of the sheets. "What?"

"This." She went to the other room and came back with a

framed painting. She held it up so he could see it. "Framed in gold leaf. It came out stunning."

"A Bullock's Oriole?"

"Is that what kind of bird it is?"

"Yes. A songbird not common to Pennsylvania, but sometimes found as vagrants." He looked at it more closely. "Wait. Is this Penny's Bullock's Oriole?"

"Yes. There's a client, you see, an influencer. She's always been drawn to Amish collectibles—quilts, mostly. And then I remembered that she's just as crazy about birds. Imagine how she'd react to a bird painting by an Amish artist . . . irresistible! I just had to show her a sample of Penny's work. When I brought her this framed piece, she offered me five hundred dollars for it. When I hesitated, she upped it to one thousand. She said she wants more, wants one for every room in her house."

Ben looked at her as if she had told him she'd joined the circus. "When did Penny show you her work?"

"Well . . ." She drew out the word. "I kind of . . . borrowed it."

"You did what?! Without asking Penny?"

Slowly, she nodded.

"How could you? When did you take it?"

"The day you went out bird counting together. The farm was empty . . . and I just couldn't stop thinking about her watercolors . . . and then . . . well, you know the rest."

He stared at her. "So that's why you had to suddenly go to Philadelphia?"

"Yes. So, here's the thing. I need your help."

"Me? You've gotten yourself into this. You can get yourself out."

"Stop looking like you just chewed a cactus. Please help, Ben. I don't want Penny to be angry with me."

"Angry? Natalie, you went into her house and took her artwork without her knowledge and without her permission. She has every right to be angry with you. You stole something from her."

Natalie was flummoxed. Stole from Penny? Way too harsh. She *borrowed* from Penny. She tried a pleading expression on him. "Don't you want to hear my offer?"

"Your offer? Back up for a minute. Penny *hides* her watercolors! Clearly, she doesn't want anyone else to know." His eyebrows drew together. "What are you hoping to get out of this? A commission?"

"No! I want my career back. But I also want others to enjoy her watercolors. They shouldn't be in the closet, hidden away. They should be seen." She paused. "What should I do?"

"Tell Penny the truth, Natalie."

She scrunched her forehead. "How?"

Ben rolled his eyes. "That's up to you to figure out."

Natalie frowned. "Ben, you're the one who says that birds don't always act or play according to the rules."

"Birds?"

Natalie and Ben both wheeled around to discover Boyd standing at the open bedroom door. "Birds?" he scoffed. "Birds act on instinct. People act on moral principles."

Oh no. "Boyd," Natalie said.

"I knocked but no one answered the door. I heard your voices, so I came in."

"Then . . . ," she said, feeling a flush creep up her neck, "maybe you heard . . ."

He turned and left, not waiting for her to finish.

~

Micah collected all the bird count results from the volunteers and compiled them. He called the Audubon president and went over the results on the phone. At first, the president didn't believe him, and as Micah repeated the results, she grew silent. Then she asked him to repeat the results for a third time.

Fortunately, he had written them down, so he was able to read them easily. Smoothly. "Over a twenty-hour period, fifteen birders found a total of seventy-four species, including an exceptional number of lingering migrants, a few accidentals, and one outstanding rarity." The White-winged Tern.

It broke Micah's heart to hear that Birdy had spotted it swooping for insects over Blue Lake Pond. Absolutely gutted him. Everyone seemed to be able to see that bird . . . but him. He cheered himself with the knowledge that at least it was still here, and that Birdy, an entirely reliable source, had confirmed it. He wasn't done yet.

"American Crow was our most prevalent bird—184," he continued reading, "Evening Grosbeak—64, Pine Grosbeak—2, Rough-legged Hawk—8, Red-headed Woodpecker—31, Golden Eagle—5, Great Egret—3, Red-necked Grebe and Eared Grebe—1 each. Baltimore Oriole—3, Bald Eagle—2, Eastern Phoebe—8, Yellow Warbler—1. Eight species of Warblers, in fact. Loggerhead Shrike—1, Blue-headed Vireo—1 . . ." He kept reading until he finished the list.

Again, the response from the Audubon president was disbelief. "Really? A Yellow Warbler?"

"Yes. S-seen at a b-bird feeder on Windmill Farm."

"You had that high a count with just fifteen birders?"

"Yes. One was B-Ben Z-Zook. He had the highest c-count." Ben and Penny together counted over half the birds, and found some accidentals that Micah doubted he could've identified: a Pacific-slope Flycatcher and an immature Harris's Sparrow.

The president gasped. "Ben Zook? *The* Ben Zook. The author of *Rare Birds*?"

"That's h-him. He's s-staying with me." Micah wasn't exactly trying to name-drop. He was telling the truth. But it did give him some delight to tell her that particular truth.

And with that additional bit of information, everything changed. Her tone softened, grew animated. "You'll mail in the paperwork today? Send it by registered mail so it'll get here before the new year." She had complained often that Micah didn't have a computer to email everything in, pronto.

Too bad, Micah thought. *This is how we roll here.*

"Well, I didn't think you'd be able to deliver, Micah. I admit that and I stand corrected. Your territory ended up with a higher, more thorough bird species count than any other territory in the county. If I wore a hat, I'd have to take it off to you."

Micah left the phone shanty feeling pretty good. His teams had followed his instructions carefully, had taken seriously the first Christmas Bird Count for Stoney Ridge, and ended up outperforming other teams in the county. Ones, unlike the Amish, that used their phones to call in birds. It might not please the Lord to feel so proud about his teams' achievement, but he did. The first Christmas Bird Count in Stoney Ridge had been a success.

It helped ease the hole in his heart left by Shelley Yoder.

He let out a deep sigh. It still smarted, everything about her. Using him as a cover, lying to everyone, pretending she was interested in birdsongs when she was really just interested in her own songs. Mostly, the fact that he was naive enough to believe she might care for him.

A gust of wind lifted his hat off his head and he went running after it. The sky had a grim look to it, and there were hardly any birds in the trees. Winter was bumping its nose with autumn. It would be here soon. And that meant any lingering migrating birds would be heading south to their wintering grounds.

He *had* to find that White-winged Tern. For Ben's sake. Maybe even more so for his own sake.

~

Natalie was in trouble and she knew it. Boyd wasn't answering her calls. Ben was frosty to her. She knew that borrowing Penny's painting was audacious, but it wasn't like she wouldn't be handing over the money to Penny. Less, she hoped, the amount for the costly framing.

She got to her feet and started pacing in a tight loop around the small living area. She had hoped Ben would drop what he was doing and help her. Act as a go-between with Penny. She'd gotten used to Ben's coming to her aid when she was in distress. He was having none of it. She made this mess, he said. She could clean it up.

She might be indulging her overactive imagination, but she sensed something a little off in Ben. The warmth was gone; he was back to his aloof, distant self.

Just telling Penny the truth wasn't enough. A confession wasn't all that was needed here. She had to convince Penny to sell her artwork.

Hold on. She knew who could set things right. The bishop. She'd met him a few times now, whenever she popped into the Bent N' Dent for one thing or another. He was always kind to her, and often told her to let him know if she needed anything. He seemed a very reasonable man, with a low, calming voice. If anyone could help her smooth things over with Penny, the bishop could.

So Natalie took the painting to the Bent N' Dent to talk to David Stoltzfus. As she parked her car near the store's front, she found David outside, sweeping the steps. The perfect opportunity to explain the situation to him, without any nosy customers listening in. Patiently, he listened to her.

"What should I do?"

"Tell Penny what you've done."

"Right. That's what Ben said to do." She tried again. "You see, I do plan to tell her. What I need help with is the part that comes after I tell her. Here's the thing. I'd like to sell Penny's watercolors. To act as the broker between Penny and non-Amish buyers. Micah calls it something like . . . complementary species."

His eyebrows furrowed together. "So Penny has more water-colors?"

"Dozens and dozens. And David, they're magnificent. She's entirely self-taught. No formal training at all."

"All birds?"

"Yes. Waterfowl, songbirds, raptors. On and on."

David was quiet for a long time, bearded chin tucked on his chest, and she almost thought he'd fallen asleep on her. But then she realized he was praying. When he lifted his head, he set the broom against the porch post, opened the door, yanked his black hat off the wall peg, told someone inside that he'd be gone for a bit so please watch the store for him. He closed the door and set his hat on his head. "Natalie, I think we need to go talk to Penny. Together."

"Yes, let's do that," she said. *Thank heavens.*

~~~~~~

When Ben saw the bishop emerge out of Natalie's car, he practically choked on his coffee. What had she done? He bolted outside to stop them. "David, I don't know what my cousin has told you, but what she did was wrong. Penny knew nothing about this. Don't blame her."

David tipped his head, as if measuring Ben's words. "Why don't you come in with us? I'd like you to be there."

Dread spiraled through Ben's abdomen, oddly familiar. Through his mind flashed that day when the deacon and bishop and minister, all three, came calling on Levi.

By now Penny had opened the back door and stood there, a curious look on her face. "David, is something wrong? Should I get Micah?"

"No, Penny. Nothing's wrong. Natalie has something she needs to tell you, and then we'll have a talk about it."

Ben tried to send Penny a message of apology with his eyes, but that only seemed to confuse her. "Have I done something?"

"Let's sit at the kitchen table," David said. "Could I trouble you for some water?"

Without a word, Penny filled a pitcher with water and set it on the table with four glasses.

246

"Thank you, Penny," David said. "Please, sit."

She slid into a chair at the far side of the table. Such a big table, Ben thought to himself. It should be full of children. There should be a husband sitting in the seat where Ben sat. Penny would make a wonderful wife and mother.

"Penny, Natalie came to me today at the store. She saw a painting of yours and . . ." He looked to Natalie to complete the sentence.

"I borrowed it."

"She stole it," Ben volunteered.

Natalie frowned at him, then took the framed Bullock's Oriole painting out of her purse and set it gently on the table.

As she listened, Penny's face drained of color but for two red spots on her cheekbones. "Why?"

Greed. Pure greed. Ben was disgusted by Natalie, embarrassed that he'd brought her to this lovely farm, thinking it would help her to get out of her own world. Instead, she'd brought her world with her. Zu viel verreisst der Sack. *Too much tears the sack.* Wasn't greed the very reason her life imploded in the first place?

"Well," Natalie started. "You see—"

Penny's cheeks were now flushed. "Why didn't you just ask me?"

"Well, I did. I told you I wanted to see them, but you seemed very lukewarm about it."

Ben snorted. "This is exactly why."

Natalie gave him a *look*, then turned to Penny. "I have a client who loves everything about the Amish and she also loves birds. I just knew she would love your art."

Ben cringed at Natalie's cavalier use of the word *art*. Say anything but art, he wanted to point out. Say drawing or painting or sketch. Not art.

"And she did love it," Natalie continued. "Even more than I could've imagined. She offered one thousand dollars for it."

Penny gasped.

Encouraged, Natalie plunged on. "And she wants more. I'm confident I could sell them all."

"Penny," David said, "you have more of these drawings?"

Penny dropped her chin, and shame hit Ben like a slap in the face. He wondered what was running through her mind. Regret, no doubt, that she'd ever opened her home to them. She lifted her head to answer the bishop. "I have more."

"Might I see them?"

Penny rose, eyes cast down, and went to the pantry.

Ben felt furious with Natalie. Not only did she steal something precious from Penny, a woman who had been nothing but kind and generous to her, but she also ratted out her carefully hidden hobby to the bishop. Who knew where that would lead? Ben envisioned Penny having to bend at the knee, confess her sin in front of the entire church, humiliated. He had a new awareness of the despair Levi must have felt when he'd been told to confess his sin to the church. It was that night that Levi had taken his own life.

Some rummaging sounds floated out from the pantry, and then Penny reemerged, with the large sketch pad in her hands. She showed it to David. He touched the pages with care, turning them gingerly, reverently.

"Penny, has anyone ever seen your drawings? Apart from your family?"

"Once." She lifted her chin, though not in a defiant way. "And then the deacon paid a visit."

David nodded, as if he'd expected to hear that. "Some church leaders feel very strongly about artistic expression, that it can lead someone down a path of pride. But I believe that recording what we see sharpens our awareness and makes us appreciate even more God's most beautiful and varied creations." He closed the sketch pad. "Penny, you remember when the Black-backed Oriole came to visit your bird feeder?"

"Of course."

"When?" Ben asked.

"In January," David said. "It stayed . . . how long?"

"Sixty-seven days," Penny said.

"That's astounding," Ben said.

"Why?" Natalie piped in. "Orioles are all over."

"Not this one," Ben said, amazed she would even know that. "It's only been recorded in the United States a couple of times."

"As I recall," David continued, "that little bird drew more than one hundred eighty people to Stoney Ridge. They came, they ate in restaurants, they shopped. Bird-watching has been a good thing for our area."

"Ecotourism," Ben said.

David smiled. "That's what the mayor of Stoney Ridge calls it. My hope is that when people come birding, they leave us feeling a little closer to nature, and to the God behind it." He turned to Penny. "I believe in nurturing and supporting all our community—that includes people as well as land and wildlife. If you choose to sell your work, and if you would like Natalie to sell your water-colors for you, then you have my blessing. Penny, we want you and Micah to stay at Lost Creek Farm. Your brother's keen eyes and ears have brought attention to the birds in the sky. Your kindness to neighbors"—Ben knew exactly which neighbor he meant—"has brought glory to God." He clapped his hands together. "But, I'll leave the decision about selling your work in your hands." He rose to his feet. "I'd better get back to the store. I left Hank Lapp in charge."

That's all? Ben was floored. That was it? No condemnation? No judging? No finger pointing? No bending at the knee?

Even Natalie got off scot-free.

He felt disoriented, fuzzy, confused, as if hit by a wave of returning malaria. This was not the Amish church he had grown up in.

Micah Weaver, Bird-Watching Log

Name of Bird: *Brown-headed Cowbird*

Scientific Name: *Molothrus ater*

Status: *Low concern*

Date: *May 1*

Location: *A field of grazing dairy cows at Beacon Hollow*

Description: *Adult male, chunky blackbird with black body and brown head. Thick, short, sharply pointed bill.*

Bird Action: *Insects caught as cows stirred into movement.*

Notes: *Cowbirds might seem like just another songbird, dainty and pleasant like a sparrow, but appearances can be deceptive. They're one of the toughest, craftiest blackbirds around. Here's why: Not all birds make nests. Cowbirds are one of them, but there's a sly reason. Cowbirds lay eggs in the nest of another species, leaving those parents to care for its young. They're called brood parasites. Most foster parents don't recognize the cowbird eggs as different from theirs. Chicks, either. Cowbird chicks tend to grow faster than their nestmates, allowing them to get more attention and food from foster parents. Some cowbird chicks roll other eggs right out of the nest.*

But a few birds are smart enough to recognize cowbird eggs. Since they're too small to roll the cowbird eggs out of the nest, they build a new nest over the top of the old one and hope the cowbirds don't come back. That's one way to outfox the fox.

21

She knew Ben would come to her. Late in the afternoon, just after Micah had gone off hunting for the White-winged Tern, Penny saw Ben cross the yard and come to the kitchen door. He didn't even knock. He opened it and came inside. She went toward him, fighting a desire to lean into him, to feel his arms around her just for a moment.

He drew in a deep breath, and then another. "Penny, I'm sorry about Natalie. She had no right. No right at all. I'm ashamed. Of her. Also of me, for not realizing that she had something in mind when she wanted to see your watercolors." He took a step toward her. "You knew, didn't you? You sensed she had an ulterior motive."

Was that shine in his eyes from tears? "Natalie meant me no harm. I knew that. I *know* that."

"But you've been good to us, and she stole something from you for her own benefit."

"The Lord used it all for good. I've been concerned about how to hold on to this property while Micah's field work is getting underway. The taxes are more than I anticipated, but I shouldn't have doubted. The Lord had a plan to provide for our needs, all along."

"Still, I feel beholden to you. If there's anything I can do to make it up to you . . . anything at all . . . before we leave."

"There is one thing." She reached out her hand to him, surprising even herself, and he met it halfway with his own, entwining their fingers. They stayed that way awhile, touching in silence. She took in a deep breath. "Go see your father."

"Penny, I can't." His voice was raw, hoarse, as if he were being strangled.

He tried to pull free, but she tightened her grip. She had to touch him, to comfort him, and he made it so hard. "I think you can."

"You ask too much of me."

"If we can't forgive others, how can we expect God to forgive us?"

"I don't have that much forgiveness in me."

"No, none of us do. It's the Lord who does the work of forgiveness in our hearts."

"Don't." Stepping back, he pulled his hand out of her grasp. "Don't preach to me. I know the Lord's Prayer, Penny." His voice had gone flat and cold now. He turned to leave, his hand on the doorknob. "I only wanted to thank you for being so gracious to Natalie."

She suffered a moment's pause before responding. She squared her chin and looked him dead in the eye. "Forgiving her, you mean."

He stood like a ramrod, too stubborn to take the one step necessary to move forward. "Yes, I suppose I do."

～

Natalie thought getting the bishop's blessing on selling Penny's artwork would've smoothed things over. Ben hardly said more than a few words to her, Penny told her she forgave her, but she needed time to think. Ben said that meant she wanted to be left alone. And so did he. Natalie had done everything she could think of to set things right between her and Boyd—she dropped a box of cinnamon rolls from the Sweet Tooth Bakery off in front of his door. She'd left long messages on his voice mail, trying to explain. She said she'd even go fly-fishing with him—the world's most boring sport. He hadn't returned a single phone call. When she drove by his house, slowly, she saw that the box of cinnamon rolls remained untouched on the front stoop.

Was this how things were going to end between them? Ben said that tomorrow would be the last day he'd be going out with Micah to try and find the White-winged Tern. Rain was coming, and if he couldn't spot it today, well, he'd tried his best. They would leave the day after tomorrow, bird or no bird.

Natalie tossed and turned all night. Her brain was exhausted from fretting over Penny, over Boyd, and a tiny bit over Ben. Nearing dawn, she even climbed out of bed and got down on her knees to pray about everything. She wanted to trust God with the mess she'd made and experience the peace that Penny talked about so much. But she didn't feel God's presence at all, only an echoing silence. Only very cold knees.

Close to dawn, she heard Ben get up and take a hot shower, preparing to go bird hunting with Micah. By now she knew their pattern. Micah would be waiting patiently on the porch of the guesthouse while Ben packed his optical equipment bag and gulped down a piece of toast and coffee.

Natalie jumped out of bed and wrapped up in her big warm robe and stuck her feet in her fluffy slippers. She opened the door to wait for Micah, to intercept him, but he was already there, sitting on a rocker. Even in the dark, she could see the surprise on his face. She sat down in the rocking chair next to him and leaned forward, hands on her knees. "Micah . . . ," Natalie started, "I'd like to ask you a question."

Micah gave a little cough and looked like he was going to bolt.

"What is the most important thing you've ever learned?"

He cast a longing look at the door, as if willing Ben to appear so he could leave. "About w-what?"

"About anything."

His eyes darted about nervously. "About b-birding?"

254

She wanted to let out a sigh but didn't. Birds, birds, birds. "Okay, then. What's the most important thing you've learned about birding?"

His gaze swept the trees, before turning to her. "Listening."

A red flare went off in her head. It was what she had dreaded hearing.

And it was exactly what she had needed to hear.

Midafternoon, someone knocked at Penny's door. She was upstairs, going through watercolors she'd spread out on her bed, mulling over which ones she'd give to Natalie to sell. It still astounded Penny that the bishop gave her his blessing to sell them. He not only gave her his blessing, but his encouragement. Frankly, she couldn't believe they would be worth much—all she could see were errors, mistakes. But if a few could be sold, it would be a gift straight from Heaven. Another sign that coming to Stoney Ridge had been the right decision, despite the cost.

She had just pulled a few from the pile, ones of common birds, and that was when she heard the knock at the door. Startled, she hurried downstairs, thinking it might be Ben. Hoping it was Ben.

But no.

It was Roy King who stood on her front step, soaked. He held out a harness of Junco's. "I promised I'd fix it for you."

Trustworthy Roy. Uncomplicated Roy. A man who always did what he said he'd do. A man who didn't bolt whenever life got hard.

"Come inside," she said, opening the door wider. "Come have a cup of tea."

"No. I'd best be getting home." He slowly walked backward down her steps, still facing her, giving her his crooked grin, revealing a dimple in his cheek. Then he turned and hurried down the drive.

Penny glanced over and saw Ben standing on the guesthouse

porch, as still as a tree. He'd been watching her. Without thinking, without praying, she hurried across the yard. She reached the
porch and faced him, not even sure why she was there or what she
wanted to say to him.

Ben started to shoulder past her but stopped short when their
faces were only inches apart. He leaned forward, bringing his face
so close to hers that she thought he was going to kiss her. Instead,
in a raspy voice, he said, "You should marry Roy King."

A simple sentence. Yet she comprehended its weight. Head held
high, cheeks aflame with emotion, she squared her shoulders. "I
think I have something to say about that."

"Roy's right for you. He won't make your life messy and difficult
and . . ." His voice drizzled off. "Don't wait any more, Penny." He
looked away. "We're leaving. Tomorrow."

She reached out to grasp his shoulders with her hands, gripping
him tightly, almost shaking him as she looked him straight in the
eyes. "Before you leave here, go see your father."

After a long moment, he pulled away, walked around her, and
went into the guesthouse, closing the door behind him.

~

It had started to rain. Natalie walked through the mud in the
yard with her head lowered against the stinging rain. It felt like
needles against her face. She knew she needed to talk to Penny, to
apologize. To truly apologize.

When she knocked on the kitchen door, Penny looked down
at her with gray eyes that were warm and concerned. "Come in.
Come out of the cold."

Natalie entered the warm, dimly lit kitchen. At first she thought
the dim lighting rendered Amish homes cold, but now she considered it to be calming. Soothing. "I just need to know. What was it
about me that made you not want to show me your artwork? Am
I not trustworthy?"

"Did I ever say such a thing?"

The gentle reproach in her eyes stung. "No. But, Penny, I'm sure you had a reason. I need to know."

Penny took time answering. She took out two mugs and filled them with hot water from the kettle on top of the stove, and then offered Natalie her choice of tea bags. Then, and only then, did she sit down to give her answer. "Do you know what a Black Kite is?"

"You mean . . . the kind of kite with a long string and a kid attached? Oh wait . . . this is probably a bird story, right?"

Penny smiled. "Black Kites actually aren't in North America. They're in nearly every other continent, but not North America. Anyway, Black Kites fill their nests with trash. It used to be thought it provided camouflage, but it turns out that Black Kites use the trash to decorate their nests. Showing them off. Some other birds do it too. Magpies, crows, Ospreys. Just last May, Micah saw a raven carrying off Hank Lapp's wristwatch to its nest. He'd set it down just for a moment and the raven swooped in and made off with it. They're always making off with baubles to add to their nest."

Natalie knew where this bird trivia was going. "So you think I was trying to show off by using your drawings."

Penny remained quiet. It was a loud quiet.

Natalie used the silence to sip her tea, pondering what Penny was getting at. "I suppose you're right. After our business fell apart, and then my husband Joel left me, well, I think . . . I've been grasping for something to hold on to, something to keep me upright. Something significant. Your artwork . . . it seemed like the answer I'd been looking for." She blew out a puff of air. "Ben told me no. You, by not showing me your artwork, that was your way of saying no. But I didn't listen."

Penny rose to get the kettle from the stove top and refill their mugs, now tepid, with hot water.

Natalie watched the steam rise from the mug. "I must seem pathetic to you." Ben, too. He was every bit as pathetic as Natalie—

stuck in his woundedness. They were like two hurt birds flying back to the nest to heal. Strangely enough, they were finding solace in Penny's nest. She knew enough to keep that thought to herself. If Penny already thought she was pathetic, that remark would convince her that Natalie was certifiably crazy.

Penny dipped her tea bag up and down in her mug. "Natalie, God can't guide us if we insist on finding our own way. It's like someone has offered you a flashlight to walk at night but you refused it. Instead, you just strike a match, one after the other, fumbling your way in the dark."

"You think I'm fumbling in the dark?"

Penny turned pity-filled gray eyes on her. "I think the Lord might be trying very hard to get your attention."

Surprise froze Natalie for a long moment. "What is he trying to say?"

Penny took a long time to answer. "I think, perhaps, that you're at a fork in the road. One road will take you down the same path you've been on. Success and significance and all the glittery, shiny things the world can offer to you. It's safe and familiar, though nothing will ever change."

Tears started pricking Natalie's eyes. Then one tear after another rolled down her cheeks.

"The road will always look just like it's looked all along, always beckoning you to venture farther down it to find what you're looking for. There will always, *always* be one more bend in the road." Penny's expression grew more serious. "The other path, now that's the one that will give you what you've been searching for. That's the one that leads to the Lord. It might seem frightening to you, unknown, but it's the one full of possibilities. Full of true and lasting satisfaction."

Natalie was really crying now. Sobs racked her body and tears streamed down her face, falling from her chin onto her expensive azure cashmere sweater. Her favorite sweater and she didn't even care. She'd blamed Joel for so much of what went wrong in their marriage and work, not wanting to admit that she'd pushed him so hard. There was a deep hunger in her. She'd done all she could to fill that need, but it always led right back here. To an aching emptiness.

She'd been trying to fill that need with everything *but* God, when all she'd needed *was* God.

"That road . . ." Natalie sniffed, wiping her nose with her sweater sleeve. "That's the road I want, Penny." Then the strangest thing happened: Sweet peace flowed into her, unlike any she'd known before.

Micah Weaver, Bird-Watching Log

Name of Bird: Common Raven

Scientific Name: Corvus corax

Status: Low concern

Date: May 8

Location: Stick nest, wedged into a tree crotch near Hank and Edith Lapp's house

Description: Adult female, large, sooty black plumage. Entirely jet-black—legs, eyes, and beak.

Bird Action: Over nine days, female broke off sticks to make nest base, piled on more sticks and branches, then wove them together into a basket. For the interior lining, she started with mud, added wool, fur, bark strips, grasses, and plastic trash for finesse. She finished it off by snatching Hank Lapp's wristwatch, for some very odd reason.

Notes: Most people confuse ravens with crows. Ravens are larger, as big as a Red-tailed Hawk. They travel in pairs, while crows are usually seen in murders. A Raven's tail is a wedge. A crow's tail spreads like a fan. Ravens croak; they scream bloody murder. Crows caw; they click and purr. Ravens soar. Crows flap.

    Both are cunning, adaptable, super-sneaky birds.

22

Ben stalked along, studying the ground. He stopped just outside the door to his childhood home, and he let the old feelings come and settle deep. If it were anyone but Penny who asked, he would never have returned to this house. He had taken pains to never return.

But Penny had asked.

There were so many arrows she could have flung at him. For nearly a year, she'd been bringing his father hot meals to make sure he ate, cleaning his house, caring for him while Ben selfishly pursued birds around the world—yet all she wanted was for Ben to make peace with his father. It was the only thing she'd asked of him. He couldn't *not* do this for her.

He took in a deep breath and knocked once, waited, knocked twice more, then opened the door that led into the kitchen. The room smelled of stale coffee and woodsmoke. Ben's eyes swept the large room, almost expecting echoes from long ago to reverberate through the house.

There was a man seated at the kitchen table, but he wasn't Ben's father. Zeke Zook was big, tall, straight as an arrow. Not in their father's hearing, Levi and Ben referred to him as L.C. *Large and in Charge.*

This person at the table was bent over.

His father had dark brown hair and a full, thick beard, whereas this man was gray, and his beard was straggly, wiry.

His father had been confident, authoritative, whereas this man looked slightly bewildered.

He couldn't be Ben's father. Yet it was him.

Zeke Zook was in his regular place at the kitchen table, seated perfectly still, framed by the afternoon light. It was the same spot where his father sat three times a day for meals during his adult life, the same exact place where he'd told Ben that Levi's name would never be mentioned again.

Ben could easily picture himself and Levi sitting at the table, as they'd done for hundreds of meals. Levi would dutifully eat whatever was set in front of him, even broccoli, which he hated. Not Ben. He would stuff the broccoli in his pockets to toss to the pigs later.

Bowls of breakfast cereal came to mind. Ben would wait until his father's attention was diverted, then add a spoonful or two of sugar onto his cereal. Levi wouldn't dare, though he loved sugar on his cereal. Even as a boy, he always seemed to act as if he had a lot to make up for.

"Hello, Dad."

No sound came, but Ben knew he had heard. His father blinked a few times, as if he was trying to make sense of this man standing in his kitchen. Ben was conscious suddenly of how he must appear to his father. Thoroughly Englisch, in clothing and shoes and appearance. It was odd, for he felt thoroughly Plain right now, standing in the very home where he'd spent so many years.

His father's eyes were the first thing that struck him. They were dull, flat, watery, but mostly they were lacking animation. He had never before realized how much came through a person's eyes.

Then his father said something in such a weak, scratchy voice that Ben wasn't sure he'd heard correctly. He went to a chair and sat next to him, his hands grasped tightly together as he leaned forward to listen. "Dad, tell me again."

His father reached out and covered Ben's hands with his own. Such an old man's hand, rivers of blue veins, covered in brown age spots, fingers thickened from a lifetime of hard work. His father tried to speak again but his throat locked up, his mouth opened but only sounds came out, reminding Ben of the way Micah's words sometimes did. One tear rolled down his father's cheek, then another. His eyes met Ben's and they were no longer flat, no longer empty, no longer cold. The words came then, clear as a bell. "Levi. Levi. You're home. You're safe."

Ben opened his mouth to correct him but then stopped, changing his mind. His vision blurred beneath a wash of unexpected tears, and his chest was suddenly choked with feelings—feelings of anger and regret and sorrow. And love.

For once he saw his father not as a patriarch full of stern and pious thoughts but as a broken man who longed for his son's well-being, who desperately wanted him to be safe and sound and whole and home. And in that one piercing moment, Ben knew his father's pain as if it were his own.

Something soft brushed against his pants leg and he looked under the table to find a kitten, curling around his father's ankle. His father pushed back from the table to let the kitten jump up into his lap. He cradled the kitten in his arms like it was a baby, gently stroking its head, and the kitten responded by purring.

Astonished, Ben could only stare at the sight. This . . . from a man who had once firmly believed all animals belonged in the barn and punished his sons severely when they tried to hide a puppy in their room. How strange. Dementia brought out a tenderness in his father that he didn't think was in him.

⌣

Natalie saw Micah head to the buggy and rapped on the window to get his attention. He stopped, saw her waving frantically to him, and crossed the yard to the guesthouse. She met him at the door. "It's so cold in here. Would you help me get a fire started? One last fire to warm the guesthouse while I pack up."

Without a word, Micah pivoted on his heels, went to the woodpile, and brought back an armload of wood and kindling. He knelt in front of the woodstove, opened the small door, stacked pieces of wood together in such a practiced way that they clacked, and tucked kindling in between the logs. He looked around for a matchbox. With sure hands he took out a single matchstick, struck it, and then the smallest of fires sprang to life, sputtering, then crackling as it grew. She wondered what was going through Micah's mind as he stared at the flames. There was a gracefulness to him, Natalie thought, as he worked. An ease in movement. The awareness surprised her. She liked Micah; she got a kick out of his awkwardness, his acute self-consciousness, but she'd never seen him like this. Confident, comfortable. Maybe this was what he was like when he was out chasing those birds. Maybe this was the Micah who had so impressed Ben.

He rose, dusted his hands on his thighs, and turned to her. "Anything else b-before I g-go?"

Just as she opened her mouth to ask if he could get down her suitcases from the top shelf in the closet, he lifted his hand to shush her. He cocked his head. "Do you hear that?"

"No. What?" Micah had such weirdly good ears. She heard nothing at all.

With his weirdly good ears, Micah followed the sound out the door. She waited, thinking he would return, but then gave up on him. As she went to close the door, he called to her, and waved his arm to beckon her. She grabbed her jacket and went out to join him, to see what bird he was after now. He pointed down the hill. "Look over there."

Perched on a fence post was a huge white owl—huge, as big as a cat—peering at them with yellow eyes.

"An albino owl?"

He shook his head. "Snowy Owl."

264

"Its feet look like its wearing UGG boots." They were covered in thick, frosty white feathers.

He grunted. "Massive feet. To snatch prey." His eyes remained fixed on that giant owl with its icy stare. "We never used to have them here, but a year or so ago, there was a bad winter up in the tundra and the lemmings got slim. Some flew south looking for food."

"So this is a big deal? Like, Ben'll be excited to hear about it?" She'd love to have something to tell him that might help break the ice between them.

Eyes never leaving the Snowy Owl, Micah grinned. "It's a big deal."

She grinned right back, realizing she'd just observed another big deal. Micah hadn't stuttered.

～

Ben went out to the cemetery where his mother and brother were buried. It was bigger now than he'd remembered, with newer graves rippling outward toward the fence. The grass around the cemetery hadn't been mowed in a long time, and such neglect surprised him. As a boy, he and Levi and their dad, along with some other families, had taken turns to mow the grass and trim around the stones. The two brothers had enjoyed the task, the smell of fresh-cut grass, and especially the birds that would follow to catch the bugs that the lawn mower churned up.

He found his mother's stone beneath a tree on the edge of the cemetery. He looked for a somewhat dry spot on the ground and sat down, his knees bent, leaning on his palms. All the stones in the Amish cemetery were nearly identical, small and nondescript. Long-buried emotions were flying through him. He felt incredibly moved to be here and gingerly, reverently, reached out to touch her stone. He thought of his mother, and about how sad she'd always seemed. As if life was just too taxing, too foreign, too much. He wondered if that was the way Levi had felt when he decided to take his life. In a way, she and Levi were similar. They were both broken in the same place.

He found himself talking to his mother, telling her about his life, about seeing his father. He thanked her for sticking it out with Zeke Zook, despite everything. "I'm sorry, Mem, for leaving you like I did. For never coming home again. I just couldn't face coming back, not after what happened to Levi." He couldn't change his father and he couldn't change what had happened to Levi. But neither could he walk away.

"Penny Weaver said that I left and I kept on leaving. She's right, I suppose. A skipping stone, that's what she called me." Her words had been coming back to him a lot lately. His thoughts returned to his mother, of how quiet she was, as meek and mild as a lamb. Too gentle for Zeke Zook. It might have been better if his father had married a woman with a little vinegar running in her veins. Like Penny.

But his mother had chosen his father. Deep down, Ben knew his mother loved his father. And he knew his father loved her, loved him, and even loved Levi. Somehow, love was the thread that ran through them all and it couldn't be cut, as much as Ben had tried.

He let his head fall back to stare up into the gray sky. The clouds were gathering, and the wind nipped at his face and hands. Something dark flashed by, a bird. Instinctively, Ben stilled.

Cemeteries, places of quiet that were uninterrupted, full of food and cover, were magnets for migratory birds. Centuries ago, no one would ever come to a cemetery to sit and reflect, like Ben was doing now. They were considered disease-ridden. It wasn't until the nineteenth century that cemeteries became garden-like, drawing birds, which drew in birders. Ever since, they'd become a favorite place to bird-watch.

Ben waited and waited, but saw nothing else. He rose, moving slowly, and went outside the cemetery to where Levi's grave was placed. Slowly, he turned his head from left to right, looking all around him. He heard the honking of Canada Geese and looked at the sky to see a V formation, coming in for a landing on a farmer's small pond across the road.

He sat on the cold, hard ground, shifting, trying to get comfortable, and turned his thoughts to the small carved slab of stone in front of him, to the brother he'd loved and lost. "Levi," he said, his voice breaking on the word. His throat closed up tight around the words he wanted to say and kept them from coming.

He swallowed and tried again. "Levi, I'm sorry life wasn't easier for you. I hope you knew that you were loved. I loved you, Mem loved you, and in Dad's own mixed-up, convoluted way, he loved you too. You gave so much more than you took, Levi. You gave me your love of birds, and it's kept me going, moving forward. I hope and pray you're at peace now. Because your life mattered. You mattered." One tear, then another, rolled down Ben's face. Crying was not his style. At all. But he couldn't stop the tears if he had tried. He cried for his brother, his poor, sad brother, who'd missed everything. For the despair and depression so severe it had taken his brother's life. For how much he had missed his brother. He wondered how long it had been since someone had sat here, remembering Levi, his boisterous laugh, his long-gaited walk, his kind face. He wanted to remember his brother's face.

He felt one raindrop, then another, a warning that his time was up, and he wiped away his tears with his coat sleeve. He glanced around, sure that he saw something, or heard something. The wind rustled branches in the tree overhead, but nothing more.

And then, far beyond Levi's stone, Ben caught a flash, a dark wing. Again, instinctively, he became utterly still. Five minutes passed. Ten. Fifteen. And suddenly he was part of the bird world. A black-and-white bird hopped its way around the side of Levi's memorial stone. It jumped to the top of the stone as Ben watched, holding his breath. A swarm of moths flew past and the bird took off, picking them off in scooping motions, capturing its prey in midair.

Ben sorely regretted his decision not to bring his optical equipment bag with him. Good grief, he lugged that thing everywhere, all over the world. How could he have left it at the guesthouse when he needed it now more than ever?

But then he thought of Penny and Micah, how they went about birding—eyes and ears were their only tools. He had grown heavily dependent on his equipment. How long had it been since he just relied on his senses to observe the beauty of birds? Far too long.

So he stopped regretting the absence of his camera, and concentrated on where he was at this moment in time and the miracle of migration that he was observing. He grinned, thinking of how he would write up this find. The First Law of Birding: When you see the bird that you have always wanted to see, it will be in the last spot you thought to look for it.

Little by little, he felt his whole self settle as he forgot about his book, his looming deadline . . . and just watched this magnificent bird. It was one of those transcendent moments that a photograph would never be able to re-create, never truly capture.

At long last, Ben had finally found the White-winged Tern. On the flip side, he had no proof, nothing to show his publisher. Yet he found he didn't really care. He really didn't. Inside him rose a joy in just being given the chance to see this rare little bird that had wandered so far off its course. He couldn't ignore a delight in birding he hadn't felt in years. It made some broken part of Ben begin to feel whole again.

Micah Weaver, Bird-Watching Log

Name of Bird: Snowy Owl

Scientific Name: Bubo scandiacus

Status: Population decreasing

Date: December 19

Location: Perched on a fence post at Lost Creek Farm

Description: Adult male. A whopper. Rounded head, large bulky body, milky white plumage, massive feet.

Bird Action: Sat on fence post for over an hour, swiveled its head now and then, watching me with an icy stare.

Notes: Easily one of the most regal, beautiful, and mysterious of all owls. This was my first sighting of a Snowy Owl. It felt kinda . . . holy.

23

Micah was on his way to the Bent N' Dent to fetch some grocery items Penny insisted she needed, right now. Annoyed, he had better things to do and told her so, but she told him that if he had any plans to eat supper, he might think twice. So he hooked up Junco to the buggy traces and hurried to the store. Still annoyed, but mostly with himself.

That *bird*. How could it be so hard for him to find the White-winged Tern? He felt like an imposter. He'd promised that bird to Ben Zook and he hadn't delivered on his promise. At the store, he pulled Junco in next to Hank's mule. Those two were friendly and exchanged nose bumps, a horse's hello. He took the steps two at a time and reached out for the door just as it opened and Trudy Yoder came out, carrying a bag of sugar in her arms.

He stopped abruptly at the sight of her, and out of him burst, "I can't find the White-winged T-tern. I've l-looked everywhere. Ben Zook . . . he's leaving soon. I promised him that b-bird. He's only here because he thought I had s-spotted it." He slapped his chest. "But I never s-saw it. I p-put it on the Rare Bird Alert without v-v-verifying."

Trudy looked down at the big bag of sugar. "That day I saw it, that first day . . . Micah, I was telling you the truth."

"I know. I t-took c-credit for it." He let out a deep breath. "It was wrong."

She held his gaze for a long time. "Micah, you told me once to put myself in the mind of a bird when I'm trying to find it. Think the way that particular bird thinks."

"I s-said that?"

"You did. When I first met you. So what's the most favorite thing of a White-winged Tern?"

"Same as m-most birds. Food." Same as him.

She nodded solemnly. "What food in particular?"

"B-bugs."

"Exactly. And it's probably looking for lots of food to feast on before it migrates." She bit her lip, thinking. "So where would lots of bugs be right now? Someplace where the cold hasn't killed them off yet."

In his head, Micah ran through the few warm places in Stoney Ridge where there'd still be plenty of bugs. Only one type came to mind. A sure thing. "C-compost heaps." Ugh. Birds had a rotten sense of smell. He had an exceptional sense of smell. But if it meant he could find this bird, he'd search every dung heap on every farm.

"Good idea."

He frowned. There was no way he could get to every compost heap in Stoney Ridge in one afternoon.

She read his mind. "I'll help, Micah. You go south and I'll go north. Let's start with the biggest, messiest, stinkiest manure piles we can find." She clapped her hands together. "Don't you worry. We'll find your bird."

Micah felt the tight knot ease some in his chest. Trudy was a good friend.

"COUNT ME IN." Hank Lapp had cracked the door slightly open to eavesdrop, missing critical information. He swung the door wide. "SO WHERE are we OFF to?" He jabbed his thumb behind him. "EDITH is in the STORE. I'll go get her and we'll JOIN the HUNT."

Micah and Trudy exchanged a look, then a smile.

~

Ben had put both of Natalie's suitcases in the trunk of her car and went back inside. He looked around the small guesthouse, making sure he had packed everything. Natalie was in the bathroom, packing up her cosmetic bag. Who knew how long *that* would take? His cousin was not one to be hurried. He plopped down on the couch and closed his eyes, as a wave of exhaustion hit him. Not the malaria kind of exhaustion. This was the emotionally spent kind of exhaustion. He still had something he needed to do.

Releasing a deep sigh, he made himself get up. He picked up the envelope he'd set aside for Penny, slipped on his coat, and crossed the yard to the big house. She must have seen him coming, for she opened the door as he approached.

Ben stopped near the bird feeder. "I went to see my father."

Penny opened the door wider. "Come in. Come in out of the cold."

He went inside, soaking up the warmth of the kitchen. The warmth of Penny Weaver. This would be the last time he stood in her kitchen.

Penny's expression was undeservedly kind, concerned. "Don't you want to sit down?"

Don't, Penny. Don't be so good to me. "No. I'll make this quick." Ben had to keep moving. If he slowed down, he might not be able to make himself leave. That wouldn't be fair to Penny. "You're right. He isn't well." That was an understatement.

She studied him with those gray eyes of hers, so piercing, so able to reach straight into his soul.

"He thought—" Ben swallowed and started again. "He thought

272

I was Levi. I guess . . ." He tried to smile, but it felt all wrong. This was even harder than he thought it would be. "I guess we looked more alike than I realized." He reached inside his coat pocket and pulled out an envelope to hand to her. "This is the money I owe you for staying at the guesthouse. For all those good meals. And I've included money for my father's care. The church shouldn't have to pay for it. Assuming, that is, that you're still willing to care for him."

"I am."

He lifted his head. "I'll come back now and then to check on my father. If there's anything he needs, just call."

She gave a nod.

"We'll be leaving within the hour. I'd hoped that Micah might be here, but just in case I miss saying goodbye to him, please let him know that I finally spotted the White-winged Tern."

Her eyes widened. "Where?"

"I was out at the cemetery when it showed up. I didn't have my camera, so I can't submit it in the book. But I did see it. Let him know. I saw it, and . . . that's enough for me. Truly it is." A few weeks ago, it wouldn't have been.

He walked to the door and turned around to face her. "Penny, I want to thank you for everything. For your patience, and also for your forgiveness." She offered him grace in more ways than he could count. Caring for his father when he hadn't, helping him recover from malaria, allowing him into her world. He didn't deserve her. He reached out a hand to offer a formal goodbye. "My cousin and I, we won't forget you."

Penny looked at him for a long moment, then she reached out to wrap her small hands around his large one as if she were cradling a wounded bird. "I hope you're leaving Lost Creek Farm finding more than you came looking for."

Her eyes were shiny, and he nearly couldn't bear it. Couldn't bear thinking that, most likely, Roy's coat would be hanging on a wall peg in her kitchen. That Penny's life would be moving on, without him.

"I'm leaving," he said, "on the mend." And that was the honest truth. Gently, he pulled her to him, cupping her face with his hands. "Promise me you'll be happy." He silenced her lips with his thumb, even though she hadn't spoken. He took her hand and kissed the palm. "Goodbye, Penny." He turned around to leave before he changed his mind.

"Ben, wait."

He stopped but didn't turn around.

She handed him a large manila envelope.

"What is it?"

"It's a drawing. This one . . . it belongs to you."

He gave her a brief nod of thanks. "I'll treasure it." And then he left.

Watching Ben cross the yard to the guesthouse for the last time, Penny brought her hand up to her mouth, pushing her lips hard on her knuckles against the pain burning in her throat. One tear, then another, streamed down her cheeks. Gone was the warmth and friendliness that usually flowed between them, replaced—at least on his side—by a guardedness, an aloof reserve. This was the Ben Zook who had first arrived at Lost Creek Farm. She could see the muscles of his jaw harden with strain. More than that, though, she could sense his inner turmoil.

Her heart ached for Ben. Her heart ached for her.

There was a little part of her that longed to run after him, to go with him. To be at his side, chasing rare birds with him all over the world. All she needed to do was take one step out the door, and he would welcome her into his life. Somehow, she knew he would.

But years ago, she had made a vow to live separate from the world. She had made that vow with joy in her heart, and she would never turn her back on that joy. Not even for Ben Zook.

Micah slapped Junco's reins one more time to hurry him up the drive to Lost Creek Farm. As soon as the horse reached the top, Micah jumped out of the buggy. He bolted over to the guesthouse and burst in without a knock. Ben was at the small sink, drinking a glass of water.

"Found it."

Ben stared at Micah for a long moment, then grabbed his coat, picked up his bag full of optical equipment, and joined him at the door. "Lead the way."

Nearly at the buggy, Ben said, "Would it be faster if we took Natalie's car?"

Micah shook his head. "I have a s-shortcut."

Thirty minutes later, they stood downwind of the dairy barn at Beacon Hollow. Trudy was the one who had suggested Beacon Hollow's compost pile first, because it was one of the largest, thanks to so many cows. Micah peered through his binoculars; Ben set up his scope and gazed through it.

"There it is." The White-winged Tern. Catching bugs, midair, over the steaming compost. Micah's heart filled with joy, with relief, with awe. He thought he might try to do something nice for Trudy, as a thank-you. He wasn't sure what she'd like, though. He really didn't know much about her, other than their shared love of birds. And Shelley.

"Think it's a juvenile?" Ben whispered. "With that black cap?"

"Looks like it." No wonder it was on its own, a little confused, thrown off course in a storm. That's what adolescence felt like to Micah. He thought about Shelley, wondering if she might return, or if her path would lead her away from home for good. He sent up a prayer, asking God to watch over her.

Ben took photograph after photograph, clicking away, until he seemed satisfied and just put the camera away. The two of them stood in the twilight, watching, listening, both full of awe.

He wondered how far that little bird had come, and how much farther it had to go. When did it first get blown off course? Only God knew. Northern European populations of the bird migrated south in large flocks to Africa for the winter. Those east migrated to China, Myanmar, even Australia and New Zealand. A migration miracle.

"Well done, Micah," Ben said, shaking his hand.

"It's my job," Micah said, pride deepening his voice just a bit.

Micah Weaver, Bird-Watching Log

Name of Bird: White-winged Tern

Scientific Name: Chlidonias leucopterus

Status: A very scarce vagrant (must have been blown off course on its way from Northern Europe to Africa)

Date: December 20

Location: Beacon Hollow's compost pile

Description: Juvenile male, winter plumage, mostly white-bodied with darker wing, black cap. Contrasts to summer plumage when its body would be mostly black with pale white wings.

Bird Action: Flew slowly over the pile to pick off prey, catching insects in flight. Impressive.

Notes: Serious long-distance flier. These birds see more sunlight than just about anybody else. In fact, this little guy enjoys two summers a year. Every year he flies from his breeding grounds of Northern Europe right down to Africa. After he relaxes and sunbathes, it gets too hot and he'll have to head back north.

This round-trip journey can cover up to 56,000 miles. That is a whole lot of flying.

Formerly, my nemesis bird. Now, my lifer. My best one.

24

Natalie was back in Philadelphia, back in her small, cozy house. This time was different, though. The house wasn't a refuge anymore, because she didn't need an escape. She felt ready to face her life. To make a new life. To create a life she loved.

Penny had given Natalie five additional watercolors to frame, so she did, and Sophia Parker was over the moon. "Get me more," Sophia told Natalie. "Get me every bird."

But Natalie didn't promise her any more of Penny's beautiful birds. She was dismayed by Sophia's insatiable appetite, probably because she recognized that quality in herself. Besides, she had something else in mind for Penny's artwork. Something she had prayed about, something she had talked on the phone about with Penny. Something even bigger than supplying Sophia Parker with her Amish fix.

Natalie had been waiting for the right time to tell Ben about her idea. He'd finished his book, submitted it, and was trying to decide where he should go next. She had never, ever known him to have trouble deciding about the location of his next book. Not once. He was usually raring to pack up and go once he'd finally delivered a manuscript. Not this time. He spent a lot of time looking out the window. She wondered if he was depressed since they'd left Lost Creek Farm, for he was even quieter than usual, but when she brought it up, he brushed that thought off as ridiculous. She didn't think it was at all ridiculous.

Natalie had wanted to give Ben time to work out whatever was going on inside his head, but she couldn't hold her tongue until the cows came home. As the sun set on Christmas Eve, she felt fed up with the gloomy atmosphere in the house. "Oh, come on," she said, "let's lighten up around here. Christmas is coming! Let's go do something."

He surprised her by closing his computer, bolting to his feet, and grabbing his coat. "You're right. I'm heading to church."

"I'll come too," she said, surprising him right back.

They went to a nearby church and sat in the back row, enjoying the Christmas hymns, the sermon about the nativity. More than enjoyed. They let the wonder of worship sink into them.

Natalie wondered if Boyd was at church tonight, and if his service was similar to this one. And if he thought of her anywhere as often as she thought of him. She said a prayer for him, asking God to watch over him.

After the service, they stopped at an upscale grocery store to pick out a premade dinner. Back at home, they set the table with fine china, complete with long tapered candles that Natalie had found stashed in a drawer. "What do you think? Do you like this food?"

"It's good," Ben said, spooning cranberry relish onto the turkey.

"It's good enough," Natalie said. "Not great though. I think Penny kind of spoiled my palate."

Lately she noticed Ben stilled whatever he was doing whenever she said Penny's name, almost visibly recoiling, as if she had given him a sharp jab with her elbow. She had *thought* there was something brewing between them. Once or twice, sitting around the firepit at Lost Creek Farm, she'd thought she'd caught Ben looking at Penny with that sappy expression on his face that a man got when he was falling for a woman. The way Boyd looked at Natalie. The way Boyd *used* to look at her.

Man, she and Ben were two of a kind, a pitiful pair. They, both of them, needed to make a change. A big change.

She picked up their plates to take to the kitchen from the small dining room. Ben had bought a pumpkin pie for dessert from a bakery, so she brought it back to the table, set it down, and looked at him, jiggling on the balls of her feet. "So . . . I have news. Guess what?"

He gave her a quick glance. "What?"

"I'm considering moving to Stoney Ridge."

He jerked his head up. "You *what*?"

"More than considering. I've spoken to a real estate agent about selling my house, and she already has a buyer who's interested."

He leaned back in his chair. "Is this because of the vet?"

"No! Not at all." She hadn't heard a word from Boyd since they'd left Lost Creek Farm. Not a call, not a text. Nothing. "Never mind." She shouldn't have told Ben. She knew how he'd react the moment she uttered it.

"Hold on. I'm sorry. Why would you consider moving to Stoney Ridge? I thought you loved city life."

"I think it's time for a fresh start. And . . ." She slid into her chair. "Penny gave me an idea. When I told her about the design work I'd done, she said it sounded like I enjoyed helping people build their nests."

One of Ben's eyebrows lifted. "So what exactly does that mean in an Amish community?"

"Maybe . . . opening a little home goods store. Furnishings and the like. Penny even came up with a name for it. 'Habitat.'"

Ben kept his eyes down. "You've been talking to her." It wasn't really a question.

"Yes. I've been talking to Penny every day. Also, to a property manager in Stoney Ridge. Turns out, there's a retail location just across from the Sweet Tooth Bakery that's available starting January first. Great location, big empty space, good parking, and excellent visibility on Main Street. It's just waiting for a tenant. There's even an apartment above."

Ben picked up a knife and cut two slices of pumpkin pie. "Is that why you wouldn't let the Sophia lady have any more of Penny's watercolors?" He handed her a slice. "Ah. Now I get it. You're planning to use Penny's artwork to entice customers into your store."

She frowned at him. It bugged her when he connected the dots. "I don't deny that it would be amazing to have Penny's work on the walls of the store. I can just see them"—she spread her hand out—"like a story unfolding." She wished she could convince Penny to sign the watercolors. All she would agree to was to add her initials and the date on the back.

They each had a piece of pumpkin pie, then one more, but not much more conversation. Ben had gone sullen, back to his taciturn self, and Natalie knew it was pointless to try to get him to talk when he was in a sulky mood. After they finished cleaning up dishes in the kitchen, he said he was headed to bed. Still a little tired from malaria, he said, but Natalie wondered if there was more to it. If she sold her house, it meant he would no longer have a home base, even if he just popped in a few times a year. She'd given that some thought, but she knew this was right for her, and she knew Ben needed to make some changes too. "Ben, I think moving to Stoney Ridge is the right next step for me. I just think I need to embrace what comes my way for as long as it lasts. If I let fear interfere, I'll miss it."

He didn't respond. At the kitchen door, he turned to her. "Are you going to patch things up with Boyd?"

"That, I don't know." She hoped so, though.

~

Late that night, Micah went to Trudy's house—a two-story white frame house that shone in the moonlight—and threw a pebble at her window. He hoped it was her window, anyway. Really, really hoped so. Her father scared him. A flashlight went on, and Trudy appeared at the window, looking down at Micah.

Suddenly she was opening the sash, whispering loudly, "Give me a minute. I'll be right down."

He cupped his mouth. "Wear a c-coat." He stomped his feet, tucked his hands under his armpits to keep them warm, and listened for the sounds of night as he waited for Trudy. He was cold. Winter had come to Stoney Ridge.

Not two minutes later, she was climbing out the open window, onto the roof, shimmying down the rose trellis, to appear in front of him. "What's up?"

He started walking and she followed. "I'm s-sorry." He blew out a puff of air. "About t-taking credit for the b-bird."

"It's okay, Micah. I know you're trying to get your field-guiding work up and going. I'm glad I could help."

She let him off too easy. What he'd done was wrong. Selfish. He kept going, cutting through the corner of a farmer's field. "My s-stammer . . . it can s-stop me from doing what I should d-do. B-being the m-man I should be."

"I never noticed."

He stopped abruptly to let her catch up with him. Was she mocking him? He gave her a cautious look, surprised to realize her face was completely guileless, her eyes were innocent. She meant what she said. He smiled as he heard the hoot of a certain owl, low and harsh, almost like a dog barking. "Merry Christmas, Trudy."

"Merry Christmas to you."

The owl screeched, a way to claim its territory. "That's my thank-you g-gift to you. For helping me find the b-bird."

She lifted her chin. "A Burrowing Owl?"

"No," he said, his head tipped, listening. "A Snowy Owl. Been t-tracking it all evening." They stood in the field, listening, for a very long time, holding their breath. "There!" He lifted his lantern to shine on the Snowy Owl, perched on a branch in a tall pine tree not far away, preening itself.

Trudy stared at it for a long time, hardly breathing. Then she turned to him with a look of awe on her face. "I think that's the best Christmas gift I've ever been given, Micah."

～

Ben woke on Christmas morning before dawn and stayed in bed, staring at the ceiling. Natalie's decision to move to Stoney Ridge astounded him. Impressed him. He was proud of her. Here was someone who'd dared to love and had experienced heartbreak. Even so, Natalie was willing to dive in again. Stoney Ridge, Boyd the vet. She was fearless.

He went to the window to find a light sprinkling of snow covered the rooftops, just enough whiteness to make it finally feel like Christmas.

Nice. Fitting.

He wondered what Penny thought when she saw the snow this morning. He remembered one night around the firepit when she'd mentioned that the first snowfall of the year was always the best. The smell of the air, she had said, was like none other. Crisp, clean, fresh.

He groaned. Uninvited thoughts of Penny came to him whenever he let his guard down. He'd fill his coffee cup in the morning and he'd suddenly remember her arriving at the guesthouse, carrying a tray, a cheery smile on her face. He'd be sitting at his computer and he'd think how she would stop halfway as she crossed the yard to peer up at the trees, having heard birdsong.

Today he'd even had another strange thought. He worried about that kitten that Roy King had given to her. She was always fretting about it getting out of the kitchen, and then suddenly, one day it was gone. He'd never thought to ask. He'd never learned what she had named it.

Stop it, Zook. Stop thinking about her. The whole time since he'd left Lost Creek Farm, he'd been trying to make himself stop feeling so consumed with Penny Weaver. Not thinking about her would make his life a lot easier, would help him keep his priorities focused on his work.

He thought a run before breakfast would help, so he dressed in his sweats and went downstairs. He smelled coffee and popped his head in the kitchen. "Merry Christmas. I'm heading out for a run. When I get back, I'll make you an omelet."

Natalie looked up from the coffee maker. "You're sounding pretty cheerful."

"It's Christmas. That's a good reason, isn't it?" He leaned against the doorjamb. "More importantly, what's happened to your cheerful attitude? Last night you seemed downright chipper."

"It's your fault. You got me fretting about Penny, about asking for more of her watercolors. I can't deny how reluctant she was to let me see them. Not me, not Roy. Why she let you see them, I'll never understand."

"Roy?" Ben's head shot up. "She never let Roy see her watercolors?"

"Nope."

"What makes you think that?"

"Because I asked. She said she hadn't. She just kept them hidden away, in that box with all your books."

"What? My books?"

"Yes. With her artwork. It's all in a box on the bottom shelf of the pantry. Every book you've ever written."

He slapped his palm against his chest. "My books?"

"Yes. I thought I told you."

"You never did." He crossed the room to look out the window at the little snowy yard. "You're saying she has my books in her box filled with drawings, hidden in the pantry." He wheeled around. "*My* books?"

"Every one. I don't even have them all."

"Roy's kitten!"

"What? What are you talking about?"

284

"She gave it to my father." A smile spread across his face. "To keep him company."

She looked at him as if he might be coming down with something contagious. "Look . . . can we please stay focused on the matter at hand? I'm making this huge decision. Uprooting my life. I just hope I'm not asking something of Penny that I shouldn't. You know? I mean . . ."

Ben had stopped listening. He took the stairs two at a time and went into the guestroom where he'd been staying. Out of his optical equipment bag he pulled the manila envelope Penny had given to him. He had yet to open it. He knew she had picked out this bird she'd drawn for him, their last connection, and he just didn't trust his emotions. Slowly, he pulled the drawing from the envelope. It wasn't a bird, after all.

It was a sketch of Levi.

Ben stared at the drawing. Penny must have drawn it the summer when she first met Levi, when she was only twelve years old. It was a rough sketch, unskilled, yet hinted at the talent of a budding young artist. She had captured Levi, if not in specific detail, then in his winsomeness, his gentleness. Even the sadness and conflict that marked his soul.

This sketch was the only likeness Ben had of his brother. The only one in existence. Tears streamed down his face and he wiped them away with his sleeve so that they didn't fall on the sketch and mar it.

He noticed the corner of a paper peeking out of the envelope. He pulled it out and read Penny's note: *I've said my goodbye. I hope this helps you say yours.*

His heart began pounding as he sat motionless, the sun streaming through the window onto his face and chest. Then the truth struck him like a blow to the gut and the tears started streaming again.

She knows me. She cares about me.

Not the man she thought I was, not an imagined version of me, but me. The real Ben Zook.

I'm not competing with a memory.

And I care about her.

Care about her? *Admit it, Zook, you love her.* He'd been determined not to love Penny, but in the end, he'd been unable to stop himself. Just being around her this last month had opened his eyes to how he had closed himself off from everyone, stuck inside a hard shell of grief and blame. It was as if he'd been living in a black-and-white photograph until he met Penny Weaver, and suddenly he was living in full color. How could he go back to his stark reality?

Going through his days without Penny, without hope of seeing her or talking with her, made him feel like malaria had returned, draining the joy out of life like water from a sink. He should be checking global Rare Bird Alerts, making travel arrangements, planning his next book, but he couldn't make himself care. The air left his lungs.

He missed Penny.

What an idiot he'd been.

He scraped both hands over his face, coming to grips with the fact that he'd been roaming the earth searching for rare birds, and the only one he really wanted was right there, in Stoney Ridge.

～

Natalie wasn't exactly sure what triggered Ben's insistence that they drive to Stoney Ridge this morning. He said he wanted to drop in on his father, and thought it might be nice to drive past where she wanted her shop. She was delighted that he seemed supportive of her Habitat store idea, because last night he had zero interest in it. Nada.

Still, it seemed a little weird that he was in such a hurry. They stopped at his father's farm, but the house was empty. No smoke coming from the chimney, no lantern light glowing, no answer to his knock at the door. Exasperated, Ben returned to the car. "*Church.* Blast. I forgot."

"That's not a very good attitude on Christmas morning, Ben."

"I just meant . . . there's always church held on Christmas morning, no matter what day it falls on. I completely blanked."

"Let's go down to Main Street and I'll show you where the store will be." On the way to town, they would pass Boyd's house. She wondered if her box of cinnamon rolls was still there, on the front porch. Frozen. Ignored.

As Ben turned down Boyd's road, Natalie told him to slow down. "There's his truck. Wait! There he is!" Boyd was just getting out of his truck. "Should we stop? No. We shouldn't. Or should we?"

Ben slammed on the brakes.

The car screeched and Boyd wheeled around. He stopped and stared when he saw Natalie.

"Go," Ben said. "Talk to him."

"But . . ."

"Natalie, it's Christmas. Go. Call me if you need me. I won't be far. It's a very small town."

"Where are you going to be?"

"I'll be . . . driving around."

Boyd was on his way to the car, so Natalie took in a deep breath. "Cross your fingers." She opened the car door and stepped out, closing the door behind her. Ben, the traitor, drove away.

Boyd stood about ten feet away from Natalie. He had a slightly bewildered look on his face. "I thought you'd gone back to Philadelphia."

"I had. I did. I'm just here to . . . wish you a merry Christmas."

"You could have just called. Or texted."

"But you don't answer my calls or texts."

"Look, Natalie—"

"Before you say anything, please listen to me. I need to ask your forgiveness."

He shook his head. "Not from me. It's really Penny who has to forgive you."

287

"I've asked. She's given it. But it's also you whom I need to ask forgiveness from. I broke your trust, and I am well aware that trust is a fragile thing." Had she learned nothing from this last year but that lesson? It shamed her that she didn't even consider the consequences of broken trust. How they splattered.

"Why?" He took a few steps closer to her. "Why did you do it? Why would you take something from Penny Weaver? Something that she obviously valued and cared about and wanted to keep private?"

"I think . . . because I wanted to hold on to something that God wanted me to let go of."

"And now?"

"I think I'm finally learning how to trust God." She held her gloved hands together. "So, what I'm asking of you is, can you forgive me? I'm not expecting things to go back the way they were. I'm not expecting anything. But I do want your forgiveness."

He folded his arms and stomped snow off his feet. She thought he was stalling. Finally, he dropped his arms and took a step closer to her. "Natalie, do you read the Bible much?"

"I tried a long time ago, but I didn't understand it. I'll try again, though."

"A lot of it is hard to understand, but one thing is hard to miss. It's pretty clear that Jesus wants us to forgive others."

She smiled. "So does that mean that you'll forgive me?"

"I guess it does," he said, but he said it softly, gently.

She ventured a step toward him. "Boyd, I don't deserve you. I've known that from the start. But I want to be the kind of person who does."

He watched her, listening thoughtfully. The wariness was gone. In its place was tenderness.

There was something happening here, Natalie could sense it.

Warmth lit his eyes. "Yeah?" he said, taking a step or two to close the gap between them. "So . . . what are you doing for New Year's?"

He slid one arm about her waist and drew her to him, setting his forehead against hers. They stayed that way for a long moment. Then he bent his head, and his lips met hers.

Ben drove around the country roads, trying to figure out which Amish farm was hosting church this morning. The sun was shining on the snowy fields, a beautiful sight. Corn shocks, like small teepees, were dusted with snow. Turning down one winding road, he caught sight of a long row of gray-topped buggies, lining the large drive like LEGOs. Ah . . . Windmill Farm. He glanced at the clock in the car dashboard. By now church would be over. Today, families wouldn't linger. They'd be heading home to celebrate their own Christmas.

He parked along the road and watched. One buggy left, then another. And another. He spotted Micah leading Junco out of the pasture to hook him up to the buggy traces. Then he saw Micah walk quickly into the barn and come out again, this time, holding on to Zeke Zook's right arm. On his dad's left arm was Trudy Yoder. He felt a surge of pity for his father, along with love. A prick of guilt too. He knew he should be the one helping him to the buggy. Even that thought amazed Ben, that he would want to be the one to help his father. It was amazing, the reversals that occurred in life.

Gratitude filled him, for a little church that cared for a difficult, cranky old man. For so many helping hands.

But where was Penny?

He saw Roy walk to a buggy, with two bonneted little girls running behind him. His breath hitched. Was he too late? Had Penny taken his advice about Roy? But then he saw Roy help the girls into the buggy and drive off, and still there was no sign of Penny. Ben let out the breath he'd been holding.

He waited and as he waited, he wondered. He prayed. *Lord, am*

I really going to do this? Give up my camera, if not my future book contracts? The travel? The freedom? The modern conveniences? All that and more.

Because . . . this was it. The watershed moment of his life, and he knew it. If he left now, he could never return. If he chose to stay, he would never leave. "God, you've got my attention. If this isn't the right path, tell me now." The Lord's blessing on this choice was something he craved.

A long-legged boy loped over to the pasture to get a horse, and something about that boy's gait struck him, reminding him so much of Levi during happier days. He squinted, trying to focus in on him, but then couldn't find the boy again amidst all the other boys. His breath was tight in his throat, his heart pounded, but the sweet feeling the vision had brought to him remained. Ben had the strangest awareness that his mother, his brother, they were not far away. And that shouldn't surprise him, for they were with God. And Ben knew, without a doubt, that God was with him.

Why had God bothered with him? Brought him all the way back to a little Amish community in Pennsylvania just because of a little rare bird who blew off course.

He didn't know why. He only knew that, incomprehensibly, God did love him enough to create the one circumstance in the world that would coax him back. To face what he was running from. Who he was running from.

A handful of bonneted women moved out of the barn and slowly made their way toward the buggies. Ben got out of the car and crossed the road to stand under a weeping willow tree, its roots firmly grounded in a stream that ran along the base of the farm. His eyes were on those bonnets.

The women parted, and then he saw her. He would know Penny anywhere, even among a clump of Plain women who all dressed alike, with black bonnets and black capes. She was the one who lifted her face to the trees, scanning for birds. She was the one who noticed a flock of Canada Geese skidding across the sky.

290

He had thought her unremarkable when he first met her, but no longer. How beautiful love could make someone's face.

Penny turned in a half circle, following the geese's path. Her attention swept past Ben, then stopped. Lifting a hand to shield her eyes, she zeroed in on him. Even from this distance, she knew it was him. Joy—deep, simple, pure joy—pulled his mouth into a grin.

And just like that, a part of his heart—the biggest part, the one that had been gone missing for the last twenty years—locked back into place.

Horses and buggies, families were moving all around her, and Penny didn't think anyone else noticed Ben standing down by the road, almost completely hidden under a weeping willow tree. Not Micah, who was involved in an animated conversation with Trudy Yoder. Not Zeke, sitting in the buggy, with his chin dropped low, a sign that he was nodding off. No one would mind if she made them wait, even on Christmas morning.

No one saw Ben, no one but her. She sensed his closeness before she even spotted him.

She walked down the driveway and crossed a small piece of yard to reach Ben. He stood at the edge of the stream, his hat in his hand. Her gaze traveled over his familiar features with wonder, as if she couldn't believe he was really here. "You came home," she said.

He gave her a soft, slow smile. "Is this my home, Penny?"

"It's always been your home, I think. It's always been waiting for you."

He took a step toward her. "That kitten from Roy. You gave it to my father, didn't you?"

She dropped her gaze. "Well, no one should give a cat to someone who loves birds."

She looked up as he took another step toward her, then another. His eyes shone with joy, straight into hers. "I love you."

291

Her heart froze for an instant, then restarted with hard, drumming beats. Tears filled her eyes, blurring her vision. He *loved* her. She had thought the caring had all been on her side. He loved her! She really hadn't expected him to come back again. Of all days, he came home on Christmas. The Lord's Day. The day that brought hope and peace and joy into this world.

He reached out his hand, and she took it, feeling the warmth and strength in it. She wove their fingers together. Their eyes caught again and held. This time they both knew that neither one was letting go.

Epilogue

The humid air of the steamy August morning held the sweet smell of freshly cut grass. Ben and Micah had just finished mowing the lawn in the Amish cemetery, the way Ben and Levi had once done.

Ben took off his hat and wiped the sweat from his brow. It was getting too hot to do much more, but before they left, he wanted to trim the grass around his mother's grave. Around his father's grave, too, though it was a fresh grave and wouldn't take much trimming. His father had died in late June. Two months ago today, while in his sleep.

Ben had moved in with his father last winter to be his caregiver, committed right to the end. He would never regret that time with his dad. As Zeke's mental condition had deteriorated, his prickly spirit had become gentler, calmer, more accepting. Zeke and Ben, after a life of conflict and estrangement, had ended well.

And throughout it all, Penny had been there. Every time he needed her, she had been there.

He finished trimming around the stone and rose to his feet, sliding the trimming shears into the tool bucket he'd brought to the cemetery. He took care with the shears, because also in the bucket were three pairs of binoculars. Just in case something interesting flew by.

A twig crunched behind him and he turned to see Penny, not far outside the cemetery, kneeling to wipe away leaves off Levi's small, insignificant headstone. The stone wasn't much, even by Amish standards, but his brother's life had been significant. Very. His life had mattered. He mattered to Ben, and he mattered to Penny. Most importantly, he mattered to God. Of that, after all that had happened this last year, Ben had no doubt. Levi, he believed deep in his heart, was safe with God.

Watching Penny take such care with his brother's grave, Ben experienced a sudden rush of gratitude toward her. This fall, after migration, Ben and Penny planned to marry. One fine summer morning, they'd gone birding up at Wonder Lake, her favorite place. He'd proposed and she said yes.

They considered living in Ben's childhood home, until Micah surprised them both by asking if he could live there. On his good days, all during the winter, Zeke had taught Micah how to repair shoes. There were times when Zeke forgot how to do something and Ben was able to fill in. Some things, you never forget.

Micah wanted to use Zeke's workroom to open a part-time shoe repair shop. Open for business only when birds weren't flying.

Ben wasn't sure he'd get a lot of customers with that tagline. But he was also aware that his father's farm shared a corner with the Yoder farm. Trudy and Micah had been spending a lot of time birding together this spring.

Penny came over to join him and smiled in a way that caused his pulse to skip. He reached for her gloved hand and squeezed it. "You look especially pretty today, Penny Weaver."

She blushed, smiling a little, embarrassed, for she didn't think she was at all pretty, though she was. To Ben, she was the most beautiful woman in the world. He should know—he'd traveled the globe.

A whistle startled them and made them turn. Micah was pointing to a branch at the top of a tree. They squinted, searching limb by limb, but were too far away to see anything more stand out than a dray, a squirrel's nest. Suddenly a large brown bird shot off in the air.

Shielding their eyes from the sun, they watched the bird make a large circle. "A hawk?" Penny said. "They're on the move in August."

"I don't think so. Not the way it shot off."

Micah bolted toward them. "Did you see that?"

"Was it—" Ben started.

"A Gyrfalcon?" Penny finished.

Micah nodded. "I think so."

The three of them looked at each other, then lifted their chins to watch the falcon soar overhead, searching for an unlucky field mouse or mole. As if on cue, all three dropped their leather gloves into the bucket and picked up their binoculars.

They had a rare bird to chase.

Questions for Discussion

1. The plot of *A Season on the Wind* revolves around the hunt for a rare bird appearing in Stoney Ridge, yet the rare bird is also a metaphor. How would you describe its elusiveness?

2. Hold on to that rare bird metaphor for a moment. Each of the main characters—Ben, Natalie, Penny, Micah—are chasing something. What keeps evading them?

3. How many rare birds are there in this story?

4. What aspects of Penny's bedrock faith were used by God to alter Ben? Natalie?

5. There are a few different themes in this novel: the power of healing, the mystery of nature, and the ability of God to reconcile even that which seems unreconcilable. Which theme held the most intrigue to you?

6. Ben Zook is an interesting guy. Smart, successful, independent. Yet dig a little deeper and there's a carefully hidden depth of hurt, of pain, of regret, of bitterness. In a way that may not be apparent to others, he's stuck. How did the bout of malaria—the one thing that grounded him—reveal just how emotionally paralyzed he'd been?

7. What were some of your early theories about why Ben did not recognize Penny? Did the answer surprise you?

8. The author added Micah Weaver's Bird-Watching Log to the end of each chapter. How were they helpful in getting to know shy, stammering Micah? Did they spark your interest in birds?

9. In a typically Amish way, providing good food was one of Penny's ways to care for and nourish others. Why do you think Penny's cooking forged a connection to Ben?

10. During the course of the story, Natalie reflected on the choices she'd made that put her in such a bleak position. She had some awareness of the consequences of her choices, yet when she was faced with changing her trajectory, she ended up making the same kind of choice. Why? How could you relate to Natalie?

11. The breakthrough moment for Natalie comes when she asked Micah what's the most important thing he's learned about birding. "Listening," he said. Why did that one word strike her like a lightning bolt? Why is listening, truly listening, so hard to do?

12. Ben and Natalie, for different reasons, needed to give up something valuable and make radical changes if they wanted to find fulfillment and meaning in their lives. When has the Lord asked you to make a change and follow him into something new? What's happened since that pivotal moment?

> Forget about what's happened;
>> don't keep going over old history.
> Be alert, be present. I'm about to do something brand-
>> new.
>> It's bursting out! Don't you see it?
> There it is! I'm making a road through the desert,
>> rivers in the badlands.

Wild animals will say "Thank you!"
  —the coyotes and the buzzards—
Because I provided water in the desert,
  rivers through the sunbaked earth,
Drinking water for the people I chose,
  the people I made especially for myself,
  a people custom-made to praise me.
                    —Isaiah 43:19–21 MSG

Author's Note

Interested in becoming a birder?

Wherever you live, birds live there too. They're everywhere, which is part of their magic. The first step is to simply pay attention. Start locally—your own backyard, no matter how small, is the perfect place to start looking. Putting up a feeder (a suet basket is my favorite) will help bring the party right to you.

When placing a bird feeder in your yard, try to think like a bird. Hang it where birds will see it and feel safe coming in for a quick snack. If possible, place your feeder near a birdbath. Keep it clean and restock it frequently.

Some additional tips: Keep cats indoors. Prevent painful window strikes (ouch!) by putting decals on large picture windows.

Consider adding plants to your garden that attract birds. Hummingbirds love salvias, for example. Sunflowers are a favorite for many birds (and squirrels). Say no to pesticides and insecticides in your backyard.

You might enjoy adding an owl box. I have them attached to redwood trees in my yard. A Great Horned Owl returns each year to raise her owlets. I have small birdhouses in my vegetable garden that are claimed by bluebirds each spring. I watch, with pleasure, as those little birds tirelessly schlep in materials to build their nest.

Invest in a bird guide so you can identify the birds at your feeder. Keep a running list. You'll be surprised at the visitors who flock to your yard. Have patience, and enjoy! Birds are a wonderful reminder of how connected we are to each other.

History of the Audubon Christmas Bird Count

Prior to the turn of the twentieth century, many Americans still engaged in a holiday tradition known as the Christmas "side hunt"—contests to kill the most birds in a single day. The winner was the one who brought in the biggest pile of feathered carcasses.

Conservation was in its infancy, yet many scientists were becoming concerned about declining bird populations. On Christmas Day, 1900, an Audubon Society ornithologist named Frank Chapman proposed a new holiday tradition. Instead of hunting birds, Chapman said, why not count them? On December 25 of that year, twenty-seven bird lovers found ninety species of birds, but most importantly, these bird lovers discovered each other. The first continental bird-watching network was born.

Audubon's Christmas Bird Count began as a way for birders to meet and greet others with the same quirky obsession. Each year, from December 14 through January 5, tens of thousands of volunteers brave the elements to count birds. Audubon and other biologists and wildlife agencies rely on the collected data in this census to assess the long-term health of bird populations and to help protect species and their habitat.

Today the Christmas Bird Count has become a birding tradition, with more than 2,615 different counts across North, Central, and South America (2019 stats). You don't have to be an expert in birding to join in on a bird count. If you might be interested, go to the Audubon website (www.audubon.org) and check it out.

Acknowledgments

All this because of a bird.

Years ago, while researching *Amish Peace: Simple Wisdom for a Complicated World* (Revell), I came across a true story of a rare Arctic bird, a Northern Wheatear, that got blown off course in a storm and ended up on an Amish farm. I interviewed Cheryl Harner, the president of the Ohio Audubon Society (at the time) and we became friends. I've never forgotten that little bird.

Many thanks to those who helped turn *A Season on the Wind* from an idea about the Amish and their love of birding . . . into a book about an elusive, wily rare bird.

To my family, who has (generally) supported my craze for birds. Even while in Honduras, I dragged my husband and son to an early morning bird-watching class. They started the class with a little bit of an eye-rolling attitude. They ended it spellbound. The ears come first in bird-watching, they discovered. Both felt shocked by how much they enjoyed the experience.

To some Old Order Amish friends in Ohio and Pennsylvania, who shared their reverence for birding with me.

To my daughter, Lindsey, for her wisdom and encouragement and excellent editorial suggestions.

To my editors Andrea Doering and Barb Barnes, front and back of the house, who provide so much talent and experience. I've always been touched by how much you care about each and every manuscript. You both make me a better writer.

Thank you to the Revell team—Michele Misiak, Karen Steele, Brianne Dekker, and so many others who help bring the book to life, and then get it into readers' hands.

And my gratitude, as always, goes to my agent, Joyce Hart of the Hartline Literary Agency, for her steadfast enthusiasm for my work.

Most of all, I'm so thankful to the Lord God for providing over 18,000 species of birds to enjoy, to discover—nearly twice as many as previously thought. The endless variety of birds makes my heart sing. If this is Earth, imagine what Heaven will be filled with!

One of the things I love about writing is to learn new things. I'll discover all kinds of information to use in a book, and then I'll move on. This time, though, I don't think I'll be moving on. My love of birding is here to stay.

All this because of a bird.

Turn the Page for an Exclusive Look at

SUZANNE WOODS FISHER'S

NEXT RELEASE!

COMING SUMMER 2022

1

Never ask a woman who is eating ice cream straight from the carton how she's doing.

–Anonymous

Dawn parked in front of her childhood home in Needham but couldn't make herself get out of the car. For this brief moment, the terrible news belonged only to her. As soon as she told someone, especially her mom, it would make it somehow more real. More true.

Maybe it wasn't real. She reviewed the conversation she'd had with Kevin last night. Was it possible that he'd suffered from premarital jitters? Just a case of cold feet. Cold, cold feet.

Tears flooded Dawn's eyes again. It wasn't just cold feet. Kevin said he wasn't sure he was in love with Dawn, not the way he thought he should be. Or the way he used to be. She looked around the car for a clean tissue, but all she could find were scrunched-up soggy ones. How in the world did she end up in a situation like this? Dawn Dixon was known as a levelheaded, objective, logical woman. Her nickname was Teflon Dawn. She could handle anything. Prepared for any crisis. Yet she'd missed Kevin's growing vacillation about getting married.

The front door opened and Mom stood at the threshold, the obvious question on her face. Why had Dawn come home, to Needham, on a weekday when she should've been at work in Boston? Dawn dreaded this conversation. Calling off the wedding, after all her mom had done to make it unique and one-of-a-kind, would devastate her. Dawn thought of the hours her mother had spent making origami doves that would hang from the enormous and expensive rented tent. Oh . . . the tent! Dawn cringed, thinking back to the huge argument she and her mother had had about that tent. Even though the wedding and reception was going to take place in a beautiful outdoor setting, Dawn had insisted on the tent because she wanted to be prepared for any kind of inclement weather. This was Boston in April, after all. Spring storms were part of life.

Another image of Kevin popped into her head—one from just a few weeks ago. They were at the wedding venue to finalize some details. Dawn and her mom were talking to the wedding event planner. Like always, her mom had some new ideas, and the wedding event planner was listening with rapt, wide-eyed interest—Marnie Dixon had that effect on creative types. It was like opening a shaken can of soda pop and the fizz spilled everywhere—and Dawn turned to ask Kevin a question, but he had slipped away. She found him close to the bay, facing the water. As she approached, he turned to her, his sunglasses hiding his eyes.

Something was off, she thought. "Are you feeling okay?"

"I'm fine. Just thinking about things."

Things. Like canceling their wedding. Their marriage. Their happily ever after. Those kinds of things.

Gag. Dawn felt queasy thinking of what a cliché she'd become. Jilted. Just two months before the wedding. Maybe not left at the altar, but pretty darn close.

Mom stood on the front porch, arms folded against her chest.

Dawn slowly got out of the car and closed the door. Steeling herself, she walked up the brick-lined path. "Mom," she said, her voice breaking. "There's something we have to talk about."

"She told you, didn't she?"

Dawn jerked her head up.

"I told her not to tell anyone. Blabbermouth. That's what she is. That's what I'm going to call her from now on. Maeve the Blabbermouth."

"Aunt Maeve?" Dawn scrunched up her face. "Maeve told me—"

"I didn't want anyone to know. At least not until after the wedding. I just wanted to get this surgery taken care of. I don't want you to worry, honey. It was caught early. I promise. That's the thing about cancer. Catch it quick and take care of it. So I did. And I have plenty of time before the wedding for treatment. The doctor promised. Come April twelfth, I'll be just fine."

Dawn stared at her mother. "Cancer?"

"Breast cancer. Very common. Very run of the mill. I hope Maeve didn't get it wrong and make it sound like something worse than it was. I'm sure she meant well, but she's in big trouble."

"You have . . . breast cancer?" Dawn's voice shook and broke and then stopped.

"Had. It's gone. I'm fine, honey. I promise."

For one dreadful, disorienting second, Dawn's mind emptied, stilled. Then denial roared in—loud and large. *No! No way. Not my mom.*

"Caught early. Taken care of. Gone." She snapped her fingers, like it was no big deal.

But it *was* a big deal. "When did you find out?"

"A month or so ago, I had a routine mammogram—and you know how much I hate going to doctors—but I went. And they called me back in." She shrugged. "That happens. I wasn't concerned. Not until they wanted the ultrasound. Then the biopsy."

"Biopsy?"

"Yes. On the day you were getting your makeup done for the wedding. You didn't want me there, remember? You said I would get in the way."

"I said you would turn me into someone I didn't recognize."

"Well, it all worked out, because that was the day of the biopsy. And then things happened fast, honey. Surgeon, oncologist, boom. Surgery. They move fast when they find cancer."

"When?"

"A week ago."

"Mom . . ."

"I know, I know. Maybe I should have told you, but I just want this wedding to be perfect. I was going to tell you after you got back from the honeymoon. I promise. I'm not trying to hide anything from you."

"You had surgery and didn't tell me? You went under general anesthesia?"

"I left a letter for you that Maeve was supposed to give you . . . just in case something went wrong."

"But . . . how are you feeling?"

"Not bad. A little sore. Like 'I don't want anyone to accidentally bump into me' kind of sore. But relieved. And grateful. I had good doctors who helped me make decisions."

"All alone? You didn't talk to anyone else?"

"I told Maeve about the surgery. And she took me to and from the hospital. She's brought me food and checked on me. I suppose I will forgive her, eventually. But I really didn't want you to know about any of this yet. I was so clear with her about that. What is the point of having a best friend if they go behind your back and tell your daughter that kind of news, right before her wedding?"

"Mom. Stop talking and listen to me. Maeve didn't tell me anything. And Kevin doesn't want to marry me. There isn't going to be a wedding."

Mom finally stopped talking.

There wasn't going to be a wedding. And her mom had cancer. Dawn and her mom stared at each other in a mixture of shock and disbelief.

Suzanne Woods Fisher is an award-winning, bestselling author of more than thirty books, including *On a Summer Tide* and *On a Coastal Breeze*, as well as the Nantucket Legacy, Amish Beginnings, The Bishop's Family, The Deacon's Family, and The Inn at Eagle Hill series, among other novels. She is also the author of several nonfiction books about the Amish, including *Amish Peace* and *Amish Proverbs*. She lives in California. Learn more at www.suzannewoodsfisher.com and follow Suzanne on Facebook @SuzanneWoodsFisherAuthor and Twitter @suzannewfisher.

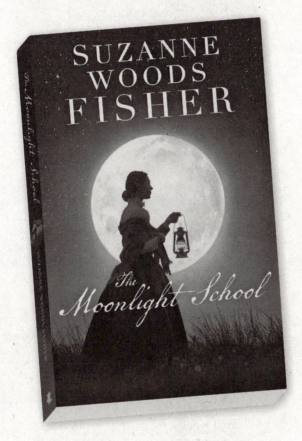

"There's just something unique and fresh about every Suzanne Woods Fisher book. Whatever the reason, I'm a fan."

—SHELLEY SHEPARD GRAY,
New York Times and *USA Today* bestselling author

Connect with SUZANNE

www.SuzanneWoodsFisher.com